Single Again

A
Rod Cornelius
Novel

Single Again
A Rod Cornelius Novel

ISBN 0-9708517-3-1
Library of Congress Control Number: 2006904075

Book Cover Illustration by Rod Cornelius

Soft copies of this book are available at www.rodcornelius.com and Amazon.com. All soft copies purchased from www.rodcornelius.com will be shipped autographed by the author.

Acknowledgements

I'd like to Give Thanks To God

My Wife,

My Son,

My Parents,

My Siblings and All Family and Friends

More Books By Akirim Press

Books by Rod Cornelius

Diggin' Gold

The Trusted

Ghetto Eyes

The Best Kept Secrets

Ugly

Books by Mirika Mayo Cornelius

Secret

Colored Lily: Poppa Took My Innocence

Ain't Quite What I Thought

Sunny Sides of My Shade

Murders At Gabriel's Trails: An Alexis & Bain Love Story

Murders At Gabriel's Trails Sons Sacrifice

Books by Cyan Deane

Dead Man's Mayhem

Execution's Karma

Chapter One
In the Beginning...

A wise man once told me that a man needs a woman in his life like a turtle needs the shell on his back. Well, he wasn't all too wise. As a matter of fact, he was this old, drunk guy that I met at this bar a couple years ago, weeping about his wife leaving him with nothing but the shirt on his back. At the time, I couldn't understand what in the world would make him come up with such a weird comparison–turtles and relationships. I just took it as the alcohol talking. Besides, that was when I was in the prime of my mac-daddy days. Relationship jargon was just that––jargon! And in reference to what my Uncle Jim once told me, I was young, dumb and always trying to find some. By no means was I trying to feel any kind of a relationship, or more blatantly, anything lasting longer than a one night stand. So at the time, I didn't know what that guy meant, why he was saying it, or why in the hell he was saying it to me.

But like I stated earlier, that was back in the prime of my player days, which virtually ended when I met Brandi Brown. Brandi, by far, was the woman of my dreams. Never in my life had I met a lady like her. To me, she was all that a man could want in a woman. But out of all the places in the world I could've met her, I met her at a club. I first laid eyes on her in the midst of celebrating my boy Rex's birthday at this little club we hit frequently called the Hot Spot. We walked in, chillin', like we normally did, and unexpectedly, we both spotted her at the same time.

"Man, look 'a here!" yelled Rex as his eyes zeroed in on her in the middle of the dance floor. "You ever saw her in here before?"

"Hell nah," I quickly replied.

6

She was dancing all by herself wearing this tight, black body skirt that revealed every perfectly placed curve on her body. She had long, thick, black hair that dangled down to her shoulders, a lightly tanned complexion, and luscious, plump lips. She freely swayed to the jazzy tunes that played as if she was the only soul in the joint. This chick was so hot, not a guy in the club had the nerve to approach her. You could literally look around and view every guy in the house sneaking peaks at her when their women turned their heads, or if they were by themselves, they just lustfully stared. I even caught a glimpse of a couple of envious females looking her way with frowns on their faces.

"Damn!" I grunted under my breath.

"Now that's dangerous," proclaimed Rex.

"You gonna holla', birthday boy?"

"Hell nah, she's too damn scandalous!" he replied. "You holla'."

I grinned, "My game's good, but I don't know about that."

"Just do it for me. Show me what I taught you."

"What *you* taught me?"

"Yeah, you know I taught you everything you know about the opposite sex."

He was just scared his ego was going to get hurt. "Whatever, Rex." As I continued to stare at her, something overwhelmed my body, perhaps just hormones, but I became strangely determined to meet this lady. Not just that, but something was telling me that I had to say something to her as if it was my destiny. Suddenly, I became transfixed on kissing those luscious, full lips of hers while sliding my hands up and down her slender back, drawing her firm, naked body against mine. Yes indeed, I was going to approach this precious victim of Godly beauty. I truly felt it would've been an opportunity missed if I'd done otherwise. "You know what?" I took a deep

7

breath. "I'm gonna do it."

He smiled, "Do that thang, pimp-a-licious."

"Pimp-a-licious, gonna do that thang, man!" If only I was as confident as I sounded. But I had to do it. I had to meet this lady. So I loaded all of the mental weapons that my brain harbored, and I strolled to my destiny.

I began bobbing my head to the music, trying to look as hip and slick as I possibly could. I'd bagged many fine females in the past but not as gorgeous as this one. As I drew near, she noticed me approaching her. "Hi!" I nervously blurted out.

She gave me a slight nod, still grooving to the tunes. I quickly realized she was going to be an arrogant one. "So, are you dancing by yourself?" Sometimes the obvious should never be put into question form. Again she said nothing. I looked back at Rex. He had grabbed himself a chair in the corner, steadily observing my actions like a gospel stage play. Man, I couldn't let him see this woman get the best of me. I would never hear the end of it from him. I quickly turned to her. "Do you mind if I dance with you?"

She stopped dancing and examined me from head to toe. A petite smile appeared upon her face. Nervous and dumbfounded, I smiled right back at her. And that's when she approached me. Before I knew it, her lips were against mine. Instantly, my mind went haywire.

"I don't feel like dancing anymore," she softly replied into my ear. Her sweet voice had a hint of an English accent in it.

With my mind on sabbatical, I could only come back with, "Well, what do you wanna do?"

She grabbed me by my hand. "Come on, love."

I looked over to Rex whose mouth had virtually fell in his lap as my feet mindlessly followed this woman off of the dance floor. I didn't know what to do next as I simply followed her lead. In a matter of seconds, we were outside in the middle of the parking lot.

"I hope your friend drove tonight," she threw a set of keys into my hands as we walked down a row of cars.

"He did," I said. Really it didn't matter who drove, because if I did, he was gonna be out of luck this night. And I knew he'd do the same to me. If he were me in the same situation and he was walking out of the club with such a beautiful lady and I was going to need a ride home, he would just leave my ass hitchhiking. But fortunately for him, he drove because I would gladly return the hypothetical favor.

We stopped at a red convertible with the top down. I opened the passenger door for her, and I anxiously jumped in on the driver side. Never had something so spontaneous happened to me with such a beautiful lady. I just wanted to get to wherever she wanted us to go, however quickly we could get there and see where things would go from there.

She gently placed her hand on my thigh. "Go straight down Main, take a left on Brenton, and pull into the driveway of the third house on the right."

Straight and direct, just what I liked. As I pulled out of the parking lot, I realized I didn't even know what this woman's name was. She just stared out of the window like she didn't even care. I could've been Charles Manson for all she knew, but even worse than that, she could've been.

"Hey, do you have a name?" She didn't answer. She blatantly ignored me, just like she did when I first approached her in the club. Now see, it's things like that, that makes a man think with his brain and not his jimmy all of the time. But then I took another glance at her body and quickly realized how much more powerful a man's jimmy is than his brain. As a matter of fact, it is his brain. Besides, this chick was a perfect ten. A ten, then some.

And those are just too hard to come by at times.

Her directions led me straight to a two-story brick house smack-dab in the middle of Brenton Avenue. "Keys," she chillingly requested. A brief thought of being stranded in the middle of nowhere swiftly raced through my mind. I gave her the keys. "Come on," she said. Thank you, Jesus. I couldn't bare the thought of walking all the way back to that club and trying to quickly compose a lie to Rex as to why I was perspiring so badly.

I jumped out of the car and shadowed her tracks like a starving dog sniffing for a meaty bone. She opened the door to the house and flicked on the lights beside the entrance. As I stepped into her crib, I began to instantly think that this experience had to be some kind of cruel joke sponsored by my subconscious and somehow, I was sleeping and couldn't wake up. And the way it was beginning to feel, this was gonna be a wet one.

She glanced back at me, "Close the door." I shut the door and followed her up the stairs. The house really didn't have much in it. In fact, it looked unlived in altogether. The walls were neatly entangled with an assortment of oil paintings but not much furniture consumed the home. Nonetheless, my primary concern rested on just one piece of furniture in particular–the bed!

We walked into what had to have been the master bedroom. It was humongous. An exquisite Persian rug laced the floor. There was a huge floor-length window open, and the nightly breeze blew her finely-silk draperies into the room. Most significantly of all, she had this massive king-sized bed in the center of the room.

I looked around, not trying to seem overly-amazed. "So this is yours?"

"Nope!" she said as she walked alongside her bed, slowly sliding her fingers across the satin sheets.

Damn! I knew she had to have a man, somewhere.

"Well, it is for now. My agency is leasing this

place for me until I find some place to live down here," she said.

"Oh," I said relieved that there was no sign of any manly presence in her life so far. "All this for you, huh?"

She grinned. "Yeap."

I walked over to the window and gazed down at the dimly lit street. I didn't want to seem too anxious for what she had to offer. "Nice view."

"I'll say," she replied.

I could almost feel her eyes cutting through my back. I turned around, thinking maybe I could slip a little bit of my own arrogance in there. "I was referring to the street."

"I was, too. What else would I be referring to?"

Ooh, low blow, and can't say that I didn't deserve it. As she took a seat on the bed, I just stared at her, not having a clue to where things were headed. But if I knew anything, I definitely had to have them go the direction I wanted them to.

"So," I took a deep breath. "Why did you bring me here?"

"Why did you come?" she quickly combated.

"What? You grabbed my hand and led the way."

"You're a grown man. I'm quite sure you could've stopped me."

"I could've, but why would I want to stop you?"

"Uh, because you have respect for yourself and you wouldn't want to become victim to a one night stand."

Playing it witty, I quickly turned my head acting as if I was surprised, "Is that what this is, a one night stand? Well, I have never..."

"This is not a one night stand," she said, really surprising me.

"It isn't?"

"No."

"Really?" I threw my hands up, looking side to

11

side. "Then what is this?"

She grinned. "It's a show!"

"What, you talking about like Candid Camera, or something?" I began looking around, searching for any hidden cameras I hadn't noticed. I knew the whole get-up was too good to be true.

"No, silly," she laughed.

I was severely intrigued. "Then what type of show are you talking about?"

"A strip-show."

Suddenly I had a smile the size of Texas on my face. "Oh, for real?" I quickly planted myself onto a chair next to the window. "Go ahead."

"You don't get it, do you?" she walked to me and stood in front of me.

I looked up at her like a little boy, waiting for his mother's response to a request to go outside and play. "What am I not getting?"

She pulled me up on my feet. "I'm not stripping, silly. You are."

"You must be outta' your mind!"

A blank look posted upon her face.

"How can I just take my clothes off in front of you? I don't even know your name. I mean, don't get me wrong, you do look good and all, but..."

She placed her finger on my lips. "My name is Brandi Brown. I am a model for the Black Friday Modeling Agency. I was born in Long Beach, California. I spent a majority of my childhood in London with my mother. I'm twenty-four years old, and I picked you out of a club full of yearning men to be my private entertainment for tonight. Now you can either do as I request or you won't have to worry about getting any more of these ever again."

She gently removed her finger and pressed her lips against mine. I just stood there, frozen, enjoying the unbelievable softness of her lips. After a few moments of her allowing me to sample heaven, she backed away. I took a deep breath, wondering what was it that I had gotten myself into. I was always accustomed to being the one in charge, but that just wasn't the case this night.

"The choice is yours." She walked to the bed and spread out on her side with her face resting in the palm of her hand.

Her eyes stayed glued on me. She knew that she blatantly left the ball in my court. By no means did I have a problem with how my body looked. I was a fairly fit brother although I could stand to do just a few extra sit-ups every now and then.

"My name is Darrel, by the way. I just thought I'd throw that at you." She knew she had all the cards in her hands, and that's what was killing me. I had never been the pupil, always the teacher. But this lady was teaching me something new. Something I was very unfamiliar with. And even though I was down in unfamiliar territory, I remained intrigued. Very intrigued. "So let me get this straight. You just want me to take all my clothes off for you with no questions asked? Might I ask what's in it for me? I know it's got to be more than a kiss. I mean, I got that from you just by asking for a dance."

"Me. Your prize will be me."

Being ever so clever, I asked, "What part of you? The neck, the rib, the thigh–what? You can't leave a brotha' in suspense like that 'cause I gotta know what I'm getting. I don't know about you."

"Your prize will be all of me that you'd like."

I smiled, "Well if that's the case…," I turned to the window to close the curtains.

"With the curtains open."

I immediately turned around. "Say what?"

"I don't want you to close the curtains. Don't you like the breeze it brings into the room?"

"Yeah, but there's like, peeping-toms and stuff like that out there! I can undress just fine without the wind coming in and strange folks staring at my rear end."

She nods her head. "You are a confident black man, aren't you?"

"Hell yeah!" I announced. "But that doesn't have anything to do with having my ass being exposed to all of the Atlanta night life.

"Well, love, I only get involved with confident men," she explained. "And the way I see it, if you want someone as precious as I am, then you can't be bashful about it. Because once you've gone Brandi Brown, you never come back."

For a moment, I thought my penis had ears. Instantly my manhood rose to the occasion–literally. Speaking on behalf of most men, we just love it when a woman talks dirty to us. "Alright, Brandi, I guess I'll just have to give you what your little demented eyes have been dying to see. The Darrel Walker show, brought to you live from Brenton Avenue. Get ready, baby!"

Quickly, I submerged into her little strip-tease game. I started by sliding my belt off, slowly, while giving her this calm, demanding stare. Hell, if I was going to make a total fool out of myself I decided I might as well have fun doing it. Next, I unbuttoned my shirt.

"Now that's what I'm talking about, love," she yelled as she fanned herself.

I never stripped before, but obviously I was doing something right–I hoped. In a matter of moments, my shirt was off and I was unzipping my slacks. "You ready for the main event, baby?"

"Yeah, love, momma's ready for the main event." she responded while licking her lips.

I was beginning to get off on the little show. I pulled off my slacks and threw them against the wall.

"Take it off. Take it off," she demanded.

14

I blew her a kiss . "You don't wanna see this."

"Oh, yes I do. Yes, I do."

Then I did it. I stripped off the boxers.

"Oh, yes!" she yelled. "Yes!"

I knew I was straight, but ole' girl was blowing it out of proportion. But I loved it. I heard a car cruising by, and someone yelled, "Nice ass, buddy!" Yeah, it was embarrassing, but I was about to get something that nosey passerby wasn't–laid.

"You ready for some of this?" I asked, knowing that she had to be ready to feel the total Darrel Walker experience.

"No, baby," she groaned, "Not quite yet."

"What?" I was totally baffled.

"You can have all of this, love," she said as she rolled over on her back and divided her legs while holding herself up on her elbows. Her beautiful brown eyes tastefully observed my every motion. "But I want you to do one other thing for me."

"What? What else do you want me to do?"

"Boo, I want you to do…'The Bird'," she quickly blurted out.

"Say what?"

"I want you to do 'The Bird' for me."

Suddenly my manhood began to sink. "Oh, hell nah! Butt-naked?" I shook my head, positively final with my decision.

Then she rose. "Oh, you're gonna do it."

"Baby girl, it's been fun, but I ain't doing no shit like that," I commanded. I looked towards the corner of the room trying to catch a glimpse of where I threw my pants.

"Darrel," she purred. In an instance she regained my attention. "Can you really say no to this?" She pulled off her blouse, slid off her skirt and held her hands out like 'what?' My mouth dropped like a full sack of potatoes. "The bra and the panties will definitely be next. Only if you're man enough to earn them."

With no mind control needed at this point, my brain played the beat to the Morris Day classic, and my feet and hands did the rest. My God, I was doing 'The Bird'! I even did a spin. My eyes pleasantly rested on her beautifully tanned body as the song repeated itself within my mind. She playfully nodded her head as she hummed out the beat of the song while she sat on the edge of the bed.

"*You fuckin' pervert!*" yelled someone in another car passing by.

She fingered me over. "Come over here, love."

I danced all the way to her, still in rhythm. She got up, put her arms around my neck and kissed me. That's when I stopped. It was time for me to do my thing, and I couldn't say that it wasn't well deserved. I had literally made an ass out of myself, but I knew what laid ahead of me was a night of passion with the sexiest woman I had ever laid eyes on.

"Take me, love," she whispered into my ear.

I picked her up, placed her on the center of the bed, and the love making began.

By far, that was the most outrageous night of my life, and it certainly was the best sex I'd ever had. It was so good that my way of thinking completely changed. And after a few weeks of exclusively dating Miss Brandi Brown and having her move into my crib, she easily became the butter to my bread, the cool to my breeze, and the slickness in my step. And to the surprise of all the great players before me, all bets were off. I got whipped!

Now for folks who don't know, there ain't nothing worse than a player that suddenly gets whipped. He starts doing stupid shit like waiting by the phone all night, asking dumb questions like, "Do you think about me when I'm away, baby?" or "I know you love me–do you love me, girl?" I was doing all of the above and much, much more. That lady just messed me all up. But I didn't fall into critical status until that night I decided to finally hang up the jersey and asked her to marry me. I got all on my knees and did it. And the story didn't stop there. Uh-uh, the story was just beginning.

After four months of being in a relationship with Brandi, I popped the question and asked her to marry me. We were the definition of hot and heavy. There wasn't a moment when we were together that we weren't in each other's face, either about to have sex or doing everything we could to get 'bout it. And I think the one thing that veered me towards thinking that I wanted to be with this woman forever was the simple fact that she was everything I thought I ever wanted in a wife. She was sexy, hard-working, and had a good head on her shoulders. And of course, she was sexy again. So against everybody's who was close to me wishes that actually knew about the situation, I popped the question and at a small reception in Las Vegas, I married her.

And the aftermath…. I think it was the great R&B artist, Percy Sledge, who sang that song, 'Take Time To Know Her'. How stupid we men are when we let our penis do all of our thinking. Just like that song Mr. Sledge sang, Momma didn't like her, was totally against the marriage, and about two months after our wedding, I caught this dread-headed bastard on top of my woman in my very own king-sized bed. And one of the many things that I've learned from being whipped is, you just don't have any damn sense whatsoever. When I stumbled into that bedroom, she looked towards me while the Rasta-man was all on top of her, huffin' and puffin'.

"Darrel, you wanna join in?" she asked with her nails gripped into his ashy-ass back.

The dude looked over to me, smiled and said, "You

can have her next, mon. I'll only be another minute, dear boy."

And I just stood there, dumb-witted, with my mouth wide open like I just missed the ice cream truck. I couldn't conjure up enough intelligence to say not one damn thing. I just froze as they just kept on doing it as if I wasn't even there. Then suddenly, I finally broke out of that suspension of disbelief and yelled, "Get the fuck off my wife!"

And the brotha' paused and looked at me. He eased up off of her and said, "I wasn't finished yet, but you know the shit's good, you can go 'head, mon. I'll join in after I get a breather."

Now at that moment, I do believe that's when all realization of being an ass-kickin' black man overwhelmed my body because I blacked out for a moment, and when I came back to reality, the police had me in cuffs, sitting on my living room sofa, and they were wheeling the brotha out on a stretcher. He wasn't dead or nothing, but I demandingly kicked his ass and unfortunately couldn't recall any memory of it. Wasn't that a bitch? Then Brandi walked out of the bedroom, fully-clothed, with one of the officers. She looked at me and couldn't say a word.

The officer approached me. "Mr. Walker, would you please stand up and turn around?" He relived me of the handcuffs. "I'm going to ask you to leave here when we leave." He looked over to Brandi. "In some states, he could've killed Mr. Williams and got off like a fat rat. He wouldn't have served not a day in jail."

I tried to hold back my tears as I stared at her. She looked as if she wanted to cry, but didn't have enough nerve to do so.

"Mr. Walker, you're free to get a change of clothing," he said.

I walked towards the bedroom.

"No," she yelled. "I'll go." She rushed into the

bedroom.

"Well, vice-versa, it makes me no difference," the cop nonchalantly replied. "As long as one of you leave. I don't wanna have to make another trip here tonight. Adultery and fornication tends to bring the worst out of couples. Especially when some stuff like what happened here tonight goes down."

Unfortunately, all I could do was look at her. I was too damn dumb to say anything and too damn whipped to tell her she needed to get the hell out and never come back. I had it bad. She returned to the den and to my surprise she had her things packed already. Bags in hand, she gave me one last stare and proceeded to the door. But before she left, she turned around and said, "Darrel... I wish I could say I was sorry, but I was only being me, love."

I turned my eyes towards the ceiling, not wanting to hear anything she had to say. She hurt me badly, and I was afraid that if I looked into her face I would've done something stupid like break down. It was bad enough she played me for a fool. There was no way in the world I was gonna let her see a tear drop from my eyes. I was content with the idea of crying behind closed doors, but definitely not in front of her. I wouldn't give her the courtesy. So after she stood there for a moment, waiting for me to reply, which obviously wasn't going to happen, she sighed and walked out.

Honestly, I wish I knew what the hell she meant by what she said. I thought I knew her. I thought she loved me. I knew I loved her. Why'd she do it, I kept thinking. Was I not doing something right? For the life of me, I couldn't understand what went wrong.

Within a few weeks I was able to get an annulment. That process went by fairly quickly, since she didn't deny the fact that she was the one that actually committed the adulterous act. We set up a meeting to sign the necessary paperwork and that was the last time I saw Brandi Brown.

I told myself I would be through with women for a very long time. Something inside of me, I felt, was irreplaceably lost. And to my sudden surprise, I had become single again.

Chapter Two

Six months passed by in no time. I had landed myself on an emotional roller coaster that had no ups, just downs. I never understood what being hurt was until I signed those annulment papers. I never realized what disgruntlement was until I blacked out while kicking that Rasta-dude's ass. Yeah, Brandi Brown had turned my life upside down and every which-a-way. It was literally heartbreaking when I finally realized she was actually right when she told me that once I went Brandi, I would never come back.

After she left, I didn't want to do anything anymore. I didn't go out with the boys. I barely ate. And I virtually cut myself off from all family and friends. It was just me, my job and my couch. It became an every day ritual. I knew things had to change, but I didn't know how to make them.

It was a Saturday morning, and I was lying in bed when I heard my phone ring. I knew it could only be one of two people—my mom or Rex. I didn't want to talk to either. I knew my mom would call me just to tell me "*I told you so*" for the nine-zillionth time, and Rex would call me just for some player recovery. After a couple of rings, my answering machine picked up, and undoubtedly it was Rex.

"Hey, nigga, get up! I know you're in there. Get your whipped ass up out of that bed. Darrel! You know what? You're a sad sight to all mankind. I mean, how are you just gonna' let some trick put you in playa-comma? Huh?" It was Rex at his finest, and he was in the midst of leaving one of his many recovery lectures on my answering machine. By now, I had gotten used to it. I simply laid in bed as he released all his anxieties of being a hunter suddenly alone to catch his prey. He no longer had me by his side to venture out with him on his nights of mischief and deceit, and it was killing him. "Man, get the hell out of bed. A brother is sick and tired of calling your monkey-ass every freakin' weekend for you to just leave me hangin' like this. But guess what? I'ma fix your ass this Saturday morning. Guess what, nigga? I'm outside!"

My whole body jolted off of the bed as I looked towards the window.

"Get your ass up!" he yelled as he began to obnoxiously blow his horn in unison with each word.

I threw on a shirt and ran to my front door. I opened up and saw him standing up in his convertible, repeatedly blowing his horn with one hand and his mobile phone in the other. *"Get your ass up! Get your ass up! Get your ass up!"*

"Rex!" I yelled as I stomped out to his car.

He quickly refrained from all the racket. "Oops, look who has risen from the dead," he said, smiling. "Damn, bra', when was the last time you shaved?"

"Have you lost all of your damn senses?"

"No," he said as he jumped out of the car. "You kept dissin' a brotha', and I didn't appreciate it one bit. And all over some broad. Nobody tell you to marry that chicken-head anyway. You should've listened to some of those messages your momma left on that machine of yours."

"No one asked for your opinion," I replied. "Nor my mother's."

"Well, I'm giving it," he said as he bypassed me and walked towards my front door. "Shoot, what you got to eat up in there—a nigga hungry! Got me waking up nine o'clock on a Saturday morning."

"Where do you think you're going?"

"In the crib, where you think?"

I followed him into the house.

"Damn," he immediately said going through the

door. "When was the last time your ass cleaned up in here?"

"It's been a while," I said scratching my head.

I wasn't big on cleaning up since Brandi and I broke up. My den consisted of gigantic mountains of clothes, shoes and newspapers. It didn't matter much to me. I wasn't trying to impress anyone.

Rex pushed aside a stack of my clothing on the sofa and landed himself a seat. "Man, I don't want nothing to eat from here no more. You don't seem to be as clean as you use to be. Let's go to the Waffle House."

I sat across from him. "Man, I'm not going anywhere."

He shook his head, "Ah man, when are you gonna let that chick go? I know this is gonna sound harsh as hell, but she cheated on your ass in your own crib. Forget that trick."

"I know. I know." It actually pained my ears to hear anyone talk negatively about Brandi or the situation. Even though she did me wrong, I didn't want to hear anyone speak badly about her. And the incident–I think it's safe to say no one likes to play the fool. Rex was just trying to help, so I didn't want to go off on him.

"Let the chick go, Darrel," he sighed. "I mean, you're not even the same person anymore. You don't hang out no more. You don't holla' at the ladies no more. You know, you don't do nothing but eat, sleep and shit! Now, you tell me what kind of a life is that for anybody to live? And I'm sorry but I gotta say this…"

"I know. I know. You told me so."

"Well, yeah," he smirked, "But I wasn't going to say that. I was gonna say you need to get yourself together. Look at yourself. You need a shave. You smell bad. Your house is all messed up. Man–*you*, two years ago, you'd beat the crap out of yourself if you could see this."

I couldn't do anything but nod my head. I knew he

was telling the truth. Somewhere in the mix, I lost myself, and I didn't even care anymore. Only the Lord knew how I was going to recapture the grace I once had. "I don't know what's wrong with me."

"I know what's wrong with you. You need some coochie."

I shook my head, immediately disagreeing, "What makes you think you know what I need?"

He tilted his head with a huge frown plastered on his face, "Fool, when was the last time that you had any?"

"What does it matter?"

"*What does it matter?*" He jumped off of the sofa and placed his hand on my shoulder. "It's the reason why you're in here acting like you're an Eddie Munster clone. With all these damn curtains covering up the freakin' daylight. Are you out of your mind?"

I rolled my eyes as he continued on with his boisterous speech.

"Coochie is your cure," he said as he waltzed around my den opening all of my curtains. "You are a victim of the most atrocious crime ever committed."

"And what is that, Rex?"

"The crime of not getting any poo-nanny when your lady done crept out on you."

I rolled my eyes and sighed as his speech began to take on new proportions. Rex was well known for his attempts of getting people to do things that they don't necessarily want to do. And there were so many times in the past that I fell victim to his ploys. I think half of the trouble that I've gotten into in the past would've been significantly down-sized if I would've listened to myself and to none of his ill-witted schemes. But I decided that this day was going to be different. There was no way in the world he was going to get me out of my house.

"You, my man, are serving hard time, and you don't even know it," he pointed his finger at me, "I'm your

24

Johnny Cochran. I come to free your ass. I came to slide you the key to the cell. And the only way we can be successful is to get you to wash your ass, put on some clean clothes and haul ass to the nearest club."

I jumped out of my chair, having heard enough, "Rex, I'm not going to any club. As a matter of fact, I'm not going anywhere at all."

"Why not?"

"Because I don't want to. I don't want to be around anyone. I barely even want to be around you. To tell you the truth, I just want to be left alone."

"Well, that's a damn shame."

"Well, that's what it's gonna have to be," I said a little upset. I began to stack all the clothes on the floor into one pile on the edge of the sofa.

"Well, I guess I tried," he said as he walked towards the front door.

"That you did."

He opened the door. "I guess Brandi is free to do all the clubin' with that Jamaican dude she wants, while you're stuck in here like some chump watching lost episodes of 'Roc.'"

I paused. My throat began to dry as I had suddenly became lost for words. "Brandi?" I mumbled as I turned to him.

"Yeap, Devon and I spotted the happy couple the other night at Club 112," he said as he shut the door. "They were bumpin' and grindin' and all that good stuff."

Heartbroken all over again, I dropped onto the sofa.

"And me, I was like that's fucked up. I was about to confront their asses, but I saw this shorty that was looking so blazed that I just couldn't pass her by. And I was like, if Darrel can't handle his own damn business, why should I? That nigga don't even answer the phone when I call!"

I looked down at the floor feeling like I was going

to burst into tears. The only thing stopping me was the fact that Rex was there with me. In front of him, I had to be strong. I didn't want all my manhood to dwindle away. So I tried to look tough and unaffected, but on the inside, the news was killing me.

"Hey, you're my boy," he said as he sat on the sofa beside me. "I know that half of the shit I tell you don't be right, but you've always been wise enough to know which way to go. The simple idea of you sitting in here after some chick just played you for a fool just don't sit right with me. And plainly, I don't like it."

I raised my head and looked him dead in his eyes. There wasn't a smile on his face as he was more serious than I had ever seen him. And although he may have brought more confusion into my life than Brandi Brown ever could've imagine, he was my Johnny Cochran. He had come to save my ass.

I nodded my head knowing that finally it was time for a change. "You know what? You're absolutely right. I've been sitting in this house, dead to the world, while my ex-wife is out having the time of her life," I shouted as I jumped off of the sofa and paced around the den. "While she's out there with the lost member of Bob Marley's band, I'm in here moping like I'm on a Keith Sweat video. I can't go out like that!"

Rex jumped up. "Hell no!"

"I don't need her. Who in the hell does she think she is? Going around town with that ashy-ass Wyclef Jean imposter!"

"Is pimp-a-licious back?"

I stopped walking and folded my arms. "I mean, for six months I've been acting like a straight-up punk, crying over some woman that played me for a sucker!"

"She did play you for a sucker, now."

"I'm the heart-breaker! I'm the house-rocker!" I yelled. "I don't get played, I play the game!"

"Damn that! Is pimp-a-licious back?"

"She let the best thing that ever happened to her slip through her tiny, little, high-yellow fingers." All my juices were flowing as I realized how much of a loser I had become. The news Rex gave me lit something that desperately needed to be burning inside of me. At last, I felt like myself again. I was finally ready to take on the world once more. I looked Rex dead in his eyes with a huge smirk on my face. "And yes, pimp-a-licious is back!"

"That's what the hell I'm talking about," yelled Rex as he got so excited he embraced me with a hug.

"Alright, alright," I said. "There's no need to get all affectionate."

"You just had me scared, man. I thought you were never gonna snap out of it."

"Well, I'm back now and thanks. I was so stupid." I said as I observed my filthy den. "And look at this place. It's a mess." It was almost like I was in a coma for the last six months. Everything around me looked foreign.

He looked around, also. "Yeah, it is pretty fucked up in here."

I sat down. "How did I let things get this bad?"

"You just got whipped, that's all. I heard that it happens to some of the best of us."

"But I never thought it would happen to me."

"But it did, and, brother-man, she got you good, too. She got all up in your mental."

"Amen."

"Speaking of amen, when was the last you talked to Momma Walker?"

"Ah, Ma," I slouched in the chair cringing at the mere thought of my mother.

"Boy, I saw her in the store the other day and she was fuming mad with you and getting on my case about it. You know she's still upset with you for leaving town and marrying ole' girl in the first place. What in the hell were you thinking about when you did that anyway?"

I shook my head, "I don't even know. Damn, I do some dumb things."

"You sure 'nuff do. Momma Walker was like, *'When you see that boy of mine, you tell him Lord knows I got some few choice words for him.'* She was like, *'I know he's not married to that little hussy no more, and I know he be listening to me on that machine when I call.'* Man, I think if Momma Walker could still get you over her knee she'd beat the black off of your ass right now."

"I know she's mad. You wanna go over there with me?"

"Hell no," he shouted. "I get my share of shouting when I visit my own momma. *'You know you need to find you a good woman and settle down. Why you ain't got me no grand kids yet?* Blah, blah, blah.' And then, your mother is bigger than mine."

I looked at him, slightly offended, "You trying to call my momma fat?"

He sucked his teeth. "No, you know I wasn't trying to say that. It's just that Momma Walker takes up a little bit more space than my mother. You know what I'm saying."

"Yeah, I know. Just don't get knocked out." I kicked back on the sofa as I realized I was guilty of committing the worse crime any child could ever commit towards their parents–not coming by to see them! And Rex's butt didn't want to go with me. I couldn't blame him though. My mom was always kind to Rex, but she often advised me to find a friend that would help me do something more productive with my life than chasing different women all the time. *'You lie down with dogs, you gon' get fleas on you,'* is what she always told me when discussing my relationship with Rex. I think every child has that friend their parent's disapproves of, and on the down-low, the parents repeatedly tell them not to hang with that friend because they think they're nothing but trouble. Sure enough, Rex was mine.

"I tell you what," said Rex, "I'll go with you to Momma Walker's house, if you go with me and Devon to the Hot Spot tonight."

"Devon!" I yelled.

"Yeah, it's that cat's birthday today. I told him I'd take him out to the club with me tonight."

I shook my head, totally against any conceived notion of going out in public with his younger, more immature cousin, Devon Stewart. Devon wanted to be everything that Rex was, but somehow, he just couldn't seem to get it together. "Rex, you know I don't like going anywhere with Devon. He just ain't right."

"D, I know that, but I promised the guy."

"So that's who you've been hanging out with during my absence?"

He shrugged his shoulders, "Well, some of the ladies think he's kinda funny."

"Of course, right before he says something that makes them wanna kill him."

"He's gotten a little better."

"Yeah, right." Rex knew he had me stuck between a rock and a hard place. There was no way I was going to survive the wrath of my mother without him being there. She'd never go off on me at full capacity if I had company with me. "How's he gonna be dressed?"

"Oh, man, let me tell you, he's gotten a whole lot better."

"I still remember the last time we went out with Devon and his yellow blazer and fish-heeled boots. We almost didn't get in. Not including the fact that before we ditched him, we were the laughing stock of the entire night."

"I know cuz has some issues, but I think he's ironed them all out. He's not down with that outdated pimp gear no more. He's modernized now."

I stared at him, virtually not believing a word that came out of his mouth. I simply knew better. "If he's dressed like a retard, Rex, I will pay you back one way or the other. Just the thought of going out in public with Devon brings chills down my spine."

"Don't worry, D. Cuz has adjusted his gear and his attitude. So are we on?"

I took a few seconds to think about it, knowing just like he did that I didn't have a choice. "Yeah, we're on. Just let me jump in the shower and get some of this musk off of me."

Rex giggled, "Yeah, go ahead and do that. I'll watch a little bit of television while I'm waiting." He grabbed the remote and flicked on the set.

I stood up. "Alright, just give me a half hour and I'll be ready."

"Cool," he replied.

I strolled out of the den and made my way to the bathroom, not knowing what laid ahead of me for the remainder of the day. But I did know that it was time for a change. No more could I let this breakup with a woman that seemed to forget everything about me dictate how I lived. It was time for me to take another route. Time for me to move on. It was time for Darrel Walker to be reborn.

Chapter Three

After a long, hot shower and a much needed shave, I was cruising down Peachtree with my buddy, Rex. Sunny day, blue skies and car top down, I was feeling kinda good. The only thing bothering me was the fact that I was about a half hour away from a lethal showdown with my mother. Now my mother was the most religious woman I've ever known, but all hell was gonna break loose the minute I stepped foot into her house. Mainly, because I disappeared when Brandi and I got married and it didn't help matters any further when I decided to stay away even longer after the split up. I knew she would disapprove of me marrying anyone that quick, and Lord forbid if she found out that the whole marriage was an offspring from a one night stand. Nevertheless, with or without Rex with me, Mom was gonna put her two cents in as soon as she got the chance.

"You got some money?" asked Rex.

I briefly glanced at him as I broke out of my train of thought. "Yeah, why?"

"I need some gas."

"So I guess you want me to pay."

"Well, I don't have any money on me, and we are driving to *your* mother's house."

"That's cool. I was gonna give you something for the ride even though *you* insisted on driving. My Maxima drives perfectly fine, you know? Nobody can help it if you want to floss all day with the Lex."

"Are you kidding? You ought to feel fortunate I'm driving this bad boy. The ladies love this shit," he grinned.

"Hey, I'm not disputing that. It's just if you're gonna volunteer to drive next time, make sure you got a full tank."

"Whatever! You just pay for the gas."

Rex asking for gas money was a sure sign that his

money stash was running out. And I couldn't say that I wouldn't be surprised neither. He hasn't worked on a real job since college. Did I say college? I meant, since I was in college. By no way am I knocking him for dropping out because school isn't for everybody, but he dipped out after only one semester. His uncle put him down with some real estate deals where they bought up some foreclosed homes somewhere in Florida and made a killing in profits. Rex's father died when he was eight, so he used the money his father left him in a trust fund to invest. Before he actually quit school, I tried to get him to consider doing real estate and school at the same time. But not Rex. His head is about as hard as a peeping-tom spying behind the wall of the women's restroom. Anyway, he pulled off a couple of deals and fattened his bank account and stopped working and school altogether. His uncle took his share of the proceeds and moved out to L.A. to pursue his never-will-happen dream of becoming a famous porn-star. Rex is my boy, but he has some mixed up folks.

"So, are you looking for a job?" I asked directly.

"A job! What the hell?," he chuckled. "I dare you say that word in my presence ever again. Why in the hell would I need a job?"

"I don't know, I guess it's just the fact that you haven't asked me for gas money since college."

"No more job for me. You know that. My debit card isn't working, and I'm waiting for the bank to send me a new one. Now if you don't have the cash, I do have the Visa. I just don't like buying gas on that damn thing."

"Nah, I got it. I was just checking you out," I said as he pulled beside a pump at the gas station.

"What makes you think you should check on me and my finances?"

"I don't know. I just thought that maybe the well was running dry. I was just making sure you were alright, you know?"

He giggled and shook his head. "Three hundred and sixty-five grand, with no less than five percent interest each and every month. No, the well is nowhere near dry."

"Okay, okay. You don't have to shoot out all those figures, baller. I believe you. You pump and I pay, alright?"

"That's cool."

I jumped out of the car and strolled into the station. I didn't mean to offend him, but I needed to make sure he was alright. The love for a homeboy goes deep, but there's nothing that strains a friendship worse than a friend with no job or money. Taking care of myself was a huge enough obstacle in itself. I didn't make enough to supply funds to a friend in need, too.

I grabbed myself a drink and paid the attendant. As I walked outside, a green Pathfinder flew by me and that damn dude that I caught in bed with Brandi was behind the helms. I dropped my drink and immediately attempted to run down the vehicle.

"Hey you—hey!" I childishly yelled as the car zoomed out of the lot. I was sure it was him, and my soul had a score to settle with him. No matter how childish it was, I wanted to put my foot in his rear end again—consciously! I stopped running as it became apparent to me that I wasn't going to catch him and he wasn't going to stop. Suddenly, I felt like a total ass. My heart just wasn't gonna let it go. Mr. Lover man and me were going to have our day, one day. I turned towards Rex as he stood at the pump, staring at me with his jaw dropped.

"What in the hell is wrong with you?" he yelled.

"Nothing," I replied as I shook my head and began walking towards his car.

Unexpectedly, the screeching sound of skidding tires pierced my eardrums. I spun around, and I was about six inches from getting pulverized by a red Ford Explorer. A new model at that. My heart almost jumped out of my chest from all the excitement. The lady driving quickly jumped out of the truck.

"I'm sorry, I didn't see you," she frantically yelled. "Darrel?"

I looked up, and my mind began to familiarize this beautiful mocha-brown goddess. It was Veronica Bethal. "Veronica," I said softly.

"Darrel, what are you doing walking out in front of cars?"

I was totally mesmerized by her stunning beauty yet still a little shaken up by all the commotion. However, I did manage to settle down enough to notice how good she looked in those tight jeans and pink tank top that exposed her cute, little belly-button.

"Veronica," I mumbled, "I thought you moved to New York."

"I did, Darrel. Now I'm back here, and I'm running late for an appointment. Now, if you would, could you please get out of the way?"

She still had that spunky attitude I adored so much. "I'm moving. I'm moving," I said as I dashed out of her way.

"Thank you." She jumped back into her vehicle.

"Wait," I said as I ran to her window. "Why are you trying to be so mean? You almost killed a brotha' out here, and all you can say is get out of the way? That ain't right."

"I'm not being mean, Darrel. I just have to get somewhere, and I'm running late. I'm sorry for almost running you over."

"Well that makes me feel a lot better," I said sarcastically. "I thought we were tight, though." I didn't want to sound like a chump or anything, but a few moments catching up shouldn't have been out of the question.

"We were, Darrel. What else do you want me to say?"

"What's up with the attitude?"

"It's no attitude, Darrel. I've moved on with my life."

"So that's how it is?"

"Yes, Darrel, that's how it is. I wish you the best, okay?"

"Dag, I thought we had something."

"Well, Darrel, we could've, but not every woman wanted to be a pawn in the games you played."

She charged out of the parking lot. I was frozen by her comments and devastated by her tone. The games I played? She acted as if I was the dirtiest man on the planet. As friends, I knew we had our ups and downs, but the way she acted was something totally new to me. I couldn't imagine what idiotic thing I could've done to her back then to make her act that way. We never even dated!

I strolled to Rex's car as he stared at me shaking his head with a big grin on his face.

"What?" I asked as I got into the car.

"I didn't hear one word, but I could easily tell that chick was pissed off at you."

"Well you're wrong and nosey."

"Hey, it happened right in front of me. I couldn't help but see it."

"I mean, really, are you gonna drive? I did pay for the gas." I was more than upset. I was genuinely embarrassed. Rex's analysis was by no way making me feel any better.

"You don't need to get an attitude with me," laughed Rex. "I'm your dawg. I didn't do you like you did her."

"I didn't do anything to her."

"It sure looked like you did."

"I didn't, okay?"

"Ooh-wee," he chuckled. "Somebody's catchin' cramps."

"Can we just change the subject? That's all I'm asking. Can we just change the freakin' subject? "

"Hey, I'll respect that. It's an improvement that you're even talking to a woman right now. So getting chewed out by one isn't that bad. At least you're making progress."

"Just drive, that's all you have to do, Rex."

"Driving the car."

Rex was gonna make his jokes, and I knew I was just gonna have to deal with it. I mean, I couldn't expect anything more or less from him. I was more concerned with my confrontation with Veronica and her surprisingly hostile attitude towards me. That almost surprised me more than spotting my ex-wife's lover.

I met Veronica my senior year in college. She transferred from some small university out of California. We never had a relationship or anything, we just kicked it a bit. She was one of those opposite sex friends that you confide in because you feel so comfortable around them. I was truly comfortable around her. To tell you the truth, I couldn't understand why in the hell she was so mad at me. I couldn't say that it didn't bother me, because it did. I was even more confused by that commitment statement she made. We both knew we were never involved like that. With the exception of a kiss we shared that one night we had too much to drink, but we blew it off as if it never happened. We were too tight to fool around with each other like that.

"Momma Walker got you scared over there, don't she? I can tell," Rex joked.

"Nah, just thinking." By no means did I want to discuss my issues with Veronica to him. He would only give me that playa' advice. *'Fuck 'em and leave 'em, don't think about 'em when you don't sleep with 'em.'* In his mind, she's just one of the countless chicks I scored with that I never called back the next morning. If I decided to let him know anything that differentiated from that, he would only give me that think with your penis lecture. I knew it by heart and I didn't want to hear it again.

"Don't get scared now," he laughed. "I know Momma Walker used to skin that ass with a switch. You better get ready, 'cause it's about time for her to get it out today."

"You know Ma." I replied with a phony smile.

We pulled into my mother's driveway. Home-sweet-home, I thought to myself. To my surprise, my Uncle Jim's gold firebird was parked alongside the road. The good Lord was definitely blessing me this day. My mom was probably too busy arguing with him to have any time to even consider blessin' me out. Whenever Jim was around, she was always occupied with arguing with him about his infamous womanizing ways. Uncle Jim was a player in the purest form. Ever since I could remember he was like that, and I never could recall seeing him with the same woman. His game was just that tight, I guess.

"Those your Uncle Jim's wheels, aren't they?"

"You know it," I answered as I stared at the firebird trying to compose the type of scenario that laid ahead of me once I entered that house.

"His cool ass," laughed Rex. "I bet he's still big pimpin', too."

"I don't doubt it."

"Well, let's see what he's talking about up in there."

"Hold on there, partner." I grabbed Rex by his arm. "Don't go in there and get Jim started with telling those stories about all of his exotic escapades with those women of his. My mother hates when we get him started with that mess. And I don't need her faulting either one of us with that crap. This is a peace mission."

"But D, your uncle has some smooth ass stories to

tell."

"I don't care. I don't want to hear anymore of my mom's complaining than I have to. Besides, we have a deal. You do this for me, and I go out with you and Devon tonight."

He nodded, "I understand. But hey, if he volunteers it, I'm gonna listen. Half that shit your uncle told me in the past worked for me, personally. A player never stops taking notes. Maybe you need to take a notepad in there. You are a bit rusty."

"No thanks. My playing days are over. And I definitely don't need to take any notes from my Uncle Jim. Once upon a time I thought I wanted to be just like him, but not anymore. There's more to life than all those games."

"Like what?" he snapped.

"Like love, man."

"Nigga, if you don't shut the hell up," he yelled. "Get your ass up out of my car, talking about love."

We jumped out of the car and walked towards the front porch.

"That's that wife shit you coming up with again. That shit's for the birds. It's gotten your thinking all messed up."

"Hey, one day…"

"One day, hell! I'm never getting married. Mark my words!"

"I'm gonna mark 'em, too."

"Email 'em, fax 'em, draw 'em, I don't give a damn. Rex ain't never getting married. Rex ain't never falling in love," he contested.

"Okay," I said as I knocked on the door.

"Shoot, it's more than okay. That's the way it is. I can't believe you. "

"Chill, I hear someone coming."

The door swung open. It was my mother. As soon as she saw me, she placed her hands on her waist and frowned. "I don't know why you decided to pop up here today."

"Hi, Momma Walker," said Rex.

My mom glanced at him and sucked her teeth. "Good afternoon, Rex." She stepped aside. "Y'all come on in."

All of the sudden, I was thirteen again. I sluggishly walked in with my head down, as Rex followed me in.

"I don't know what you're walking in here like that for. You're a grown man Darrel Walker." Her voice rose as we walked into the den. "You don't have to worry about me lecturing you about the wrongs you're doing or have done. You know exactly what you're doing. It's not for me to judge. Never has been."

We walked into the back of the house where the den was. I wanted to at least plead my case to my mother, but I was too smart for that. Everything that I was doing was wrong from her point of view, and bad things were only happening to me because I asked for it. And maybe she was right. I just didn't want to hear her say it.

We entered the den and Uncle Jim was lying on the couch with a huge bandage across his forehead.

"Dag," yelled Rex.

My uncle quickly rose up. "Fellas, what's going on?"

"Uncle Jim, what happened?" I asked.

"Man, that bitch got me," he said as he shook his head. "You fellas come and have a seat."

Ma breezed in. "Yeah, y'all talk to him. Birds of a feather, flock together. Lord Jesus, please save 'em all!" She stormed into the kitchen while looking towards the ceiling, thrusting her fists in the air.

Rex and I took a seat beside Jim. "So who did this to you?" I asked.

"Man, Charlene did it, acting all crazy and shit."

"Don't be cursing in my house Jimmy!" my mother

yelled from out of the kitchen.

"Damn, your mother got some good ears," he whispered.

"I heard that, too," she yelled. "Don't play with me around there. This house has all the Lord's blessings, and I don't allow no foul language in here."

Uncle Jim just rolled his eyes. "Darrel, I love your mother but if I only had somewhere else to go."

"So, what happened? Did your lady kick you out of your own crib?" asked Rex.

"My wife kicked me out of my own crib."

"Wife!" Rex and I yelled simultaneously.

"Yeah, fellas, ole' Unc got hitched."

"When did this happen?" I asked.

"About two months ago. You know, it was on the down low. I was getting too old for all that skirt chasin'. Too much stuff out there you can catch and can't get rid of. Much different than back in the days when your father and I held things down."

"Dag, Jim," said Rex, "I can't believe that you hung up the ole' pimp gear."

"I couldn't either." He said as he smiled and looked straight ahead as if was enjoying the sights of something only he could see. "But she caught me off guard. Her dark chocolate self, with them gorgeous brown eyes. When I saw her, it was the first time I ever fell in love with a woman. I wanted more than just that treasure between her legs. All that womanizing didn't mean a damn thing anymore. She hooked me like a fish."

"Well things couldn't have been too perfect. She slapped you over the head with something." I interrupted.

"Man, she knocked the hell out of me."

"Why?" Rex asked.

"Because she thought I was courtin' time with somebody else."

"Well, were you?" I asked.

"Yeah, but that don't give her no right for knocking me over my head with that damn frying pan."

"She clubbed you over your head with a frying pan, Jim?" asked Rex.

"One of them old cast iron ones. Got my head aching."

"How'd she find out that you cheated on her?" I asked.

"Yeah, because you've been in the game too long to make any simple mistakes. I know that for a fact. Cats like you don't get caught slippin'," Rex preached.

"I've been in the game a long time, but sometimes, you get caught off guard. And that's exactly what happened to my ass when I met that red bone at that courthouse."

"Did she look that good?" asked Rex.

His eyes almost jumped out of his head. "Man, hell yeah! Nice little red bone with those pretty, full lips. She was around your age."

"Really?" I replied.

He chuckled. "She was fine. Too damn fine. I mean, fellas, it was so easy it scared me."

"How easy, Unc?" I questioned.

He shook his head. "Man, this chick must've been a nympho. 'Cause I was just sitting in the lobby, sipping on my coffee, waiting on court to start back up 'cause the judge was out to lunch. I came there in the afternoon. But she must've been in there for something, too. And this chick walked by me with this tight, black skirt and just eyed me the whole way pass. I mean, I know the chick was in her mid-twenties, and Unc don't normally go that young no more, but it was something about this chick. Something that just made you do stupid shit. 'Cause my mind was so bent on her, I went and spilled my damn coffee on my slacks," he sighed. "You know I spent ninety-five dollars on those pants?"

"Yeah, Unc, what happened next?" I asked.

"Oh, yeah, well she went on and disappeared into one of those offices. I jumped up and rushed to the restroom. I had to get that shit out of those slacks. Ain't nobody got no money to be wasting."

"I hear you Unc," replied Rex, with a hypnotized look on his face, solemnly following every word uttered out of my uncle's mouth.

"Well, I went in there and started wiping myself off at the sink. After I got as much of the stain out as I could, I realized I had to take a piss. So I went around the corner to the urinal and handled my business, you guys know. And that's when the shit hit the fan. Suddenly, I heard the door swing open.

"Oh no, please don't tell me," yelled Rex as he put his hand over his mouth, overly amazed.

"Now, let me tell you. Normally you don't pay much attention to somebody coming into the restroom. But I knew something was fishy from the get-go because when that door closed, I heard heals tapping into the joint. So, you know, I zipped my stuff up and looked around the corner towards the door. And that's when the damn'est thing that ever happened to me happened. That red bone was standing right at the door. Would you guys believe I couldn't say nothing? My mouth was just numb."

"No, Jim," laughed Rex.

"I couldn't say a thing! I just stared at her," he shook his head with a clueless look on his face. "Then she locked the door and approached me, slow and cocky. I mean this broad just knew she was bad. But most of all, she knew what the hell she came in there for. So she stood in front of me and stared into my eyes and said, *'I thought I heard someone call me. Was it you?'* And guys, I tried again to say something, but I just couldn't. I just stood there like a dumb ass dog, nodding my damn head up and down."

"What she do next, Unc?" I asked, all caught up in the drama.

"Man, that chick grabbed me by my head and hit me with the most erotic kiss I ever had. I mean, just tongue's and carrying on. I could barely keep up," he laughed. "And Uncle Jim may be married, but he sure was glad he never got out of the habit of keeping a rubber on him. 'Cause when that chick jumped up on that sink, I started laying down some serious pipe, you hear me?"

"Go 'head Jim." yelled Rex.

"Right in the court restroom, Unc?"

"Hell yeah! I always believed in seizing the moment. And that definitely was the moment."

"But..." I suddenly stopped myself.

"But what?" he asked.

I stopped myself because I was gonna tell him he didn't even know her. Then my mind quickly flashed back to Brandi and my first night together. The events were just the same. And in a sense, too much the same. "But you never told us what her name was?" I eloquently switched the direction of the question, hoping desperately he'd at least drop the name of this woman. I knew the odds were zero to none, but the whole incident seemed so Brandi Brown-like.

"Cause she never gave it. I wanted to ask, but after I handled my business, she walked out and disappeared," he leaned back and folded his arms. "Just like she was a ghost or something."

"Why couldn't something like that happen to me, just once?" Rex griped.

"So you didn't get any inclination of her name, Unc?"

"I wanted to get her name, but like I said before, when I got myself together and walked back into the lobby she was gone. Man, that thang was good too!" Suddenly the small grin on his face turned into a huge frown. "At least at that moment it was good."

"What do you mean, Jim?" asked Rex. "Hitting something off like that must've kept you on cloud nine all that day."

Jim took a deep breath and shook his head, "I wish like hell it did. You see, fellas, when you got a good woman that invests all of her time and energy in you, she learns things about you. Things you don't even realize she knows. Things your ass probably don't know."

I could see the tears wanting to come out of his eyes, but the pride of being a man sucked them right back in. He was hurt. "What happened, Unc?" I asked.

"Man, Charlene, she knew I kept rubbers on me. I got home thinking I was nine-sharp, but she saw some lipstick on my collar. Then words exchanged. We started scuffling over my wallet 'cause she knew that's where I had the rubber. Then somehow she managed to get the wallet and didn't see the rubber. And that's when more hell broke loose," he gasped. "It ain't worth it fellas. It ain't! While it's happening, it's all good, but afterwards–shit! If you know you got somebody good and that person loves you and you know that's the person you're suppose to be with, all that other shit is small. I messed up, fellas. There's no other explanation. I messed up bad."

I was truly amazed. I stared at my uncle in awe, because I knew he was in love and that's the one thing I never thought would be possible for him. With all the shenanigans I saw and heard from him while growing up, I thought he would never settle down. But I guess I was wrong. Unfortunately, he just couldn't shake the ghosts of his past habits. "So that's how you got that bump on your head, huh?"

"Yeah, I'm mad as hell, but I guess I deserved it. Damn, I know I deserved it. Maybe you really can't teach an old dog new tricks."

I got up and put my hand on his shoulder. "Change takes time, that's all, Unc."

"Man, you guys falling in love, I just know the world is coming to an end. You guys don't even see all the trouble getting sprung is getting you into. Walking around all sad. That's not the way a man should be. We're the dominant factor. We break the hearts," Rex said.

"Rex, I guess you'll have to find out how it feels when it comes knocking at your door," I said.

"It's not coming because I'm not gonna let it in. Player for life, baby!"

I grinned, "I'm going in the kitchen to check on Ma." I left the room as Rex immediately began to lecture Uncle Jim about why it's so good to be single. My friend had so much to learn. I remember not long ago when Unc was giving us both those same types of lectures. I guess things change when you least expect it.

I walked into the kitchen and Ma was standing at the sink washing some collards. At this point, I didn't care what she was going to say. It had been so long since we had a chance to sit down and talk, the *'I told you so'* didn't even matter to me anymore.

"Hey, Ma," I cracked out of the back of my throat.

"Darrel," she calmly replied not looking at me.

I took a seat at the table, as my mind relived those days in my youth where I knew I did something wrong and awaited the punishment she was going to hand out to me.

"So how have you been, son?" she asked.

"Fine," I replied. It felt so good just to hear her ask me a question. I quickly thought, maybe it wasn't going to be so bad after all.

She grabbed a dish towel, dried her hands and turned around. Then, she looked at me with a straight face. "So where have you been?"

"Working, you know…the television station, and all."

"So, you work at the television station twenty-four hours a day now?"

"No mam, I..."

"Thirteen hours, Darrel," she interrupted. "It was precisely thirteen hours. For thirteen agonizing hours I pained in labor with you. Sweatin', hollerin' and calling out every four letter word the Lord will never hear come out of these lips again. And they trust to say a woman never remembers the pains of labor, but I certainly beg to differ, I'm telling you right here and now."

I gulped, knowing that the showdown was about get started and rowdy.

"I differed so much that after you called yourself popping up out of me, I knew, before my God Almighty, that you were gonna be the first and the last to ever come poppin' out. And never in my wildest dreams would I ever come to imagine that my *only* son would ever stray from his home for any reason."

"Ma," I replied, as I jumped up to get near her.

"*Sit down, boy!*"

Not being foolish, I planted myself back in that chair immediately.

Rex quickly ran in from the den. "Everything alright everybody? I heard screaming."

Momma looked up and closed her eyes. "Boy, I 'clare, the Lord knows you got about three good seconds to get out of my kitchen while I'm talking to my son or it's gonna be some serious trouble."

Rex immediately began to tremble. "I think I'ma go back in the den and finish talking to Uncle Jim."

"*Get out!*" she yelled.

Rex's feet almost left the rest of his body, he dashed out of there so quick. Momma then gazed at me with her eyes squinted and her mouth all balled up. She pointed her finger at me and waived it up and down. She was totally, totally pissed.

"I raised you Darrel Walker, not to be a whoremonger but a man. Not just any kind of man, but a man of God. And I don't know what point in your life that you decided to stray away from that, but you better get back on track. There's a broad way and there's a narrow way, Darrel Walker, and right now your tendencies are veering towards that broad way. So I suggest you check yourself, buckle up and find your way back to that path that's righteous and narrow, and do it with some haste."

"Ma, I know that I've been…"

"Shut up!"

My mouth zipped itself shut.

"And you know good and dern well, I don't want you to be laying down beside no hussies and on top of that, calling yourself marrying none of 'em. Me and your father, bless his soul, worked too hard at raising you for that."

"Momma, I…"

"Shut your mouth, Darrel Walker! I will let you know when you can say something. And right now, I don't want you to say nothing. And frankly, I don't want you to think nothin' either. And I know that should be easy for you to do because obviously you haven't been using that brain of yours for the past couple of months or else I wouldn't be in here now trying to set you straight." She took a deep breath and sat in the chair across from me. "All I've ever had for you were dreams, Darrel. Dreams of you making something out of yourself and doing what's right."

I felt like I was ten again. My mom never laid me over her knee when I was growing up because she never had to. All she ever had to do was sit me down and talk to me. The way she put her words together about whatever it was that I did wrong was more than enough punishment for me. Now my pop, that's another story. Just the thought of him and that infamous black belt brings chills down my spine to this day.

"What are you doing out there, messing around with all these different kinds of women, calling yourself getting married and ain't telling nobody? What are you doing with your life, son?"

"I don't know, Ma. I don't know." I looked down. "I know I was wrong for not telling you that I got married and not introducing you to my wife. But I guess I was scared. Scared of how you were gonna respond to it. I know Rex's big ole' mouth, and I know everything that gets to him, gets to his mother. And when it gets to his mother, there's no way it's not getting to you. So I knew that you knew I didn't know her for nothing but for a few weeks before I married her. I also knew you weren't having it and I tried to avoid coming over here as long as I could. But I was going to let you meet her one day, but then it all ended before I knew it."

She shook her head. "One night of passion can only lead to a lifetime of heartache."

"I know that's the truth," I blurted out.

"Darrel, just because you can do something, it doesn't mean you have to do it. Son, you need to learn how to control your emotions and stop acting off of impulse. Think before you delve into things. There's too much going on out there. I don't want you to be like your Uncle Jim, and have to worry about where you're gonna be able to rest your head the next night just because you can't commit to something or somebody."

"I know, Ma"

"Well you better act like it, boy." She reached across the table and grabbed my hand. "And I may not like all the decisions you make, son, but there ain't nothing in this world that you should feel you have to keep from me."

"But, Ma', I knew what you were gonna say."

"Then maybe you should've let me have the chance to say it," she replied as she squeezed my hand. "And maybe, Darrel, just maybe, things wouldn't have gotten this far."

I nodded my head. "But I'm a man now, Ma. I have to start making my own decisions. I can't sit down and consult my every move with you when things aren't clear. I'm a man, Ma."

"Darrel Walker, I would never deny the fact that you are a man, because you definitely are one," she smiled with a proud look on her face. "But you don't know everything in this world. You may think you know, but you don't know. All I can do is try to help you the best way I know how. So if that means checking you on something that I don't think is right, well that's my job as a mother. I love you, son. I'm just here to help you."

I smiled and jumped up. My stomach began to curl because hearing my mother say those words made me really feel good. I made my way around that table and tightly wrapped my arms around her soft, cushiony body. "I love you, too, Ma."

She pulled away and stared into my eyes. "Darrel, you're gonna find the right one, if you haven't met her already and turned her off by your childish games. But when you do find her, everything about the way you see women is gonna change."

"But it has, Ma," I walked to the fridge and grabbed some juice. "I don't wanna be a player no more. I want to find a good woman, settle down, and start a family with that same magic you and dad had.

"Is that what you thought you had with Miss Brandi?"

I paused for a moment, stunned by the fact that Ma knew her name.

"Well, is it Darrel?"

I poured the juice into the glass. "I don't know what I thought I had. I don't even know what I was thinking, Ma."

"You see, Darrel, if it was real love you would've known. Your father and I knew. Love is not difficult, but it can be tricky. Say, I knew your father for about three whole years at that factory, and I never batted an eye at him. He tried to approach me with his little smooth talking every now and then, but I wasn't paying it no mind. I suppose he didn't know that I knew he was dating that totally loose child named Francine, that just bounced her oversized booty all over that factory as if it were a basketball."

"Y'all had chicken heads back then, too?" I laughed.

"Where do you think the ones waltzing around here today come from?" She snapped, just a little ticked that I interrupted her again. "But anyway, she was all wrong for your father, with all that flirting and carrying on. But that's what your father thought he wanted at the time. And he really thought he had something, too," she blushed. "But there was this one night that it was raining something awful, and I was waiting outside of that building for your grandfather to pick me up. Everybody was finished getting off and your father was always the last one straggling behind at night. He walked out of the door and looked at me and asked *'Are you okay?'* Me, being the proud, yet feisty, young lady I was, blurted out *'I'm just fine!'* out of the back of my throat, knowing that in my three years of working at that plant, my father was never late picking me up. Something was surely wrong."

"You were trying to play hard to get," I added.

"Not hard to get, Darrel, hard-headed! I didn't want to see that it was fate's hand shoving us together. You see, I wasn't fond of Francine just because she was nasty and obnoxious. I didn't like her because she was nasty, obnoxious and she had your father. And he was a good man. And I didn't wanna take a ride from him because I didn't want to truly find out how good he was."

"Well thank the Lord you found out somehow, because if you hadn't, there wouldn't have been a me." I most certainly added.

Momma continued her story as her face told me that she wasn't in that kitchen with me anymore, but back on that rainy day she fell in love with Pop. My two-bit comment about getting conceived probably didn't even graze her eardrum.

"Fate wasn't gonna let me be bull-headed that night, Darrel. No it wasn't," she smiled. "Why, your father walked to his old beat-up Chevy and drove back to the front of the building, and jumped out of that car steadily getting soaked from head to toe. He just stood there staring at me. After a few moments of me looking up at the rain, trying to pretend he wasn't there, he finally yelled, *'Look, your father's never been this late since the three years you've been working here. Now, it's getting late and nobody else is in that building, so you can either let me take you home or make me stand out in this here rain so I can catch pneumonia and die tomorrow. But I'm gonna tell ya', it's gonna be all your fault if I die tonight from that pneumonia. 'Cause I'm not leaving until you get home safely!'* Why it was the sweetest and the dumbest thing I'd ever heard all at the same time. I didn't know if I was more surprised at him knowing how long I worked there or him talking about he was gonna stand in that rain and die later on, unless I let him take me home."

"So did you let him take you home, Ma?"

She blushed. "Not without him answering a few good questions, with my trifling self. I asked him, *'Where's Francine? Don't you take her home every night?'* And he said to my surprise with his deep voice *'We don't see each other no more. She started courtin' one of the supervisors. I guess I wasn't good enough for her.'* And son, what rolled out of my mouth after that was something that continues to shock me to this day. I don't even know how my lips even formed themselves to say it, but I looked at your father and said, *'You're definitely good enough for me.'"* she giggled.

"*Momma,*" I yelled, "I know you didn't."

"Child, you of all people should be glad I did."

"But it's so, so..."

"Human!" she interjected. "Darrel, I was young once too, you know. But I certainly knew what I wanted, and your father was definitely it. And I didn't have to shop all around and do all these taste tests to find out what I wanted. You gotta know what you want before you go into the store, Darrel, or you're gonna end up taking all kind of produce back home with you."

"What did he say when you told him that, anyway?"

"What could he say? He knew he wanted me all along. He just wasn't ready."

"So, Ma," I interjected, "How did you so elegantly figure out that Pop was ready for you?"

"Because he wouldn't leave me. Only a real man would assist a woman in distress with such persistence. Persistence is the absolute key to love, Darrel."

"Persistence? Now that's a pretty bold statement there, Ma." I said. The comment made me take a moment to think. It baffled me. I always thought being persistent was the wrong thing to be. The laidback approach was always my way of getting what I wanted. But then I took another second to think about all of the relationships I've been involved in with respect to the laidback approach and I realized not one of them resulted into anything. "So do you really think persistence is the key to love?"

"It's the key to everything, Darrel. Without persistence, how can you commit to anything? Persistence and commitment work hand and hand, son. Do you think if your Miss Brandi had to have stayed persistent in keeping your relationship together you would've found her in bed with another man?"

There was Brandi's name thrown all in my face again. Rex's mother gave her the full blow-by-blow no doubt. I had my mind set on ramming my foot completely up Rex's rear end for being such a tell all Momma's boy. "I don't know, Ma. I don't know why Brandi chose to get her freak on with that dude. I can't blame it on persistence because it could've been something I did."

She sucked her teeth, "The only thing you did wrong, Darrel, was marry that woman. You didn't even know her."

"So I guess we can't blame it on persistence, then."

"Don't think I can't smack you so hard that your teeth won't come flying out. Your smart tail mouth." She quickly pulled away from the table and headed for the sink. "Maybe if you were as persistent at finding a descent woman than you are at being hard-headed, you wouldn't have to get so offensive when I try to tell you wrong from right."

I jumped up and stood beside her. "Ma, I'm sorry. I don't know, maybe you're right. Maybe persistence is what I need. I just get so on edge when anyone mentions Brandi."

"For what, Darrel? She slept with another man in your own house, honey."

"But, Ma!"

"What, Darrel?" she said with her hands on her hip.

I knew I was about to say something bold, so I hesitated a bit, but I quickly decided to just let it loose. "What if you had caught Dad cheating on you? Would you had left him?"

She smiled and shook her head. I was certainly surprised that she didn't slap the taste out of my mouth for asking it.

"Son, you just can't let things go, can you?" She turned to the sink and began rinsing her collards again.

"It's not that I can't let things go. I just want to know what you would've done, that's all."

"What I would've done was told whomever he decided to make time with that they better get missing, and do it fast. Then I would've sat down and asked your father exactly what he wanted."

"That's it? You wouldn't have been so mad at him that you wouldn't have asked for a divorce?"

"For what?"

"For cheating on you, that's what."

"So he could leave me and go to the other woman? I don't think so, Darrel."

"But if he cheated on you, that means he didn't love you. What's the purpose of talking? There's no talking needed for that situation."

"Darrel, you have so much to learn, son. That's exactly what's wrong with this generation now. Every marital problem is always answered in divorce." She paused and shook her head. "If there had ever been a day that I caught your father in the act with someone else, we simply would've talked about it."

"Why? The relationship's over when that happens."

"No, it's not. If what you have is important to you, then one mistake wouldn't end it all."

"But that's a huge mistake, Ma." I replied. "Besides, you don't mistakenly just sleep with someone."

"But it all boils down to what's important to you," she said. "Just like with your Miss Brandi. If that relationship was worth a commitment before God to you two, y'all would still be together."

"Huh," I was confused. I loved my father, but if he had ever cheated on my mother, I wouldn't have blamed her one bit for leaving him. But here she was practically saying she would've talked it out and stayed with him.

"Darrel, when you find that person that you're

suppose to be with, everything I'm saying right now will make perfect sense to you. And you will quickly find out that a mistake in true love is worth forgiveness. It's all about persistence."

"Persistence," I softly replied under my breath. "Ma, I've never doubted you, but I'm gonna have to see about that one."

"You can see all you want," she pointed her finger. "But don't see too much, because too much seeing leads to a lack of doing. Don't watch Miss Right pass you by because of your own stupidity!"

I laughed, "I won't, Ma."

Suddenly we heard a harsh cracking sound from outside.

"What in the blazes?" said Ma.

"I don't know. It sounded like it came from the front yard," I replied. I tried my best to peek out of the window but the kitchen was angled to the side of the yard and not the front where the ruckus came from.

Mom grabbed a dish towel and dried her hands. "Oh Lord, let's go see what done happened out here."

She opened the backdoor, and I followed. We walked out onto the car porch and saw a middle-aged woman standing on the side of Uncle Jim's Firebird with a baseball bat.

"Who's that?" I asked.

Momma stood there with her mouth wide open, "Charlene!"

"*Jim, get your cheatin' ass out here, right now!*" The woman yelled. "*Jim!*" She smashed his trunk with the bat one good time.

"I gotta stop her," I said as I stepped forward.

Momma grabbed me by my arm. "That's Jim's business. You ain't got a thing to do with it."

"But she's messin' up his ride. I can't just standby and watch her do it."

"Jim is messing up his ride," she said firmly.

"*Woman, what in the hell are you doing?*" yelled Jim as he stormed through the front door with Rex. Rex stopped on the edge of the porch and looked at me with a small smirk on his face.

"*You wanna hurt me —now I'm hurting your sorry ass,*" screamed Charlene as she bashed out the passenger window with the bat.

"Woman, you better stop that shit," Jim demanded, pointing his finger at her. "What in the hell are you trying to prove? Stop this shit right now!"

"Why? *What the fuck are you gonna do?*" she yelled.

"Lord, somebody please put a muzzle on their mouths," Momma said to herself, looking towards the sky.

"Woman, you gonna make me stomp a mud-hole in your ass. You better put that damn bat down."

"*Fuck You!*" she yelled as she ran rampant on the car with the bat.

"Bitch!" he screamed as he squeezed the sides of his head with both hands, responding as if the bat was hitting him and not the automobile.

She stopped after a good thirty seconds of ransacking the vehicle and stared at him with a huge grin. "Now," she said gasping for air as she slammed the bat to the ground. "There you go, Jim—the real love your life. There she is, make love to her now, lover boy." Tears made their way rushing down her face.

Unc just stood on the side of his car and stared at it. He had no expression on his face whatsoever. He took a deep breath and turned to her. "You had enough?" he asked.

She wiped her eyes. "Maybe… Maybe not."

"Well, I've had enough," he said. "I've had enough of this shit. All this playing around I've been doing all my life. I'm sorry, Charlene."

My mouth just dropped as I looked to Rex, who was stunned, also. I never saw or heard of my Uncle hitting any woman before, but I thought for sure he was gonna jump on her for this crap. I was getting prepared to pull him off of her, too.

"What are you trying to say, Jim?"

"That I'm sorry for what I've done."

She shook her head. "Why'd you have to do it? Why'd you have to cheat on me, Jim?"

"Stupid as hell," he gasped. "Charlene, I was a fool and I'm sorry. Can you just forgive me and give me another chance? I can get another car, but I can't get another you."

"I can't *just* do anything, Jim. How can I trust you again, Jim? Tell me how?"

"If you think I'm worth trusting, just a little, that would be enough for me to make up for the rest. I don't wanna lose what I got."

She quickly snapped, "Well, did you think about that before you laid up with her, Jim? Did you think about how much I loved your sorry ass? Did you think about that, Jim? Huh?"

He bowed his head, looking as if he was gonna break completely down. "I didn't think about it until after I did what I did. I… I know I was wrong, and there ain't nothin' I can change to undo what I've done. But the feeling I feel right now by seeing how much I hurt you is something I don't ever wanna feel again. Baby, I love you, and I've never loved nobody else the way I love you." he paused. "I'm sorry, Charlene. I'm sorry."

She burst into tears as he rushed towards her and embraced her with a hug. "I'm sorry, baby." he said, as she hugged him back.

Momma just shook her head and made her way to the back door. "If people stop to think about the foolishness that they're 'bout to get into before they do it, they'd be a whole lot better off."

I glanced at Ma and then, continued to stare at my uncle and his wife as they hugged. I really didn't know what to make of it. Was Uncle Jim whipped or was it just love? Did persistence play a role in getting them to reconcile? I didn't have an answer and watching them sure wasn't gonna give it to me.

Rex approached me. "You get that?"

"I heard that they call it persistence," I replied.

"I would've called it an ass whoopin'. She tore that car up, and Unc hugging her. I know the world's coming to an end for sure now."

"Come on," I flagged him to follow me into the house, "Let's let them do their thing."

Chapter Four

The vibrant sounds of Tupac Shakur blasted through the airwaves as we made a stop in front of building four in Trinity Gardens, the apartment complex Rex's cousin, Devon, called home. No, I wasn't looking forward to seeing his face but a deal's a deal. Rex had held his part up and, unfortunately, it was time for me to do my half, and I hated it. I didn't feel like going to any club, and I certainly didn't want to be accompanied by that pain in the ass cousin of his.

"I wish this negro would come on here. It's already a quarter till' eleven," grunted Rex. "If the Hot Spot's not kicking, we need enough time to rock some other joint before all the big ballers come flashing all that ice and grabbing all the real dumb chicken heads."

I stared at him and smiled, "You never cease to amaze me."

"What?" he questioned. "Man, things are getting competitive these days. You gotta roll up with more than a Lex. All these so called rap stars and athletes hitting the club with their entourage of free loaders, taking twenty to thirty women back to their cribs at a time. It's getting tough for the average, hardworking brotha' like me."

"But you don't work," I corrected him.

"The game. The game, negro! It's a hardworking game." he shook his head. "Stop being so damn literal."

I looked up at the apartment that was supposed to be Devon's as the lights turned off. "I think he's coming."

"I wish he'd bring his ass on," said Rex as he began beeping his horn.

I quickly snapped at him, "Chill man, people do have to sleep at night."

"What?" he said reluctantly, as he stopped smacking the noisemaker. "Forget these losers. I'm trying to hit some skins tonight."

"Well, you keep on blowing that horn like you fool, you're gonna be in jail giving up some skins," I added.

"I'd like to see that go down."

I looked toward the apartments, and down the stairs and out of the shadows came Devon. Surprisingly, he was dressed neatly, with a dress shirt, slacks and a kango turned backwards–a huge improvement! This cat's original perspective on club fashion was some sagging jeans and an oversized jersey.

"What's up, fellas?" he said as he jogged to the car and jumped into the back.

"Nothing, what's going on, man?" I said as I gave him a brotherly pound with my knuckles.

"Chillin'," he said.

"Boy, I thought I told your ass to be ready by ten thirty," Rex fumed.

"Man, don't play me. You just got here. I saw you roll up all late."

"Nigga, the ride ain't never late. Only the occupants."

"Whatever," Devon brushed off the statement. "We gonna bag some bitches or what?"

Okay, and here he went, referring to women as bitches as usual. Just when I thought the brother had made a one-eighty. I guess you could clean the dog but not change his dirty habits. It was my job to check him before we stepped foot into the spot. "Hey, Devon, watch the bitch stuff around the ladies tonight, alright?"

"Yeah, don't be saying that crap around no chicks, man. I'm not trying to kick nobody's man's ass because of that garbage that comes out of your mouth."

"Man, whatever," he gasped. "As long as those broads don't start trippin' and shit, they won't get dealt with like that."

With that statement being said, I knew this night

was going to be a big mistake. Devon was one of those dudes that would sit there and say everything wrong to a lady and have the nerve to wonder why he can't get any play. He was one of those cats that walk in the mall and childishly hisses at a girl and when they look at him like he's stupid, he'll yell out 'bitch'. A dumb negro to the fullest.

"So, Darrel, I heard you was on lock for a half year with some dime piece model. I never thought I'd see the day your ass would get whipped," he giggled. "That stuff must've been some good."

I sighed and tried to compose myself from getting upset too quickly. This dude had a way of getting on my nerves real easy. "What can I say? I just got whipped, homey," I politely replied.

"Shit! To have you all locked up in the crib, not hitting the clubs no more, that must've been some platinum shit."

"Nigga, will you shut the hell up?" Rex shouted. It was a good thing, because he was about one more snide remark away from getting my size twelve shoved down his throat. "You think that man wanna talk to your non-pussy getting ass about his relationship?" Rex asked.

"Why I gotta be that? I bag plenty of skins. Y'all cats don't know."

"Yeah, nigga, your palms."

"Fuck you, Rex."

"Nigga, fuck you!" laughed Rex. "Mess around and get your ass waived outta my ride with all of that mouth."

"Whatever, man. I ain't even gonna go there with you," replied Devon, with his pride a little wrecked. He knew Rex would throw him out at the blink of an eye. It definitely happened before.

"Your punk ass better not go there. You can talk all that jazz to them marks in your hood, but you better not come at me with it."

I glanced at Devon out the corner of my eye and saw him frowning. He wanted to say something, but, unfortunately, he didn't feel like walking for the rest of the night. In genuine fashion, he got punked out!

Clubbin'. Probably one of the most exciting parts of a single man's life. The club is his battlefield. The club is his stomping ground. The club is his warehouse for more unsolicited booty that his one track mind could ever imagine. For a real player, the club is his domain. For a broken-hearted, divorcee trying to sort out his thoughts, clubbin' is like jumping into a shower and not knowing what the water temperature's set for. You know you're going in, but you're uncertain of how it's gonna feel when you do jump in.

Enter my return to what was once my favorite hangout, the Hot Spot. This joint used to be my stomping ground, my battlefield, and yes, my hub for more unsolicited booty than one could handle. But now I felt about as out of place as Jessie Jackson at a Klan rally. Rex had left me at a booth with Devon who was busily looking at every woman in the joint, pointing out any type of complaint as to why they didn't fit his criteria. And me, I nonchalantly listened as I felt as if I was doing something severely wrong just by being there. In the past, on my worst night in this joint, I could pull at least ten numbers and a guaranteed one night stand with any of the hottest chicks in the joint. But I wasn't feeling it. I felt more at ease just listening to Devon disguise his short comings by criticizing every women that walked by.

"Look at her," frowned Devon as he stared at a female passing by. "All that damn weave in her hair. Shit! Why women be doing that?"

"I don't even know," I replied.

"You see, I'm getting older now. I need an all

natural woman, Darrel. You know what I mean?"

"I feel you."

"I mean, I'm getting old. I just turned twenty-five years old today. I gotta get my stuff together. It's time for me to move out of my mom's crib and find me a good woman to move in with. It won't matter if she's white neither."

"You gotta go for it," I said, totally getting sick of hearing him complain.

"I mean, what's all the fuss about getting a sista' for, anyway?" he grunted. "All they want is money. I don't have no damn money. Shit, I ain't rich. That's all you hear from these chicks these days, '*What can you do for me?*' Hell nah, trick! What can you do for *me?*"

As he rambled on with his diluted comments about my precious black women, I wanted to break him down on the sista's behalf, despite my mishaps with Brandi. But then I took a good, hard look at him while he talked and thought to myself, ain't no sista' wanted his sorry ass anyway. They'd probably tell him to kiss their asses and keep on walking. So I decided not to even bother. I figured he'd end up talking that garbage to the wrong sista' one day, and they'd break his tail right down. So I'll save that moment for that sista'.

"Where's Rex at anyway?" he asked, surprisingly changing gears.

"He's probably making his rounds. You know Rex. He'll be back in a few."

"I wish he'd come on. Ain't nothing but a house full of skeezers in here tonight. I'd rather spend my birthday at the bowling alley, striking out."

"You're striking out just fine in here tonight," I mumbled.

"What's that?" he asked.

"I said you'll probably find you a little something in here tonight," I replied cleverly.

He looked around distastefully shaking his head. "Ain't nothing in here on my level."

I grinned, "That's the realest thing you've said all night."

"Right." At first he agreed, but paused for a moment to think about it, uncertain if what I said was a compliment or a blatant insult. He absolutely wasn't intelligent enough to figure out it was the latter.

"Oh Lord, here comes Rex with some fresh meat," I announced as Rex approached us with two fine, sparsely dressed females.

Devon quickly turned around. "Damn! Now they may just be my type."

"Fellas," said Rex with a smile from ear to ear and his arms around both ladies waists. "I would like you both to meet Amber and Nivea."

"Hi," Devon and I said simultaneously.

"Amber and Nivea, meet my main man Darrel and my cousin Devon."

"Hi guys," they both replied concurrently.

"Ladies, have a seat," Rex smoothly instructed the women.

Devon scooted next to me as the girls entered the booth. Rex sat on the end, next to the one named Amber.

"Now, we're all one big happy family," smiled Rex as he winked at me.

"Where you ladies from?" asked Devon. He attempted to deepen his voice in efforts to sound a little sexier, I guessed. It sounded a little cheesy, though.

"We're from Charleston, South Carolina," said Nivea. She seemed to be the more vocal one. The one named Amber was much sexier, but she kept giggling for no reason.

"Darrel, I was talking to the ladies, and they told me that this was their first night in the ATL," said Rex in an attempt to get me started. It would've worked in the past, but he needed to come off with something a little better than that if he wanted to get me going. I was too content with my loneliness and neither one of the girls were my type.

"You ladies shouldn't be spending your first night in the ATL all by yourselves. You girls can kick it with us tonight," Devon offered. The guy was definitely turning it up a notch. Apparently, he did learn a little something from Rex during my absence.

"Oh, we're not staying by ourselves," Amber said, valiantly trying to hide her heavy geechee accent. "We're staying with some friends while we search for a place to stay."

"I gotta place you broads can stay," Devon mumbled in my ear.

"What was that?" Amber asked, with a hint of an attitude towards Devon.

"He said, it shouldn't have to be that way," I rapidly interjected. "You know, women of your stature should have no problems finding a place to live."

"Oh," she rolled her eyes at Devon.

I didn't think she bought it, and it was quickly becoming apparent Devon's true colors were getting ready to show.

"Who the fuck are you rolling your eyes at?" Devon questioned.

"Excuse me? Who in the hell do you think you're talking to like that?" Nivea quickly jumped in.

"Ladies, never mind my cousin…" Rex tried to intervene, but we both knew too well that the damage had already been done. Devon struck, quicker than ever.

"I'm talking to your girl with the eye problem, and you too, *bitch*, if you gotta problem," Devon chuckled.

"What did you call me?" Nivea yelled.

"Okay," yelled Rex.

"A bitch! *Bitch!*"

Nivea frowned and shook her head. "That's what I thought you said." She turned to Rex. "Move, please."

"Yeah, girl let's go," said Amber.

Rex stood up as the ladies made their way out of the booth. I could only shake my head because I knew Devon and the opposite sex in the same place at the same time was only an accident waiting to happen.

Nivea turned to Devon. "I hope we see your faggot ass in Chuck-town one day," she said as she picked up a glass of beer and splashed it in his face. "Then we'll really see who the real bitch is–bitch!"

"You stupid…" said Devon as he wiped his face. I quickly held him back, as the ladies dashed away. "You see this shit?"

I looked over to Rex, who was boiling mad. "You just had to fuck that up, didn't you?" asked Rex.

"What? You saw what that crazy broad just did," Devon argued.

"Right after you just called those girls something we specifically told you not to. Boy, if I wanted to get locked up in here tonight, I would whip the black off your ass for the shit you just did."

"What I do wrong?" asked Devon.

"Everything!" screamed Rex. "You know what, I want your ass to sit here for the rest of the night until we get ready to go. And you better hope those girls don't bring some dudes back to wipe the floor with your ass because I'm gonna watch them do it. And I may even give them a hand. Do you understand me, bitch?"

"Bitch!"

"That's what I said. Do you have a problem with that?"

Devon shook his head. "Man, why you wanna play me like that?"

"Play you? Nigga, I'll…" he said moving towards Devon. I jumped up and pulled Rex out of the booth.

"Boy, you better be glad you're family."

"Come on here, Rex." I pulled him over to the bar.

"His stupid ass," said Rex. "He's always on that stupid shit."

"Man, I hate to say it, but I told you so."

"I was foolish for thinking I could take that knucklehead somewhere."

I laughed, "We all need to take time to evaluate our judgment sometimes."

We grabbed two stools at the bar.

"Man, those chicks were fine, too," he stated painfully. He wanted to get those females in his bed so bad he could taste it. Unfortunately for him, Devon messed that all up.

"Yeah, well, you can't win 'em all."

"You're acting as if I lost a softball game."

"No, they just weren't worth fighting family over," I added. "Relationships come and go. Family is there always."

"Well, why did mine have to be so damn stupid?"

"The cat has your same genes in him."

"He don't have any of my genes," he advised me, still shaking his head about the situation. "Those chicks were easy, too. And that one named Amber was so damn thick. I would've been tapping that all night."

"Well, you can't cry over spilled milk."

"Yeah, you're right. She probably couldn't hang with it anyway." He turned to the bartender. "Beer, light ice, please."

"I mean, I hate to say I told you so again. But I told you so. He's just not ready to interact with mature women."

"He's not ready to deal with any type of women."

"He'll grow out of it one day."

"He's so damn stupid, though."

"Once again, he's your flesh and blood."

"Don't remind me," he chuckled. "Darrel."

"What?"

"You got a honey staring the black off of you."

"Say what?" I turned to my side and saw a short, light-skinned diva with a Halle Berry cut. She gave me a little smile as I quickly turned my head to Rex.

"She's fine. Go talk to her."

"She's not my type."

"She was before you met Brandi. You used to love those chicks with them short hair styles. Now you're acting brand new. I think you're scared."

"I'm not scared," I looked towards the woman again and she gave me a little wave.

"Look at her, skins on a platter. She's begging for it. You're scared," he said, attempting to egg me on.

"No, I'm not. I'm just not ready for all of this."

"Boy, did you get whipped or what? I used to look up to you. Now I'm beginning to look away."

"I'm scarred, man. I don't want to rush into anything."

"Oh my God, you sound like a genuine chump, talking about you don't wanna rush into anything. Man, what's wrong with you? What is it gonna take to get you from acting like this?"

"I don't know, Rex. I just need some time. I'm just not about all of this right now."

"How about Brandi Brown?"

"What?"

"Brandi Brown," he said as he pointed towards the back of the club to the dance floor.

"Brandi..." I said as I spotted her dancing with this tall, bald, dark-skinned guy. The sight was so unexpected, it hit me like a Greyhound bus.

"I guess she's not scarred. Do you think?" Rex asked jokingly.

She was having a ball with her booty all backed up

into his crouch. And I'm not a hater, but he looked like such a flake as he did the infamous two-step around the booty swinging his hands in the air like he was really doing something. I turned away and looked at Rex. I simply couldn't stand the sight of her with someone else.

"It's your turn to play hardball, baby boy," Rex said, "Or are you too scared to get into the lineup?"

"I ain't scared, and I'm not getting played for a fool anymore either."

"Well congratulations! Now all you have to do is prove it."

I looked over to the girl sitting at the end of the bar. By this time she was looking bored, playing with the rim of her glass of wine with her finger. Determined to let my ex know that I was doing just fine all by my lonesome, I decided to make my move. "Be careful about what you wish for, Rex. You might just get it."

"Go do your thing, playboy," Rex said as I made my way to my damsel in distress.

I walked to her and sat on the stool beside her. "Hi," I said.

"Hi," she replied.

"Do you mind some company?" I asked, my eyes secretly observing her body as a whole. She was quite cute. In the back of my mind, I was hoping Brandi would catch a glimpse of me doing my thing once again.

"No, I don't mind your company. I was actually hoping that you would come over."

"You did?" I asked, not trying to seem too surprised.

"Yeah," she grinned. "I was checking you out, and I must admit, I liked what I saw."

"Oh, you did?"

"Yeah. You are about the only guy up in here not trying to holla' at everything with a pulse. I like that."

"Thanks. I just came out here to have a good time

with my boys, that's all. I'm not out here for the hunt."

"That's good," she smirked. "Sometimes it feels good to just get hunted. What do you think?"

Her statement caught me off guard. It was a long time since a women came on to me. And she made no qualms about it. I could tell she knew exactly what she wanted. "My name's Darrel Walker," I said as I extended my hand to her.

She gently shook it. "Hi, Darrel, my name's Natasha. Natasha Stanley."

"It's a pleasure to meet you, Natasha."

"Likewise" she said as she simply held onto my hand with her light brown eyes locked onto mine. "So do you come out here often, Darrel?"

"No, but if I knew there were ladies out here of your essence, I wouldn't miss a night." Suddenly, no one else in the room mattered, not even my ex. I was in that level of consciousness that folks like Michael Jordan would call the zone. "You have some very beautiful eyes, Natasha Stanley."

"Thank you. I'm glad you find them beautiful. It's not every day that a girl gets a compliment."

"Well, obviously you've never spent a day in my presence. Anything less than a compliment per minute would simply be impertinent."

She chuckled. "You are just too smooth, aren't you?"

"Not smooth, sweetheart–honest." This was all too easy. She was eating up my lines like they were going out of style.

"Well, Mr. Honesty, since you're so big on telling the truth, where's your lady? I know that a man as handsome and charming as you has to have somebody."

Immediately Brandi's name flashed through my mind. Then the cold, hard truth of her infidelity quickly followed. So I decided to make light of the situation. "She left me for a refugee."

"Well, if that's true, she's a very, very, silly woman."

I glanced towards the dance floor and didn't see Brandi. "I couldn't agree with you more."

"So I guess that means you're on the open market."

"Hopefully, not for long," I replied.

"I hope not either," she replied. "I don't believe in letting a good thing pass me by."

"That's funny because I don't believe in getting passed by."

"Well I guess we have something in common."

I moved in close, and smiled. The sparks were flying heavy. "Hopefully, we'll have a lot more."

"I'm quite sure we will."

"I'm more than looking forward to it."

"Listen, I need to go to the ladies room. Will you make sure that you keep my spot for me, Mr. Honesty?"

"It's as good as kept."

"I'll be back," she promised. "Please don't disappear on me."

"Oh, I won't. I'll definitely be waiting," I replied.

She pranced to the restroom as I eagerly stared at her perfectly curved rump through the crowd of club-goers. She was straight–damn straight! For a moment I felt like my old self again. I was still upset that Brandi was in the joint having what seemed to be the time of her life. I was determined to have a very good time myself, although the situation as a whole had me feeling uneasy. Brandi was the only real commitment I ever had. Only to her was I true. I didn't dog her out like I did the other ladies in my past. And with me putting game to another female after being married for a few months was placing a strain on my conscience. For what, I had no clue. My wife dogged me out and then left me. I couldn't help but wonder if these were the same kind of strains I had put on the women I had dated and played in the past. I know one thing for sure–it doesn't feel very good.

Suddenly, I felt a tap on my shoulder. "Darrel!"

I turned around, and to my surprise it was Veronica. "Veronica…"

"Darrel, I'm sorry about earlier today. Come here," she said as she wrapped her arms around my back and gave me a hug.

"Well, this is different." I said.

"I know," she replied. "I was just so stressed out today. I'm sorry. I had a lot on my mind. You know you're my boy."

"I thought you forgot. You were so cold to a brother today. And then you threw all that stuff at me about how I used to be."

"I apologize, Darrel. Today just wasn't a good day for a sista'."

I looked at her and smiled, knowing there was no way I could stay mad at her for too long. She was my girl, and we went way back. "I'll forgive you this time."

"Thanks, boo," she said as she pinched my checks. "You still got those cute cheeks, Darrel Walker."

I grinned, "And you still like pinching them like you're an old lady or something."

"Because they're so cute."

"Speaking of cute, girl, do you realize how good you look up in here tonight?"

She blushed, "Well a sista' was trying, you know."

"So what brings you out to the club, tonight? I know good and well this is not your steelo."

"And you know me well, too," she said as she took the stool beside me. "I'm out here with a girlfriend. Her and her man just broke up, now she's out here tearing the floor up."

"I guess it wasn't that serious."

"No, it was serious. They were engaged. She

I nodded. "You're absolutely correct. It is time to make new friends. Do you wanna be my new friend?" I slid my arm around her back and gently pulled her into me.

"Of course I do, Mr. Honesty."

I took a quick glance to the back of the club and didn't see my ex-wife nor Veronica. I didn't even care anymore. It was time for me to go back to my roots. To hell with being the good, honest guy. It was time for me to look out for self again, and Ms. Natasha Stanley was going to be just the one to help me do it.

"Would you mind if I bought you something to drink?" I asked.

"Not at all," she replied.

"Good. That's real good. I'm really looking forward to getting to know you better, Ms. Stanley."

"It's definitely the same here, Mr. Walker."

"I like that," I laughed. "I like it a lot."

Chapter Five

There's nothing like coming into work on a Monday after you've had a blast of a weekend. Sure, my weekend wasn't the greatest of all time, but it sure was better than the ones I had been having for the past six months. I strolled into my job with a light step and my nose in the sky, feeling like the doctor was finally in. I ended Saturday night by leading Natasha to believe that I was going to call her the following night, and that certainly wasn't the case. Sure, I was definitely interested in the woman, but I've learned from so many experiences in the past to never let a woman know that you're desperate or weak for her company. With most of the women that I've encountered, if they ever discovered that they had you sprung, they'd get the tendency to think that they could call all the shots, and I was always too damn selfish for that. It was certainly all about me, and no one else. I would do my best to make them think it was about them in the bedroom, but I would never show my weaker side for love that all men possess outside of it. At least not until I met Brandi, and that's when she became my prime example for me to keep my real feelings on the inside.

But indeed, I had my sights set on Natasha and her wonderfully, tight physique. I still didn't know where her mind-set was, but my interests really didn't lie with her brain–it was more her body. On top of that, it had been a while for a brother. And as wild as my ex was, I just knew she was giving the skins up like government cheese. So it was finally time for me to hand out some government cheese of my own.

I approached my desk and noticed there was a memo there left by my boss, Perry Putnam. He wanted to see me as soon as I got in. I made way to his office, dreading the thought of sitting through another one of his 'I could've done' speeches. He used to work for a major broadcasting company in New York a few years back. He let alcohol and his obsession for doing the interns get the best of him, and his ass got canned. Now he's down here in Atlanta, trying to make a dollar out of fifteen cents with APA. His dream is to make Atlanta Public Access the premier station to watch in the city, even though we're just a public access network with overly-cluttered children's and instructional programming. He wants it to be public access with a twist–as he puts it 'the twist of entertainment'. I can't say that he hasn't made his strides, even though his no holds barred documentary, 'The Legend of the Freak-nik', almost got him canned again. The uproar it caused with the parents in the local community who discovered the freakier side of their youngsters was a bit overwhelming for their eyes to see. But it sure as hell was fun doing the shooting on that bit. It was simply, all good.

I gave his office door a light knock, "Perry…"

"Come on in, Darrel," he requested.

I walked in and he greeted me with a handshake, "What's going on, my man? Have a seat."

"Nothing new. I just got in," I said as I sat down.

"How was your weekend? Did you lay any of that pimp juice on the ladies?" he asked.

"No, no pimp juice this weekend," I replied with a phony chuckle. There was one other thing about Perry Putnam—he swore on his life that he was a brother. And to be quite honest, if it wasn't for his pale, white skin, I would swear he was at times.

"Well, you know I laid my mac down at this little social Bob James had this weekend. But he had too many old white women out there with no asses. And Darrel, you know that I'm an ass man. And I just love…"

"Mr. Putnam, you wanted to see me about something. I have to jump on logging that teacher of the year footage." He was cool, but the last thing I wanted to hear was a white man talking about asses. I don't care how black he thought he was.

"Oh yeah, my bad. I called you in here for a story."

"A story?" It was music to my ears. It had been a minute since a brotha' actually had a chance to go out into the field for some actual shooting.

"Yes, my man, I got a story for you."

"Well, what is it?" I asked anxiously.

"TGIF!"

"TGIF?"

"Thank God it's Friday, as in Terrance Friday."

"Terrance Friday? What's he got to do with anything?"

"What's he got to do with anything?" Putnam sighed, "Why he's about to make the biggest announcement since the first Michael Jordan comeback."

"What, he's getting tested for HIV?"

"No, Darrel. I don't know what that has to do with anything."

"Long story!" I added, thinking about my infamous alum, Friday, and our college days.

"Don't you watch Sports Center at night, Walker?"

"Not a real big sports fan, Perry."

"Well, Terrance Friday, Atlanta's very own, will announce in the very near future who he's going to sign with. And I have a personal contact that's telling me he's going to play for LA, and I don't mean the Clippers."

"Okay," I replied, totally unenthused.

"Okay? Is that all you can say? I thought you would be thrilled."

"Well, I guess I would be if that was a story for us to handle. We're APA, Atlanta Public Access, we handle stuff like Sesame Street and Mr. Rogers."

"Walker, think outside of the box for a change. The key word in APA, is Atlanta. That's right baby! It's

Atlanta. And as long as Terrance 'TGIF' Friday is a
natural born native of this city, then he's an APA story. So
I want my best Production Assistant to team up with my
best Production Manager, and I want you guys to bring the
full scoop to the small screen as it comes out."

"You're best production manager..." I said, totally
fired up because I knew who that was.

"That's right, you and Dale Summers. Back
together again, just like Jack and Jill."

I rolled my eyes, as I tried to keep my anger to
myself. The TGIF story was okay, but working with Dale
was pushing it. I hated working with that jerk. All he ever
does is talk about what he does and what he can do. "Well,
that's just great."

"Darrel, you don't have to seem so excited," he
stated, trying to be sarcastic. He knew I didn't like
Summers just as much as he didn't. "But you do this for
me, with those fresh camera skills you possess, and the
only way you can go is up. I got my eye on you. You
know that you're my main man."

"That's real flattering, Perry."

"It's more than flattering. It's the truth. Now I
don't know if Summers is in yet, but you guys need to go
ahead and get together on what you're going to do for this
story. Friday is expected to announce his signing two
weeks from today, so time is of the essence. I'm putting
my faith in you to making this project phenomenal for our
network, Darrel."

"I will do my best," I said as I jumped up and
headed for the door.

"And that's all you've ever given me, Darrel.
Peace out, now."

I walked out of the office wanting to tell him
exactly what piece of my rear end he could kiss. Doing a
story on that jerk, Friday, was one thing, but pairing me up
with Dale Summers was another.

"Darrel!" called a voice. I turned my head and it was Dale. It's funny how you could just think up people you really don't want to be around.

"You just got finished talking with Putnam, huh?" he asked as he approached me.

"Sure did," I said as I made my way down the hall. He followed, no doubt.

"So what do you think?"

"About what?"

"The story," he answered. "Putnam's really doing it this time. He's gonna make the APA a heavy hitter with the big boys. And it's all in our hands."

"Whoop de doo!"

"You don't sound excited."

"Why should I be, Summers? The last time we got paired together on a special project, you found yourself missing, leaving me with a van to load in the midst of a bunch of screaming college students."

"And you didn't get you some out there at the Freaknik?"

"Well, not when we were supposed to be wrapping things up."

"Come on, Darrel, you're so uptight man. I was only getting me, and you of all people should be able to respect that."

"And why's that?"

"Come on, Walker, everybody knows your track record with the ladies. You're like Wilt Chamberlain Jr. around here. Well, at least until you got hitched a few months ago. And then you started acting like a real square."

I stopped in my tracks. "A square?"

"Yeah, a square."

"Summers, what does any of my personal business have to do with this job? I mean, is it anyone's business what I do on the home front?"

"No, but…"

"But what, Summers? I really wanna hear it."

"You weren't keeping anything much of a secret until you got hitched, that's all I'm saying. You slung your ding-a-ling around here like a Louisville Slugger," he chuckled. "None of this would even be an issue if you never met that chick that turned you out."

"Turned me out!" I looked around to make sure no one was coming. I stepped a little closer to him. "Did you just say that I got turned out? Summers, have you ever had a foot rammed so far up your ass that you literally felt like you could cough up toenails?"

His arrogant smirk surfaced upon his face. "No I haven't. And I'm quite sure as long as I'm the head production manager, and you just being a production assistant, I won't ever have to know."

"Well, if I should ever quit, I guess that would open the doors of opportunity for you. I mean it's not that hard to find a PA spot in this city, know what I mean?" I gave him a demented smile. I could tell by his worried expression that he felt threatened, and that's exactly what I wanted.

"You don't like me very much, do you, Walker?"

"Now what would ever give you that idea, Summers?"

"I'm gonna call Clearwater High to get some footage from some of Friday's high school games. I'll stop by your cube later, and we'll go over what I obtain."

"You do that."

He turned away and began to walk back down the hall. "It really doesn't have to be this way, Walker. We're just alike in some ways." He said as he continued trekking.

Whatever, I thought to myself. The only thing we had in common was that our paychecks were signed by the same man. And that was too much for me. I've always thought of myself as more of a lover than a fighter, but people like Summers make you put your foot down, while yearning to ram it elsewhere. The nerve of him telling me I got turned out. I might've been whipped, but never turned out.

"Someone certainly hit the sweet spot this weekend," said Ruth, the front desk secretary as she walked towards me with a bouquet of roses. "These are for you, Darrel."

"For me?" I asked as she handed me the flowers. "Who left them?"

"Don't know. A delivery guy just dropped 'em by. There's a card with it, though." She started walking back down the hall.

I opened the card, and it read 'On my mind constantly.' I smiled. Natasha certainly meant business, but I didn't take her for the flower-sending type. No, men aren't generally into flowers, but when they're received, it's quite flattering.

I strolled to my cubicle and dialed Natasha immediately. My goal was to get something set up for later so I could show her how much I appreciated the flowers. That was the least I could do.

"Hello," she answered.

"What's up, sweetheart?"

"Darrel?" I could hear her smile through the phone. "How are you?"

"I'm just fine. Did you have a good rest last night?"

"It would've been better if I had gotten a call from somebody."

"I'm sorry, my dear. I got all tied up at my mother's house yesterday until late, and I decided to just knock off there." Just a little white lie. Lord please forgive me.

"That's all good, but how are you gonna make up for it?"

She definitely knew what she wanted.

"Well, I was thinking about us going out to dinner tonight."

"Where to?" she asked.

"Any place your heart desires," I advised her. "But I was thinking about surprising you."

"That's cool. I like surprises."

"Well, I'm certainly not the one to disappoint you."

"Do you remember the directions to my place?"

"Of course I do." It's always been my number one rule to never lose directions.

"So when should I expect you?"

"I'd say around seven. I'll be there at seven."

"Okay, then seven it is."

"Alright, I'll see you then."

"Darrel," she uttered, catching me before I hung up.

"Yes."

"Don't keep me waiting. I don't think I could stand it."

"Like I stated earlier, sweetheart, I'm not the one to disappoint you."

"Good. I'll see you tonight, boo."

"See you later." I hung up the phone, smiling from ear to ear. I definitely had my swagger back. Once again, it was on, just like old times.

I pulled into Natasha's driveway around six thirty. Yeah, I told her seven, but I've always believed in showing up a little early. It was my way of letting the woman know that I really anticipated spending some time with her. I knocked on the door, and a tall, skinny, light-skinned guy with corn-rolls answered. He was wearing a white tee-shirt and some sagging blue-jeans that were damn near hanging off his behind while twisting one of the corn-rolls above his ear.

"What's up, dawg?" he asked with his mouth full of gold teeth gleaming. "You here to pick up Tasha?"

"Yeah. The name's Darrel."

"That's cool, D. Come on in," he said as he widened the entrance to let me in. "Have a seat in the living room."

I walked into the den and grabbed a spot on the sofa. It was a pretty descent sized two story house that was very well kept. I could pretty much guarantee Old Dawg at the door didn't have anything to do with keeping it neat.

"Tasha," he yelled up the stairs, "Dude down here waiting on you."

"Tell 'em I'll just be a few minutes," she yelled from upstairs, no doubt getting ready for our evening.

He chuckled while making his way into the den. He sunk into the chair across from me. "You know them females—always keeping a nigga waiting."

I put on a fake smile as I looked towards the television. This cat was watching a Yogi Bear cartoon. He looked towards the television.

"That damn Yogi Bear. His ass is always trying to get out of that damn park, just like niggas trying to get outta the hood."

"Yeah, he's always about getting out of that park."

"Shoot, my bad, man, the name's Chester," he said as he got up and gave me a handshake.

"Nice to meet you, man," I replied.

"You too. Shoot, you probably looking at me like, look at this grown ass nigga looking at cartoons. But I watch 'em, though. The damn news is so trifling these days—everybody killing everybody and shit. I just watch the cartoons to calm my nerves."

Oh Lord, not another I know life, but I ain't doing nothing with my own life jitty-bug. I glanced at my watch, thinking my early arrival had backfired on me in the worst way. I was gonna have to listen to this guy and his recollections of a thug life gone wrong. "Yeah, I know what you mean, Chester."

"Call me C-Dawg. All my niggas do."

"Alright... C-Dawg."

"Yeah," he smiled as if he accomplished something. I realized quickly his elevator didn't go all the way to the top. "But on the real, man, it's hard out there right now."

"I hear ya'," I replied, knowing undoubtedly my plan had backfired. Rampant thoughts about Natasha's mind-set began to surface. Hopefully they were just adopted.

"A nigga like me, trying to get a job at the post office. They ain't gonna hire my black ass. And just because I got corn-rolls in my head. But all the white man gotta do is splash a little water on his head with a white tee-shirt, slacks, and flip-flops, and he got the job."

"So I take it you didn't get the job at the post office."

"Nah. I didn't apply. I know them herbs ain't gonna hire me, so why even bother? I got another month of unemployment, shoot. I ain't in no rush for the man to be telling me what to do anyway. Know what I mean?"

"I hear ya."

"It's fucked up, D."

"I know," I replied, wishing this negro would just shut up.

"On my last job, my fat ass manager tried to say I was stealing steaks. Now, what the fuck do I look like stealing steaks?"

"Don't know."

"I ain't steal no steaks. Now the shrimps on the other hand, I probably lifted a few of them, but not no steaks. He called himself firing me because of some steaks. Talking about he know I stole 'em. He ain't know shit!"

"That's messed up... C-Dawg."

"It's alright. I got my unemployment now. I'll be looking for something else soon. I just hope that shit don't mess me up, though. Know what I mean?"

"I hear ya'."

"And if I ever see that punk on the street, I'm gonna bring it to him. You feel me?"

"I feel ya'." I looked impatiently at my watch. I was on the verge of just outright telling him to just shut the hell up.

"So what you do, D?"

"I work at Atlanta Public Access."

"The educational channel?"

"That's me."

"Bullshit," he laughed. "They hiring at that muthafucka, dawg?"

I quickly shook my head, "No, no, not right now. They have a hiring freeze."

"Yeah, it's probably hard to get a gig up in there." He began scratching his head. "Shoot, I remember that time they had that freak-nik joint playing. That shit was hot. I was shocked as hell when they played that joint."

"Well, we try to be different."

"Different! That joint was off the chain. That show turned my whole life around. I saw my ex-baby momma on that joint acting a damn fool."

"Ex-baby momma?"

"Oh yeah, she tried to say her little rug-rat was mine, but I got a DBA test."

"DNA?"

"Yeah, DBA. That's it. But the kid wasn't mine. It was this dude's named Calvin she had on the backburner. It was all good though, 'cause a brother wasn't trying to feel no child support. Feel me?"

"I feel ya."

"Okay, I'm ready," said Natasha as she jumped in from nowhere.

Thank God. "You didn't have to rush," I told her, totally lying. "I was getting to know your brother a little bit."

She shook her head and rolled her eyes. "He's not talking about nothing."

"Ah, why you wanna say that Tasha? Me and D was having a good conversation."

"Whatever," she said as she gave him the hand. "I'm quite sure Darrel could find a more interesting conversation with a parking meter. Come on, boo."

I jumped up and gave her brother a quick handshake. "Nice meeting you, Chester."

"C-Dawg, D. My niggas call me C-Dawg."

"Boy, shut up," said Natasha as she grabbed me by my hand and pulled me out of the house.

"Y'all have a good time," chuckled Chester, as he stood at the door behind us. "Don't keep her out too long, D."

"Boy, shut up," she replied, not looking back.

For a moment, I thought I was never getting out of that house with that nut. My attention quickly swayed to my date as I stared at her from behind as she wore this nice looking blue jean outfit that exposed her well rounded rump.

"Dag girl, you're looking good tonight."

She stopped walking and turned around blushing. "You're looking pretty straight yourself."

"Thanks," I replied as I walked around her and opened the passenger door for her. "Get yourself on up in this ride so I can show you off."

"Thanks," she replied.

I shut the door, ran to other side and jumped in. I wanted to get the party started pretty quickly so we could make time for some bonus activities if I could work things out right. When I jumped in, she was staring at me. "What is it?"

She grinned, "What if I told you I didn't really wanna go out tonight?"

"Well, I wouldn't be mad or anything. We could put something together for some other time."

"Uh-uh," she said as she placed her hand behind my neck and began gently caressing it. "I'm not talking about not going out period. I'm talking about maybe picking up a movie from Blockbuster and kickin' it at your place."

My hormones quickly upgraded to a code orange. "Shoot, we could do that."

"Really? That would be straight, for real."

"I don't have any problem with that at all."

"Maybe we could pick up Titanic. I love that movie."

The movie sucked, but it was long and boring and every man knows there's nothing like a boring, date movie. "That sounds good. That's one of my favorites."

"Really? I never met a guy that admitted they liked that movie."

And your search continues. "Yeah, I don't broadcast it or anything, but it's really one of my favorites." Okay, I know I need double forgiveness for that lie, but I was always about saying and doing whatever it took to get from point-a to point-b. And point-b was getting her out of them clothes and underneath my sheets.

"Well, can we do that?"

"Sure can." I agreed as I started my engine and began a night that was surely going to be tight.

We stopped by the video store on the way to my crib and picked up Titanic and some popcorn. I was a little nervous about taking her to my crib because it had been a while since the opposite sex had been there. My spot was cleaned up and everything because I anticipated her company for the night, but I was still nervous. To a lot of woman, how a single man's place looked determines how far the relationship goes. It could determine if she's gonna stay the night and get her freak-on with you, or make her beat around the bush for an hour or so and come up with an excuse to get the hell out of dodge. While I wasn't looking for anything serious with Natasha, how my place looked had always been one of my primary tools. I've seen many of my boys in the past get everywhere with a woman but to the promised land simply because they took their dates home and their cribs looked like Oscar from Sesame Street resided there.

We walked into my house, and I flicked on the lights. She looked all around and a huge smile spurred onto her face.

"This is nice, Darrel."

"Thank you," I said, absolutely pleased she liked it. Only time would tell if she was truly comfortable.

She made her way to my den and browsed around my entertainment system. "This is really nice."

"Well, I try to keep it right in the crib." I eased up behind her.

"I'm impressed."

She waltzed to the sofa and planted herself a seat as I placed the movie into the DVD player. I looked at her. "So do you want me to pop up the popcorn?"

"Nah," she said shaking her head. "I want you to come over here and sit beside me," she said patting a spot on the sofa beside her.

I walked over, gently taking my offered space. "So what's up?"

She smiled, "You tell me."

"Nothing. I'm just trying to be a good host."

"I couldn't imagine a better host than you, Darrel."

"Thanks."

"You're house is so wonderful. I just can't wait to get out on my own and get my place right."

"No need to rush. Stay home as long as you can because bills can get aggravating."

"Oh, Darrel, I know. But I'm twenty-two now, and I can't stand living with my mother and my big head brother. I thought I would be so much further than where I am right now."

"Well, things will come in time."

"I don't know, Darrel. You're talking to a big spender here. As soon as I get my check, I'm blowing it on some new clothes or getting my hair done."

"Well then, you know what you have to do. Prioritize. Believe me, it takes time getting it right because my money use to burn a whole in my pocket when I got it. But my mom, she used to always tell me to save, and separate your needs from your wants. She told me that everything you want, you don't need, and everything you need you don't want. At first it confused me, but I think that was what she intended on doing because it made me just a little more cautious on my buying. Then eventually, I found myself being a lot more selective, with a little more money than normal in my pockets."

"That's some good advice. I would like to meet your mother one day."

She totally caught me off guard with that comment. My mind went haywire as I questioned myself, is this the one you want to take home to momma? She was attractive, but my mother would most certainly go deeper than looks. Then a cold chill rushed down my spine as I had a more shocking revelation. Was the reason I never took Brandi around my mother was because I knew my mother would know that Brandi wasn't the woman for me?

"What do you think about that?"

"Huh?" I uttered.

"Meeting your mother. When do you think I would be able to meet her?"

"Uh… one day. I'll take you to meet her one day."

I pretty much knew the likelihood of that visit would be nil.

"Good, because I want to get to know all about you." She slid her arm around my waist, and laid her head against my chest.

I don't know what it was, but something just didn't feel right about it. It seemed to me that she wanted to know too much, too fast. So I decided to try and draw the attention away from the future and more into the moment. "Well, I'm not nobody special. Just the average Joe trying to make a living. But you on the other hand, you have got to be a princess because you're the most attractive woman I've ever laid eyes on."

She looked up at me. "You always know what to say." She gave me a little kiss.

"What was that for?"

"No reason. I just felt like doing it."

"Really? Do you feel like doing anything else?"

She grinned, "I thought we were suppose to be watching the movie."

"The movie's been playing for the last ten minutes, and neither one of us has even blinked at the television."

"So what does that mean?"

"It means this movie totally sucks or maybe we can entertain ourselves just fine without it."

"Hmmm… Now if I'm not mistaken, Darrel, I would swear you're hinting at getting your freak on with me."

"And what if I told you that you weren't mistaken?"

"Then I would say, what's taking you so long to make the first move?"

I smiled, "You ain't said nothing but a thang!" I bent over and began kissing her. She pulled me on top of her and began unbuttoning my shirt. Everything was definitely going according to planned.

She laid on top of me fast asleep, as I rested my back against the headboard. My body felt at ease from all the good loving I received, but my mind ran astray. I couldn't help but think if I was going backwards or forwards. The sex was unbelievably wonderful as we did a few rounds in every room contained within the walls of my little abode, but it just didn't feel right afterwards. I told my mother I was going to change my old habits and that I was done with playing all my games with women, but here I was again, laying up with someone I couldn't even hold a descent conversation with without sex on the brain. Then her comment about actually meeting my mom threw me for an even bigger loop. The girl was a sweetheart, but definitely not the one I could take home to momma. Or was she? I didn't even take the woman that I had actually married home because I was scared my mother wouldn't like her. And deep down inside, I knew she wouldn't. But then what did that say about me? What did that say about the validity of my marriage?

"What are you thinking about?"

"Nothing," I replied as I slipped out of my train of thought.

She looked up at me. "You don't look like you're thinking about nothing. It looks like something's bugging you. It wasn't good enough for you, or something?"

"Oh no, it was great."

"Then what's wrong?"

"It's nothing," I said as I wrecked my brain for something to deter her from asking her snooping questions.

"Are you sure? You know you can tell or ask me anything."

I suddenly came up with something. "Well, I do have a question."

"Bring it on," she said as she rose up and positioned herself beside me alongside the headboard.

"Well, what would possess a woman to give a man

flowers?" I decided to start picking her brain to find out what made her tick.

"I don't know. I know I wouldn't."

Shocked, I asked, "You wouldn't?"

"No, that's too tacky, Darrel. If I want to send a man a gift, I'd send him some cologne or something, but never flowers. No way! It's getting harder these days just to find a brother not wanting the same qualities in a man that a woman wants, if you catch my drift."

"But..."

"But what, Darrel? Would you like me to send you some flowers, boo?" she asked jokingly, as she gently bumped me from the side.

I laughed, "Hell nah, girl! What do you take me for, some kind of a chump?" I shook off my surprise briskly. "I just got this friend and his girl sent him some roses the other day. I thought that was kind of weird."

She chuckled, "It is."

"You think so?"

"Of course, Darrel. You can't just give a man flowers like that unless you're trying to toy with him. A girl just doesn't do things like that without a hitch. And if she knows what I know, she better stop doing it. Well, unless she wants him to start trying on her panties."

"You sound as if you know what you're talking about."

"I do," she said as she reached for her shirt from the side of the bed.

"How?"

"It's a long story Darrel. I really don't feel like talking about it."

"Well... I wanna hear it."

She sighed, "It's nothing really."

"I don't know about that. It looks like it's buggin' you a bit."

"Real funny, Darrel."

I smirked and shrugged my shoulders.

"Anyway, when I tell you this, don't go thinking differently about me."

"Is it that bad?" I said trying to say it as playfully as possible. But it was obvious to me that whatever she was about to tell me was indeed going to change the way I thought about her.

"No, it's not bad. Well, it's probably bad if you were Juan."

"Who's Juan?"

"Juan is my ex-boyfriend."

"Oh well, I know this is bad."

She bumped me again. "It's not bad. I call it... getting even."

"Okay, what happened between you and Mr. Juan?"

"Well, he was just one of those guys that would overly-enjoy receiving those flowers your friend got."

"Oh, so Mr. Juan had some issues."

She frowned and nodded her head. "Issues would be an understatement. I dated that guy for almost two years of my life and never caught on."

"Caught on to what?"

"The flaunting me around in front of his family, and the constant distance he kept when we were alone together. The frequent gifts he bought for me at Victoria's Secret, but him never wanting me to model the gifts for him. And let's not forget the total lack of sex!"

"The lack of sex?"

"Yeah, the lack of sex."

"Oh-oh, it sounds like Mr. Juan was a...."

"Homo!" She sucked her teeth. "The gifts from Victoria Secret got me suspicious. I kept thinking why was he always buying this stuff for me and never wanting me to show it off to him. But the truth was he always picked up something for me, when he bought himself something.

94

And I was just a decoy for his family. He didn't want them to find out about his little secret."

"How did you find out for sure?"

"This guy that they hired at my job one summer recognized Juan from a gay club when he stopped in to see me one day. He told me that my man tried to holla' at him one night. Can you believe that? My man! I would've laughed it off if it wasn't for all those signs he kept giving me the whole time we were together. And deep down inside, I knew something just wasn't right with the brotha'. So I followed him around one night with one of my girlfriends."

"Did you find something?"

"Did I? We followed him right to his honey hole for pickups, all dressed up like a woman."

"Oh, that's messed up."

"No it ain't! What I did to his car was messed up."

"What you do?" I asked, instantly thinking about my uncle's altercation with his wife the other day.

"I keyed in 'homo' all over his prized Escalade."

"You did what?"

"I keyed his car with the word 'homo' everywhere. It wasn't like he didn't deserve it, using me as a decoy. I'm not anybody's decoy. And I was so glad I used a condom the few times we did have sex. No telling what that jerk had."

Her words shook me. It was messed up how her man deceived her the way he did, but trashing his ride was just as bad. An Escalade at that. Now I knew what she was capable of, and I was less than impressed. "Did you ever verbally confront him about his secret?"

"No, I didn't have to," she laughed.

"Why not?"

"Because all that garbage he bought me from those stores was dangling right in front of his apartment door. Knowing him, he's probably wearing it all right now. And he knows I did it, too, because he hadn't called me since. He better not."

"Wow, you really got him."

"That, I did," she said as she jumped out of the bed and began collecting the rest of her clothes from off of the floor. "I'll be ready to go after I shower, okay?"

"That's cool."

She looked at me and smiled, then, eased on the bed and jumped on top of me. "Now are you sure you aren't going to go thinking differently about me because of what I did to Juan?"

"No. You did what you had to do, right?"

She nodded, "Yeah. That's what I felt like doing then, but I don't think I'd ever do something like that again. Besides, I've found a real man, now."

"This is true. Ain't nothing weak about this."

"Good," she said as she kissed me. "I'll be about twenty minutes, okay?"

"That's fine."

She left the room. After her story, I realized two things, the girl didn't like to be crossed, and whenever I decided to let her go, it was gonna have to be nice and gentle. I didn't want her to come back trashing my spot. And on a finer point, if she wasn't the one that sent me those roses, who in the hell did?

Chapter Six

I sat at my desk in a trance with my quickly decaying roses. I had them for only two days, and they were already on the way out. It's probably the reason men don't keep flowers or plants. We wouldn't give them the necessary care they would need to survive. And if we did, something would have to be wrong. I couldn't help but parallel my marriage to my decaying bouquet. When I was out playing around, not giving a damn about how I treated women, everything was just fine. Then when I decided to care, I got my heart broken. My father, if he were alive, would firmly tell me what comes around goes around. And me, being as ignorant as I could be, thought I had it all planned out. I thought I would play around as long as I wanted, and then when I got good and ready I would one day settle down with Miss Right. I had no idea the One up above had other things in mind. Now I'm back at square one with a chick that has the potential to become very unstable if I did the wrong thing. I swear, when it comes around, it just stays for a while and makes sure you know darn well that it's there.

"What's up, chief?" asked Dale as he came out of nowhere.

I looked up at him, immediately wanting him bug off, but I was at work so I knew I had to keep it professional. "Nothing, what's going on with you?"

He glanced at my roses. "Nice flowers."

"Thanks."

"Putnam and I just got finished viewing that high school piece you put together about Friday. It was good."

"Thanks."

"So are you ready for the real deal?"

"What are you talking about, Summers?"

He sighed as his arrogant smirk appeared on his

face. "Remember that fine chick I was dating last
December?"

"No!"

"Oh, you remember, the one with that nice ass and
jumbo-sized tits…"

"I said no, Summers."

He frowned and sucked his teeth, finally realizing
that I could care less about who he dated. "Well, anyway,
she's good friends with Friday's agent and they set up some
time for us to have an exclusive interview with him at his
crib."

"Really? That's great. When is it set for?"

"At four."

"Four, when?"

"Four o'clock today."

"Four o'clock today! Summers, that's about an
hour from now."

"I know, but I knew that you're always down for
the cause."

"The cause. We don't get paid for overtime. We'll
be out there well after five. What if I had plans tonight?
I've been here all morning."

"Darrel, you know this is the shot we need. This is
an exclusive."

"Ah, man, you guys act like Friday's Michael
Jordan or something. This guy hasn't even led the league
in scoring yet."

"Come on, Walker, this is your job. This is what
you get paid for, so start acting like it."

"I get paid for my work between nine and five.
And this is certainly going to go over into my personal
time. I do have a life outside of this place, you know."

"You act as if you never worked over. Get the
stick out of your ass and get with the program, Walker."

"I've worked over plenty of times, but never with
you. I guess that's what's making this shoot really

distasteful to me right now."

"Hey, I'm willing to ignore that comment. But Putnam, on the other hand, he's gonna be quite ticked off if he finds out that you were dragging your feet on this interview. Especially when he's the one pushing this entire project."

I stared at him, wanting immensely to tell him where he could take his threats. But I was much smarter than that. I knew what my job was, and it was going out there and doing that interview. I just didn't want to be there with Summers' obnoxious behind. And if he did go to Putnam, his claim wouldn't hold water because Putnam knew I was always about the business. But I would still have to go with Dale, no doubt. So it didn't matter one way or the other.

"Look, I'll have the truck ready in twenty minutes. Just go and do whatever you have to do to get ready."

He smiled, "That's more like it." He strutted to the door.

"Just remember that your threats don't mean anything to me."

His smile instantly disappeared. "Just have that truck ready when you said it will be, Walker." He left the room.

"Whatever, Summers. Jack-ass!" I added under my breath.

I loaded the truck with the camera and the other necessary items for the shoot in no time. It was going to be just a basic interview, so we didn't need too much. As I threw in the last item at the back of the van, I noticed the roar of a motorcycle approaching. I moved from behind the van and caught a glimpse of my good buddy, Rex, drawing near on a brand spanking new bike, with a half-dressed diva on the back. He pulled up in front of me.

"D!" he yelled as he shut off his bike.

"I see you got a new toy."

"Brand new Kawasaki Ninja. Just rolled it off the lot today."

"Did it come with the girl?" I asked as I gave her a little wave.

He glanced back at her and smiled, "Nah, this is Tootie. We've been kicking it for a week now. Say hi to my boy, Darrel, Tootie."

"Hi, Darrel." She winked her eye at me.

"What's up?" I replied as I couldn't help but stare at her in awe. She wore a tight yellow shirt that barely grazed her belly button, and it looked as if the shirt was suffocating her bosom.

"Hey Tootie, why don't you show my man what you got for daddy."

"Okay," she said as she jumped off of the bike. "Yo, D, you have gotta see this."

I walked closer as she began unzipping her shorts. She leaned over on the bike and pulled her shorts halfway off of her butt to reveal a tattoo that read 'Property of Rex Daddy'.

"This is mine, baby," Rex chuckled as he smacked her on the spot and gripped her buttocks. "Now put that up, baby."

She stood up straight and zipped her pants back up. I was frozen by the stupidity of this fine, young woman.

"Get back on the bike. I'm about to holla at my boy right quick."

"Okay, daddy. Don't be too long," she said as she reclaimed her spot on the bike.

Rex hopped off the bike and walked towards me. He childishly laughed as he placed his arm around my neck and guided me towards the van. "So what do you think, dawg?"

"She's straight, but a little absent minded, don't you think?

"Nah, not her, the bike! It's tight, right?"

"Yeah, it's straight, but I thought you were talking about the girl."

"Ah man, she's nice too. But she's too damn possessive."

We stopped and stood on the other side of the van, outside of his new playmate's view.

"Rex, she has your name tatted on her ass. I imagine she would be a little possessive."

"I didn't ask her to do that."

"I'm quite sure you provoked her."

He admittedly nodded, "Well, I probably gave a little input on it. But I didn't place a gun to her head. I don't force these chicks to do nothing they don't wanna do."

"Yeah, right."

"But besides being too possessive, she's alright. Oh yeah, she does this little thing with her tongue that you just gotta see."

I shook my head. "Spare me, please. I think I've seen enough for one day."

"Alright. Oh, I almost forgot. You got a little bit of action of your own now. So how have things been with you and shorty?"

"It's okay, Rex. She has her issues too."

"What? You thinking about marrying her or something?"

"No. Hell nah."

"Then what the hell are you complaining about?"

"I'm not complaining about anything. It's just this dating thing is gonna take a little getting used to again, that's all. I keep thinking about Brandi."

"Man, get off of that Brandi shit. Was the sex with ole' girl good to you?"

"Yeah. It was nice."

"Well, that's all the hell you need to be thinking

about. Her fine ass. You better be glad I didn't scoop her from you when I had the chance."

"She keyed up her ex-boyfriend's Escalade."

"Oh yeah, you can keep her."

I laughed, "Yeah, I bet."

"You always be messing with those crazy chicks. I just don't understand you."

"Well, you're the one that noticed she was staring at me in the club."

"But I didn't know she was crazy. You shouldn't have even hit that after you found out she did some shit like that."

"I found out after we had sex."

"Oh," he frowned. "I wouldn't hit it no more then."

"She had kind of a good reason for what she did."

"You must be kidding. There ain't no good reason for messing up an X."

"Her ex was sleeping with guys."

"Well, I can see her point of view a little better."

"I bet."

"You bored with her yet?"

I shook my head, not wanting to admit what he already knew. "No, not really."

"D?" he looked at me with a smirk, knowing I was lying.

"Okay, a little."

"See, man, it never fails. You don't ever know how to just have fun with a chick. You just hit it, and forget it, just that quick. You gotta change man."

"Well, I'm trying to have fun with her. You and your girl already beat us to the tattoo parlor, though."

"That shit's tight, though, ain't it?"

"It's cool," I replied, as we both shared a chuckle.

"So are we still on for tonight?"

"Tonight?"

"Pool, remember? We were suppose to go out and shoot a little cue-ball."

"Dag, Rex, I forgot all about it. I probably wouldn't even make it out tonight anyway. We're about to head out to Terrance Friday's place for an interview."

"Friday, the basketball player?"

"Yeah."

"I heard that cat's suppose to be signing with the Lakers."

"Yeah, that's what all the hoopla is about."

"I couldn't stand that chump when we were in college. He always hollered at the girls I wanted and got 'em."

"Gee, I didn't think you remembered him in college, since you weren't there very long."

"Yeah, I remember his punk ass. I heard he was still a real jerk in person, too. He always thought he was better than everybody just because he could shoot a little hoops."

"I know that's right. The general public doesn't seem to mind, so I guess he has it like that."

"The biggest assholes always seem to have it like that, too," Rex laughed. "I remember this game he was in last season and Shaq was just dunking all over his ass, and he kept staring at Friday like 'do something.' Friday couldn't even come back with anything. He is so over-rated."

"Yeah, well tell that to Perry Putnam."

"Is that your boss?"

"Yeap!"

"No thanks. I might make you loose your job," he said. "But since you gotta do this video, we can hook up this weekend."

"That's cool with me."

"I heard The Hot Spot's suppose to be rocking this Saturday night."

"No clubbin' this weekend, Rex. I pretty much got my hands full with the chick I found there last weekend."

"Ah, I hear ya," Rex replied as he looked towards the back of the building, over my shoulder. "Here comes that chump you work with."

I looked back and glanced at Summers making his way towards us. "Yeah, let me get ready to go, man. I want to get this shoot over with as quickly as possible. This dude is aggravating as hell."

"Cool," Rex replied. "I'll give you a call later."

"Alright." I gave him a handshake.

"Peace," he said as he walked to his motorcycle and jumped on.

Summers walked up beside me. "Kawasaki Ninja, almost nicer than the hoochie he has on the back."

I rolled my eyes. "Do you have everything you need?"

"Yeah, I just had to draw up a few extra questions to ask Friday at the last minute. I want to make sure I can get all that I can out of him. Any new information about his private life is worth some big bucks."

"Well cool, let's ride." I said as I closed the back door of the van and made my way to the driver's door.

We arrived at Terrance Friday's crib at a quarter till five. He had this beautiful mansion just outside of Brentwood that was bigger than some business buildings I've seen. We approached his front door, a camera in my hand and Summers with his usual notepad in his. Summers knocked on the front door, while I observed the gigantic home in total astonishment. I didn't like Friday one bit, but the brotha' was definitely paid.

"Maybe I should've focused more on a jump shot back in school," Dale stated.

"You telling me," I replied.

The door opened, and a slender Latino women

wearing a maid's uniform stood on the other side of it. "Welcome to Master Friday's abode. He's been expecting you," she greeted.

"We've been expecting him, too," Dale added.

"Follow me out to the pool, please sirs," the young woman requested.

She wasn't the typical looking maid. She was young and very attractive. I presumed handpicked by Friday himself. Knowing him, he probably had her doing a lot more than making the beds up, but having a good time with her messing them up.

We walked through the house and it was like being inside of an exquisite work of art. There wasn't a smidgen of dust on anything anywhere. There were huge portraits of Friday covering just about every wall, exquisite furniture everywhere and beautiful chandeliers hanging down from the ceiling. I felt like I was on an episode of MTV's Cribs.

We followed the maid outside where an enormous pool resided, and the first thing we noticed was Friday lying on a lounge chair with his cell phone glued to his ear yelling into it. He wore a red robe that was opened at his chest and some orange slippers hanging off his feet. He also sported a pair of shades, protecting his eyes from the blazing Georgia sun. Obviously, he didn't think too much of our interview because he wasn't dressed down in the casual gear he normally sported on the other interviews I've seen him in for the bigger stations. I guess we were just small ducks to him.

We stopped halfway to him, not wanting to interrupt. "Is good. He is ready," the woman assured us.

Friday looked towards us and flagged us to come over. We walked towards him.

"Yeah, well I gotta go, baby. You tell the people at Leno if they want me to appear next week, they gotta be talking the right kind of paper. I'm a star, baby. You feel me? Alright then, holla at you later." He ended the call and looked at us. "Gentlemen, what's going on today in this hot southern heat?" he asked as he closed his robe.

"Nothing. How are you today, Mr. Friday?" Dale asked, rapidly transforming into his suck-up mode. It couldn't have been me.

"I'm fine. I'm just enjoying this nice summer day, making things happen as usual," he laughed. He pulled off his shades and laid them on a small table beside him. Then, he stared at me closely. "Darrel Walker, is that you?"

"Yeah, Terrance, it's me. What's going on?"

"Well, son of a gun. What's happening, baby?" he asked as he jumped up and swallowed me with a hug. For a moment, I almost thought we were good friends or something.

"Nothing much," I said, slightly confused as he let me go.

"How the hell are you, baby?"

"I'm fine. Just living, you know."

"Hey, me too," he replied holding out his arms. "A brotha' came up, right?"

"Yeah, you've done good for yourself."

"Damn right," he said as he looked towards his maid. "Go get these gentlemen some lemonade, Rosa. Fresh squeeze that shit, will ya'?"

"Yes, Master Friday," she replied as she hastily made her way to the house.

His eyes followed her behind as she walked away. "Fine ass." He turned to me. "I gotta make sure they look good, know what I mean?"

"Not really, but I hear ya'."

"I can't be having no ugly help around this piece. It would mess up the whole TGIF experience."

"We definitely don't want to mess up that," Dale interjected.

Friday angled himself to Dale. "You must be Dale Summers."

"That's me," Dale replied as he extended his hand.

Friday looked down at it and looked Summers in the eyes. "I don't make a lot of physical contact with people I don't know."

"Hey, I understand you completely. My father is the same way."

"So what kind of questions you gonna be asking me, man? Rita said this is suppose to be for educational television. Are kids suppose to be watching this or something?"

"Well, it's going to be a mixture of children and adults. Primarily, we're gearing this towards the adults. We want them to get the total TGIF experience."

"What? You don't think they've seen me play or something?"

"No, no, of course not. The purpose of this piece is…"

"The purpose is to expose you in a brighter light to the community, Terrance," I interrupted, fully aware that Dale was beginning to ramble out a whole bunch of nothing. "We want Atlanta to know how important you are to this community."

"Oh well that's straight. Let's get the party rocking, baby. We gotta educate the people about my shit."

"Great! Now if we could only find the right place to shoot this interview…" Dale said as his eyes rapidly wandered around the enormous estate.

"What's wrong with the pool?" Friday questioned.

"Nothing! Nothing's wrong with the pool." It was clear from Dale's facial expression that the last place he wanted to conduct this interview was at the pool. He just didn't have the backbone to disagree with Friday about it. It didn't make me a bit of difference where we shot the darn thing, as long as we could wrap it up fast.

"Good," answered Friday.

"Your lemonade is ready, Master Friday," said the

maid as she approached us with a tray with three glasses of lemonade, all filled to the brim.

"Damn, that was quick." Friday grabbed a glass and began gulping it down. "Damn, this is good. Fellas, get some of this shit. It's good as hell."

"I'm fine," I said.

"Me, too," stated Dale.

"Hey don't be too proud. You guys are my guest." He took one last sip and placed the glass back on the serving tray. "Keep that on standby for me Rosa, will ya'?"

"Yes, Master Friday," she answered.

"You're dismissed." He walked to his chair. "Alright now, are we ready to do this, fellas?"

"Sure, Mr. Friday," said Dale.

"Wait a minute, dude. You gotta stop calling me Mr. Friday. Call me T. or something. That Mr. Friday stuff makes you sound like a chump or something. I can't have no chumps around me. It would mess up TGIF's flow, ya' dig?"

I laughed to myself because that was the same thing I've been trying to tell Putnam every time he paired me up with Summers. He messed up my flow.

"Okay, T. I'm sorry. Would you like to look over these questions I've made up for you to answer before we do the shoot?"

Friday laughed, "Wait a minute. Don't you guys have one of them machines that cut out all the bad stuff in a tape?"

"Of course," Dale answered.

"Alright then. If something's unfit then y'all gonna have to cut that shit out. Feel me?"

"Of course." Dale stated.

To tell you the truth, I don't think Summers realized how hard it was going to be to work with Friday. I mean, I knew he was a jerk ever since college. Summers, on the other hand, only knew what he had seen on television, if he knew that much. I knew well enough to be blunt, to the point, and ready to get the hell out of dodge.

"This chair is cool right here, right?" Friday asked as he flopped onto the lounge chair, not leaving any room for dispute.

"Perfect," said Dale.

"It's fine with me." I said as I turned my camera on.

"Good. Well I'm ready when you guys are ready," Friday declared.

"Are you ready?" Dale asked as he looked back at me. He pulled up a chair and positioned himself directly across from Friday.

"Yeah," I answered as I propped the camera on my shoulder and got down on one knee. "Ready." I started taping.

"Alright. First off, Mr. Friday, welcome and thank…"

"Hold up, hold up, hold up. How do I look?" Friday interrupted.

I immediately stopped filming. "Fine," I replied as calm as I could.

"You sure? A brother just isn't feeling like he's all that right about now," he stated.

"You look fine, Mr. Friday," Dale suggested.

Friday gave Dale a weird look out of the corner of his eyes. He shook his head and jumped up. "Man, you'll tell me anything. Rosa!" he yelled.

Rosa quickly dashed out of the back door. "Yes, Master Friday?"

"Go fetch me a mirror. I gotta make sure I'm looking straight."

"Yes, Master Friday." She hurried back into the house.

Friday positioned himself right back on his chair.

"I gotta be looking good, y'all understand? The public expects a certain element out of me."

I sat there eagerly awaiting his maid's return. I couldn't believe that after a few years of being in the pros, Friday's arrogance had almost tripled. It made me even more ready to leave. Rosa quickly ran to Friday with a small mirror.

"As you requested, Master Friday," she said.

"Here we go," he said as he grabbed the mirror.

Rosa just stood in front of him solemnly waiting on his next demand.

"Shit, I do look good," he declared as he carefully examined himself in the mirror. "You guys weren't lying, at all. My sexy ass. Okay, I'm straight now." He handed her the mirror.

"Will that be all, Master Friday?"

"Yeah, go back to what you were doing before."

She bowed, thanking him and hurried back into the house.

"Alright, let's shoot this thing, fellas." Friday requested

I threw the camera back onto my shoulder and pointed it towards Friday's arrogant mug. "Ready," I called out.

Dale gave me a nod and turned to Friday. "Alright, Mr. Friday. How are you today?"

"Splendid." he replied.

"Are you enjoying your summer during this off season?" Summers read directly off of his notepad.

"You know it."

"Well, Mr. Friday, one of the first questions I wanted to ask you is about your childhood. How was it?"

"It wasn't all that good. I was brought up in the ghetto, but I made good for myself. I got momma riding in a Benz now, you know?"

"So your childhood was rough?"

"Hell yeah. I almost started slinging rocks at one time when I started doubting myself back in high school. But I refused to give up, and look what happened. I'm right here today, ya' feel me?"

"Yes, Mr. Friday. Speaking of the present day, what is life like now as Terrance Friday?"

"Ah, man, I know you didn't ask that," he said as slouched back into his chair and a huge smile surfaced onto his long face. "There's only one word to explain it–marvelous. A day in the life of Terrance Friday is like winning the lottery every hour on the hour. I got the rides, the home, the game, and the fans. It just don't get any better than this."

"Could you tell us just a little bit about the contract offer L.A. has presented to you?" Summers asked.

"I can't discuss that at this moment. But rest assured, whomever I sign with is going to get the most electrifying ball-player on the face of the earth when I arrive," he giggled. "I'm the shit…. Oops, I wasn't suppose to say that on television, was I?"

"Don't worry about it, Mr. Friday. We have one of those edit-thingies you asked about back at the studio."

"Cool," replied Friday.

"So I guess we have no choice but to wait until the press conference?" Dale questioned one last time.

"You know it," Friday grimaced.

"Terrance!" yelled a voice from behind us.

I stopped taping as everyone looked towards the house. It was Veronica, and she was making her way towards us. I couldn't help but wonder what in the world she was doing at Friday's place.

"Baby! What's up?" Friday jolted out of his chair and rushed to her, totally neglecting our interview.

"I've been calling you all day," she advised him with a hint of anger.

"Baby, I've been doing my thang, you know that,"

he quickly answered, giving her a peck on her lips.

Now I just knew they weren't a couple. She could do so much better than Friday, if they were.

"I've never worked with someone so unprofessional in my life," Summers mumbled. He was mad as hell. His high-yellow complexion was quickly altering to dark red.

"Doing your thang, huh? Am I not more important than your thang, Terrance?" she asked him.

"Baby, baby, come on now. You know that you are top priority in the TGIF experience."

They were a couple! I put the camera completely down and focused totally on them.

"I don't want to be apart of no TGIF experience. I want you, Terrance Friday, to help me with this wedding," she demanded.

"You're getting married?" I shouted.

Their conversation came to a halt as they looked towards me.

"Darrel! What are you doing here?" she asked, just a little less shocked than I was of her news prior to my interruption.

"They're doing an interview on me and my life, baby. They've been here all day trying to get this thing flowing right. That's the reason why I didn't get a chance to call you," he looked to us. "Ain't that right, fellas?"

"Uh... that's right!" Summers answered. I didn't say one word. There was no way in hell I was going to take part in Friday's lie, especially to one of my oldest friends.

He grabbed her hand. "See, baby, I just lost track of time. I didn't have a chance to answer nobody's call nor make any on top of that. I've been out here creating a better image of myself to the hometown. You know I gotta represent," he said, completely lying.

Suddenly, I became an advocate of her common

sense. I eagerly anticipated her seeing right through his bald-face lies and suggesting him to go to hell, like I knew she would.

"So you've been out here all day?" she questioned, almost sounding like she was taken in by his outlandish story. I knew her too well for that, though. I expected her to tell him off at any moment.

"Baby, this is all I've been doing."

She sighed, "Oh well, I'm sorry for blowing up."

What in the hell? Stupid had obviously become a wide-spread virus. I stood there with my mouth wide open because she believed every ounce of that jerk's lies. I really couldn't believe it. What happened to my girl?

"I'm sorry for neglecting you, baby. I didn't do it on purpose," he said as he embraced her with a tight hug.

I was mad as hell, yet astonished at the same time. I knew Veronica was smarter than that. I was a much better liar than Friday back in the day, and she knew just about all my schemes and tricks. With their arms around each other's backsides, they walked towards us. Dale got up and stood beside me.

"Yes, Darrel, I am getting married," she said.

"You are? Well…" I was almost lost for words. "Congratulations!"

"Thank you," she replied.

"Now if I'm not mistaken, Mr. Friday, the general public knows nothing about this little engagement," Dale investigated, his nose quickly recognizing the scent of an exclusive story.

"Well, I guess you got yourself a TGIF exclusive, baby," Friday announced. "TGIF is getting hitched."

"This is great," Summers said with his beady eyes almost bulging out of his head like a man possessed.

"It sure is," Friday suggested as he pulled Veronica closer to him. "It's a beautiful thang!"

I couldn't say anything because I knew the whole

thing was wrong. I felt Veronica would only end up feeling the pain that I felt with Brandi when I caught her creeping if she got married to that jerk. It was bound to happen since Friday was a mere no good, lying dog in the flesh.

"So might I ask when is the big day coming?" Dale asked.

"In three months," Friday answered, "Right at the end of summer."

"That's right around the corner," replied Dale.

"It sure is," Veronica answered, looking at me, not quite making eye contact.

"Well, guys, I'm sorry we didn't finish today, but I promise you if we could reschedule for Monday morning it would be right on point. I'll even throw in a little bit of information about my contract negotiations with a certain team out west, ya dig?"

"Hey, we can't beat that," Summers instantly agreed.

"Good. I just gotta spend the rest of this day with my woman," he said as he wrapped his lanky arms around her and engulfed her with a kiss.

I couldn't stand it one bit. I couldn't understand why she couldn't see through his weak lies and games. He was such a phony. I couldn't help but wonder how in the hell they hooked up. Was she desperate? She deserved so much better than the so-called Terrance Friday experience. And there she was standing before me kissing on the ultimate scum bag. It was truly an unbearable sight for my eyes to see.

"Come on. Let's pick up our shit and leave," Summers whispered in my ear. He was back to his normal jack-ass mode. "We got an exclusive of a lifetime with this wedding news."

"Whatever, man." I grabbed my camera as we made way towards the back door to Friday's mansion. We were totally ignored on our exit as the alleged love birds lost themselves in each other's lip locking. If there ever was a day for me to pinch myself to wake up, this was definitely the one.

Chapter Seven

It was a Saturday afternoon, and I was strolling through the gorgeous Lenox Square. I was never much of a mall person, not even back in my puberty filled days of high school. I always had a habit of running into people that I really didn't want to talk to in the mall. But today's visit to Atlanta's glamorous center wasn't for shopping nor the meaningless chitter chatter with long lost associates. I told Natasha that I would pick her up from work and that we'd go catch a movie afterwards. In my mind, I guess I was trying to prove Rex wrong by attempting to have a little fun with the woman after we did the sex thing. Even though I enjoyed my sexual relationship with Natasha, I wanted to tone down the love making and do other things. So I figured taking her out to a movie would be an excellent start. And I even promised myself that I would try not to have sex with her later.

I walked into the department store that she worked in, and the outlet was packed with oodles of women pulling items off of the racks everywhere. There was a sale going on, no doubt. I cruised to the first register that I saw free, and there was a short dark-skinned chick examining the tags of some clothing.

"Hey, do you know where Natasha is?" I asked politely.

She paused and eyed me down for a second with a bit of a frown on her face. "She's at the register in the back, where the tops are," she replied, smacking fiercely on some chewing gum.

"Thanks," I replied as I headed that way.

"I don't think she's going nowhere right now, though," the woman added.

"Thanks again," I replied, not looking back. I walked on down the aisle and noticed Natasha behind a register tending to a huge line of customers. She looked towards me and quickly whispered something into the guy's ear that was standing behind the counter with her. Then, she speedily trotted over to me and dazzled me with a kiss.

"Hey, boo," she said.

"What's going on, lady?"

"Nothing."

"Are you ready?" I asked.

"Well…," she stalled, "Don't be mad, Darrel."

"About what?"

"My manager needs me to stay for another hour."

"Hey, that's cool."

"Are you sure? I know you had something planned for us to do. This isn't gonna mess things up, is it?"

"Nah, girl," I assured her. "That gives me a chance to drop in at the food court and grab a bite to eat. I'm a bit hungry anyway."

"Really?"

"Sure. It's no problem at all."

"Thanks, Darrel," she said as she engulfed me with a hug. "You're the greatest."

"I'm alright," I teased.

"It'll just be an hour," she reassured me.

"It's cool. Take as long as you like. I'm in no rush."

"Thanks, boo. I'll make it all up to you tonight," she promised.

I grinned, "Don't go making promises you can't keep, now."

"Oh you know I takes care of my man," she said as she returned to her register.

I headed out of the store and into the mall walking area. Her final statement got me thinking–her man! I think

117

she was beginning to catch feelings, something that I wasn't even close to doing. I enjoyed our time together, but there just wasn't any importance to our relationship to me. I felt as if she could be replaced by someone else, and it wouldn't make me a darn bit of difference. And even though I knew it was wrong, that's just how I felt about her. I just hoped that I wasn't making a mistake by attempting to do more than just having sex with her.

I grabbed myself some chicken fingers and fries from one of the restaurants and settled at a table near the back of the food court, away from all the incoming mall traffic. My mind was bent on my newly found relationship with Natasha. I couldn't help but wonder why I was even getting involved any deeper with the girl if I didn't have any genuine feelings for her. My mind was telling me it was just for fun, but my heart was telling me I was lonely. Then I started thinking that maybe this was the reason I was always jumping from woman to woman. I was just lonely.

My mind and heart were both equally confused. I looked up at the entrance and noticed a couple walking in holding each other's hands. They seemed to be so happy with each other. Each step they took was taken in perfect harmony. It was like they were trekking down the royal red carpet together and no one standing alongside the path even mattered. I rested my head on my fist and gazed pass them and through the window. I was sadden by the fact that out of all the women I dated, I had never walked anywhere with them holding hands. I was always too concerned about some other chick noticing me and thinking that I was in the depths of love with whomever they saw me with at the time. No matter how unavailable I was with a female companion at public outings, I always wanted all women passing by to know that the room for availability was possible.

I just shook my head. I couldn't help but think

about the number of females I had been with and the fact that just one of them could've been the one. They could've been the real Mrs. Darrel Walker and not just some skeezer waiting for the right moment to break my heart. And then I laughed because I realized I honestly deserved what I got from Brandi Brown.

"Something funny?" asked a voice. At first I thought it was Natasha, but then I looked up and realized it was Veronica, again!

"Now how in the world do you manage to keep bumping into me?" I asked her.

"Maybe it's fate," she said as she simply invited herself to my table by placing her salad down and pulling the chair out across from me. "You are alone, aren't you?"

"Yeah, for now," I answered as I looked around, making sure Natasha wasn't anywhere to be found. I would've really hated her rolling up on me again from behind.

She sat down. "Good."

"So... how are you?" I asked.

"I'm fine. What about you? I know that you're waiting on somebody because you hate the mall."

"You know me too well, don't you?"

"Well, you told me everything, remember?" she smiled as she applied the dressing to her salad, carefully, as if it was a work of art.

"Don't remind me," I stared at her impatiently waiting for the right moment to ask her about her relationship with Terrance Friday. The whole ordeal was running rampantly through my mind for the past two days.

She looked up, then glanced at my tray of food. "I didn't stop you from eating, did I?"

"No, no, you didn't. I'm not that hungry right now."

"Are you sure?"

"Yeah, I'm sure," I jumped back into my grub to

stray her away from her questions. I wanted to be subtle about my inquiry, not wanting to seem too nosey.

"I know what you wanna ask me, but I ain't telling. I can see it all over your face," she said as she dug into her salad.

"Oh, come on, Veronica. You know I just didn't want to blurt it out," I confessed. "Now you gotta tell me what's the deal with you and that character."

"Terrance is not a character," she firmly announced.

"Yeah, whatever. Now what's the deal, girl?"

"Dern! You're just all up in a sista's business, aren't you? What's up with that, Darrel?"

"Nothin'. I just wanna know, that's all?"

"Whew, you've gotten nosey, Darrel. You didn't ask a girl how she's been doing these past couple of years, where she's been at. You just bypassed all of that and cut straight to the juicy stuff."

"Are you gonna tell me what's going on or not, Veronica?"

She grinned, "Nope!"

"And why not?"

"Because I said so."

"I hate you!" I declared, frustrated.

"No you don't. You just hate not getting your way."

"You always have to make things hard. You just love dragging things out, don't you?" I said. "Some things just never change, do they?"

"You said that they do last week."

"Well, I lied," I combated.

"I knew that."

"Fine!" I yelled. "How have you been Veronica Bethal? What have you been up to since college?"

"I'm okay. I'm still pursuing my career in photography, Darrel Walker," she replied with a silly frown.

I shook my head as we both began to chuckle. "You make me sooo sick!" I joyously advised her.

"You make me just as sick, Darrel," she replied. "Now what are you doing working for Atlanta Public Access? I thought you were gonna direct music videos and stuff."

I sucked my teeth while thinking back on my failed ambitions. "I stopped pursuing that a long time ago. I did a few videos for some cats nobody has ever heard of before and probably never will. It was just too hard collecting my money from people that weren't established already. And the established cats weren't trying to feel me because I was just getting my own stuff together. So I picked up a job at APA, and I've been there ever since. It pays pretty good so I'm satisfied."

"Well at least you've found something that ties in with your studies in college."

"What? Photography isn't what it's cracked up to be anymore?"

"It has it's moments. I do a few weddings every now and then. Every once and a while, I'll sell a photo to a magazine. It's a tough living, but I love it."

"Well, Mr. TGIF should have your living expenses covered well enough."

She blushed. I embarrassed her a bit, but she knew I was going to take another crack at the situation.

"You just don't give up, do you, Darrel?"

"Nope. You couldn't stand the guy back in college just as I, but now you're about to tie the knot with him. I can't help but be intrigued because inquiring minds just want to know what's going on."

"There's nothing to know, Darrel. We just decided to get married, that's all."

"Did you hear what you just said? You referred to marriage as if it was something you just walk up and do, like going to the bathroom or something."

"Well, you did it."

I froze. "Now where'd you get that from?"

"Don't act like nobody knows about you and the infamous model, Brandi Brown. Or should I say Brandi Brown-Walker?"

"You were right the first time," I replied, totally disgusted by the comment. "How do you know about me and Brandi? She's not so big time where the whole world knows all of her business."

"Well, let's see, Darrel… she's a model, and I'm a photographer. We've met."

"You've talked before?" I asked as I became more concerned about my ego than anything. I was hoping she didn't know any specifics about me and Brandi. Back in the day, Veronica always advised me that one day I was going to get what was coming to me. The last thing I wanted her to know was that she was right.

"We never held a real conversation or anything. I was just at a shoot she had with a fellow photographer a few months ago. I presumed it was after you guys broke up."

"Was she talking about me or something?"

"Not really. I just heard her mention your name, that's all. I kinda put two and two together, though, especially when she said she had gotten an annulment."

"Really?"

"Yeap, I just knew Darrel messed things up again."

I wanted to correct her on her statement, but my ego quickly placed me back in check. If she knew about Brandi's infidelity, I would never hear the end of it. "Well, what can I say? Things just didn't work out."

"I wish you had told me you were going to marry her before you did, though. I heard that chick was wild as I don't know what."

Really, I thought. "Well I didn't, and it's over

now."

"You don't have to get feisty, Darrel. I know you probably tried to be faithful."

Tried was an understatement. I was very faithful. I literally shocked myself by the level of faithfulness I administered in that relationship.

"It just didn't work out, did it?" she asked while trying to refrain from grinning. I could tell she really believed I couldn't be faithful in a relationship.

"Now, how did we go from your situation with Terrance Friday, to my marriage with Brandi Brown?"

"Quid-pro-quos, Darrel. You want to know some of my business, now I'm asking for a little info about yours."

"Well, what you're doing is not fair. I asked you about Friday first. Now you're trying to turn the tables on me. That's not gonna work."

She let out a hard grunt. "What is it that you want to know, Darrel?"

"You know! How'd you guys hook up? I mean, he's the biggest player since..."

"*You!*"

I rolled my eyes. "You know what I'm trying to say. Don't act like you forgot about all the things he used to do in college."

"The same things you used to do. And he doesn't do them anymore, either."

"Ah, come on, Veronica. Are you that taken in by his games?"

"Contrary to what you may believe, people can change. People grow up, Darrel. Just because you don't know how to change, doesn't mean nobody else knows."

"Hey, I've changed!"

"Really?" she frowned. "Who are you waiting on right now, then?"

I sucked my teeth. "Whatever, Veronica. How

long have you guys been together anyway?" I totally ignored her question.

"About a year," she answered. "Are you waiting on that rude girl you were with at the Hot Spot?"

"How'd you two hookup?" I asked, ignoring her question again. I was through with giving out information. It was time for me to receive some.

"I was taking some pictures at a fundraiser he was attending and he remembered me from college. We got to talking, and he asked me out to dinner, and I accepted. We've been together ever since—happily together!"

"You accepted dinner from him after all of the things you knew about him in school? I can't believe it."

"As a matter of fact, Darrel, I did," she smiled. "And it was that night that I discovered there was even more to Terrance Friday than all of the arrogance and money. I discovered he was a beautiful person underneath it all."

"Oh give me a break!" I interjected. "Did he brainwash you that night, too? He is so not your type."

"Then tell me who is, Darrel? Tell me who's my type? I get so tired of people being so critical of other people when their own closets have just as many skeletons than the next person. Can you honestly tell me what's the difference in what you did to females in the past from what Terrance has done? Huh?"

I couldn't reply at all. She was right. Terrance may have been more popular and may have done his dirt to more females than me, but there weren't any differences in the things we'd done. I wasn't any better than him. "I'm sorry, Veronica, okay? There isn't a difference," I admitted.

"There really isn't, Darrel."

"I still don't think he's the one for you, though. You deserve so much better than him."

She let out a huge sigh, "Then who is the one for

me, Darrel? You? The next player after the next? Who?
You guys think women, good women, should have to sit
and wait forever on you to stop playing your games. That
we need to put our lives on standby until you start looking
for more than just sex! I don't have the time, Darrel. I'm
ready now. Terrance presented himself as a man that's
ready to make those steps forward, and that's what I'm
looking for. I don't care about the things he's done in the
past as long as he's not doing them now. That's what I'm
looking for."

"Are you happy with him?" I asked.

"What?"

"You heard me. Are you happy with him?"

"I'm with him, aren't I?"

"That's not the question that I'm asking, Veronica.
It's a very easy question. A yes or no question as a matter
of fact. Are you happy with him?

"Yes, I am," she stated firmly.

I could tell I was beginning to upset her and that
was something that I didn't want to do, so I accepted her
answer even though I didn't believe it. "Okay then, that's
good enough for me. If you're happy then I'm happy."

"I'm surprised that it is."

"It is. You're my girl, and I have to look out for
you, that's all. I just don't want to see you get hurt."

"I'm a grown woman, Darrel. I can look out for
myself."

"And I'm sorry I even interrogated you about your
relationship with Friday."

"Darrel, believe me, he's really a sweet guy."

"Underneath all of his obnoxious behavior, I really
believe he could be." He wasn't sweet enough for her,
though.

She laughed, "Okay, he is a little obnoxious at
times, but you can learn to see pass it all."

"I don't doubt it," I added, but I did doubt it. I

doubted a lot of things about Friday, including his alleged change. At this point, it wasn't my place to advise her that Friday was and would always be up to no good. And the real difference between us was that I was trying to change. And after my experience with Brandi, I knew I could be an even better man.

"Oh, what time is it?" She asked as she quickly piled all of her eating utensils on top of her barely touched salad.

"A quarter after," I answered as I glanced at my watch.

"I gotta meet my seamstress today."

I shook my head. "I can't believe you're tying the knot."

"Imagine how I felt when I found out about you. It's too bad yours was over by the time I got the news. I would've loved meeting the married Darrel Walker."

"He was the same person that's sitting before you right now."

She took a good look at me and smiled. "Something tells me that wasn't a bad thing." She took out a pen and wrote her number on a napkin. "I want you to call me some time, Darrel. I don't want us to lose touch with each like we did after we graduated."

"You know, I don't want to lose touch again, either." I took the piece a paper, split it in half and wrote my number down also.

"Thanks, Darrel. Maybe we could hang out some time."

"Maybe we can," I said as I stared at her number. "Now, wait a minute. You don't live with Friday, do you?"

"Of course not, Darrel. We're not married yet. One thing that I don't believe in is shacking up before I get married. You know me better than that."

I did know her better than that. "Oh, I was just making sure. I don't want your man to answer the phone and get mad at me for calling."

"Anyway! Call me some time, okay?"

"I will," I assured her.

"See you later," she said as she walked to the trash can and dumped her tray into the trash.

"Bye," I said, as my eyes lost her into the crowd of mall goers.

It sure was good talking to her. We never could see eye-to-eye on everything, but her conversation always got me going. Friday sure was lucky.

"Darrel," a voice called out. I looked up, and it was Natasha. My jaw dropped to the floor because the girl's hair was redder than a Chicago Bull's jersey.

"So do you like it?" she asked, as she took her super-model pose with her hand on her waist and her head tilted sideways.

"Natasha.... you've changed the color of your hair." I was shocked and not liking her new style at all.

"I cut it shorter, too. I'm sorry I lied to you about staying late after work. I just wanted to surprise you with my new flavor," she said. "It's tight, right?"

"Yeah... uh, it looks good." I stood up and examined her hair a little closer. I did not like it at all, and I didn't want to walk in public with a woman with a fireball for a head. "I'm parked right outside."

"Good, boo. Now we can get our day together started," she said with a smile the size of a whale.

We exited the mall and started hiking towards the parking garage. My pace was a little faster than hers because I honestly didn't want to be seen with her looking like that. As we approached my car, I noticed something wedged underneath my wipers. I picked up my pace, and as I gained more ground, I realized it was a rose and card.

"Darrel, you're so sweet," said Natasha as she brushed pass me and snatched the rose from the windshield.

"Huh?" She immediately thought I had left the

flower for her.

"Always on my mind," she said, reading directly from the card that was attached. With a smile on her face, she inhaled the scent of the rose while her eyes laid locked on me. "You're always on my mind, too, boo." She planted me with a juicy kiss. It was so quick, I struggled to keep up with her.

"Thanks," I said as she backed up and slid her arms around my waist.

"You're so thoughtful," she said.

"Well, you know, I just want you to know how I feel, that's all." I had no choice but to take credit for the small gift. It would've been too hard for me to explain that I didn't send it nor did I know where it came from. In other words, I didn't want to open a can of worms that I didn't have to.

"Damn," she said as she pulled away. "I left my purse in the salon. I have to go back in there and get it."

"That's cool. I'll be in the car."

"I'll only be a few minutes," she said as she trotted back into the mall.

I jumped into my car, frantically thinking about that card and rose someone decided to leave me. I was becoming paranoid since it was becoming apparent that someone was watching my every step. It pissed me off because suddenly my privacy didn't feel private anymore. I had a stalker that wanted to play games with my mind. And if they wanted to make me crazy, they were doing a darn good job of it.

Unexpectedly, I noticed a figure from the corner of my eye. As I focused in on the person, I realized it was that guy I caught Brandi in bed with. I jumped out of the car and dashed towards him. He began to run as soon as he noticed me coming.

"What's wrong, mon?" he asked as he run down an alley of dumpsters. He stopped as he realized he had ran into a dead end. He held his hands in the air. "I don't want no trouble, mon."

"I got you now!" I said, as I moved in on him.

"Mon, what is wrong with you? What do you want from me?"

I charged at him and shoved him to the ground. "Why are you fucking with me?" I yelled.

"What are you talking about, mon? I don't know you," he cried. With his dreads spread wildly across his face, he began backing away from me on his elbows.

"Oh, you don't? Well, I was the guy that caught you sleeping with his wife a few months ago. You remember, the guy that blacked out while kicking your ass!"

His eyes almost popped out of head. "My God, mon, I am so sorry. I did not know she was your wife. She had never made mention of you, mon."

"Yeah, right! You didn't make any efforts to get the hell out of dodge when I first came in that day, either. "

"I thought you were a partner. Lady Brown is into those things, you know?"

"No, I don't know."

"Yes, yes, dear boy. We have been having relations like that for the past five years now. Lady Brown is down for whatever, you know. I'm not pulling your leg here. I would never tamper with a woman that is taken by marriage."

Something inside of me was beginning to believe him as my anger cooled. I felt embarrassed because I had let my temper overrun my thinking. "Are you sending me things?"

"Mister, all that I know of you is what you have just revealed."

"You said that you've been having relations with her for five years?"

"Yes, mon, the whole time I've been in the states,"

he said nervously.

I bowed my head and held my hand out, "I apologize for pushing you down."

"It is okay. I would imagine I would do the same if someone had entered my bedroom in sin, too," he chuckled as he dusted himself off.

I placed both of my hands on top of my head feeling frustrated about the whole Brandi Brown ordeal. With his information, I soon realized I didn't know this woman at all. "You won't have any more problems out of me," I said as I started walking away.

"She is very powerful when she attempts to manipulate you by the games she plays."

I stopped and turned around. "What did you say?"

"She tries to capture your heart by playing games with up here," he said as he pointed to the side of his head. "Yes, it's been five years, but five years of confusion. I am simple, mon. I don't like confusion, but I do love Lady Brown. You mustn't fall prey to the games she plays, or you'll be trapped like me. Trapped by the lust of being hers."

I stared at him and didn't say anything at all. I suddenly realized who was sending me the flowers—my ex-wife. I walked back to my car and noticed Natasha had returned. I tried to relax my breathing as I jumped in and shut the door.

"Where'd you go? You left your door wide open," she inquired with the rose under her nose.

"I had to check something out," I replied, still baffled by the man's statements. I looked towards the dumpster area, and he had disappeared just that quickly.

"Well, it's dangerous to just leave your door open like that, boo," she said. She placed her hand on my thigh as I started my car. "So where are we going?"

I turned to her and took a good look at her horrific red head. "Blockbuster. We're gonna rent something tonight."

She started stroking my thigh. "I take it someone wants to get kinky tonight. We can definitely do that."

I didn't reply. For once, sex was the very last thing on my mind. I wanted to get to the bottom of Brandi's weird love games as soon as possible.

Chapter Eight

I laid in bed as the Sunday afternoon sunlight stretched through the unguarded vents of my curtains. My body was exhausted from the sex I had with Natasha all through the night. I know I promised myself not to do her, but with yesterday's revelations about Brandi, I couldn't resist. I needed something to relax my mind. After I had dropped Natasha off, I attempted to go to bed immediately. Initially, I couldn't rest a wink, but after a few hours of watching a flood of boring infomercials, my eyes finally found themselves shut.

In an instance, my phone's ring abruptly pierced throughout the house. I sluggishly rolled over and answered, "Hello."

"Boy, what did I tell you about spending the bulk of your Sundays in bed when you could start your day off right by visiting the house of the Lord for some worship?" It was my mother in full gear.

"Ma," I answered, "How are you this morning, Ma?"

"It's the afternoon now, Darrel," she corrected me. "And I would be fine if my son would accompany me to church once in a while."

"Ma, you know that I would, but…"

"But what, Darrel?" she interrupted. "What's your reasoning, Darrel? Make it sound good so we can beware of it next week when you *do* come to church with me."

"Ma…"

"Did I say something wrong? Did I stutter, Darrel?"

"No, Ma, you didn't stutter," I replied. "And I will go to church with you next Sunday. I don't have a problem with that."

"Good," she said as her whole tone went from

demanding to peaceful. "Now how has my young man been doing?"

"I've been fine, Ma." I wasn't fine, but I wasn't about to let my mother know what my problems were. I knew that every solution to a problem for her was answered by one person only—God! Now, while I believed the same thing, I wasn't about to look like a heathen to my mother by giving her the low-down about my relationships.

"And why are you sleeping so late? Aren't you getting enough rest, son? Darrel, are you still going out to them filthy clubs?"

"No, Ma, I told you I don't go out to them places no more."

"Well that's good for you, son," she replied. "Ain't nothing but trouble in those places. The pastor was just talking about it today. He was talking about how people will break their necks to pay to get into a club, but drag their feet when it comes down to coming to church for free. Mmm-hum, he preached that sermon this morning. You should've been there, son."

"Oh, I'm quite sure he's gonna pick up right where he left off this week, next week."

"And I sure hope he does," she said. "You need to hear the good Word, son. Get some positive things running through your soul."

"I know, Ma." I said, wanting to quickly get off of the phone. "Ma, I'm about to go now. I'm suppose to go somewhere with Rex today."

"Darrel, I don't like you going places with that boy," she said hastily. "You lay down with dogs, you get fleas on you, Darrel."

"Ma, you say that every time I mention him."

"Well if you stop being around him, I won't have to say it no more."

"Ma, his mother is one of your best friends."

"And what does that have to do with anything,

Darrel? You're my son."

"I know, Ma," I said, as I decided to not even go any further with the subject. "I just gotta go, okay?"

"Well, you be careful out there. You may be grown now, but you'll always be my baby."

"I know, Ma."

"I love you."

"I love you, too, Ma."

"See you, Sunday."

"Okay, Ma. See you later."

"Bye, baby," she hung up the phone.

"Man, she got red hair." I announced to Rex, while setting my focus on stuffing the eight ball into the left corner pocket.

"Uh-uh, not no damn red hair," he replied from the opposite side of the pool table.

We were in the midst of ending our first game of the day at a little spot we used to hit every Sunday night to shoot pool. Rex had always been the better player at the game, but the tales of my wild and crazy experiences with the opposite sex had thrown his game off tremendously.

"What in the hell made her dye her hair like that, man? Nobody wanna be walking around with no chick looking like Dennis Rodman."

"I don't know why she did it. I just wish she hadn't. I mean, I had the whole night planned out for us, and then she came out of the mall looking like someone attacked her with a bottle of ketchup. Boy, you just don't know, I'm on the verge of being through with women, completely."

"Man, you'll never do that."

"And why not?"

"Without no skins, you'll go crazy. A man needs his sex, D. It's like his energy. It's like fucking pac-man and his power pellets. The ghost will sit there and chase

134

pac-man all around the damn screen, kicking his little yellow ass, but when he gets his shit, the ghosts better watch the hell out."

"That's about the dumbest thing I've ever heard. Besides, if you play that game long enough, eventually you get caught."

"Ain't nobody ever caught my ass."

"Don't worry. Your time will come soon enough. And if you should ever go through anything like I've been through, you'd start thinking about leaving the game alone, too."

"You're talking nonsense, man. Do you realize how crazy you were getting after you and that Brandi chick split up?"

I sighed, quickly remembering my altercation with her lover the day before. "Man, let me tell you about that, too. I ran into that guy she was messing with."

"You didn't try to kick his ass, again, did you?"

"At first, I was a little hot-headed," I said as I stuffed the eight-ball in its designated corner. "I win," I announced.

"It's about time," he laughed.

"You wanna play another?"

"Hell nah, let's grab a table. I want you to give me the scoop on your ex and her Jamaican lover boy."

We laid our sticks on the pool table and grabbed some chairs at a nearby booth. "So what did you do to him?" he asked slouching back in his chair.

"I pushed him down, and started cursing him. Basically making an ass out of myself."

"You have the right to act a fool. You caught the dude in the bed with your woman."

"Man…" I shook my head. "I should've just left the house that day. I shouldn't have even attacked that guy. He didn't know."

"What?" Rex questioned. "You don't have mercy

on some chump that you caught sleeping with your wife. He better be glad it wasn't me because homeboy would've never regained consciousness after I got through with him."

"Man, it wasn't even worth all of that. I can't blame him because Brandi knew we were together. She was really the one at fault."

"Damn, that! He was her accomplice."

"Whatever, Rex," I replied. "You don't even understand. He didn't know. I sat there attacking that man, and he's just as whipped as I was for the woman. Plus they've been screwing around for over five years. He actually knew her before I did."

"How'd you find that out?" he asked.

"He told me. He told me a lot of things."

"You talked to that nigga? How can you believe anything that clown said? How are you gonna just talk to someone that slept with your wife like you're good pals or something? You're slipping, man. You are really slipping."

I paused for a second, as I doubted if I should go any further with my story to Rex. It was too obvious he wouldn't understand. But I needed to vent to someone, so I decided to continue. "Rex, she's been trying to play games with my mind."

"Games? What kind of games?"

"She's been sending me cards and flowers, talking about how much she misses me and stuff. The girl is loony."

"How do you know if she sent the stuff? Did you see her?"

"No, but he told me she plays these games with people. She does it to him."

"Man, I don't know why you're believing that mess. He's sending that stuff, messing with you. He's the one trying to make you look like an ass," he chuckled. "And if you believe any of that crap he tells you, you might

136

as well be an ass. A big ole' ass!"

I sighed, "You just don't understand, do you?"

"No! That guy's pulling your chain. Don't be a sucker, my man."

"I don't know," I replied. "I don't even care."

"You need to find a new set of skins to hit, that's all. The red head chick needs to get the boot, and you need to forget about your ex-wife altogether."

"I agree with you on both parts of that," I laid back in my chair and stared at the ceiling. "I know I need to go ahead and get rid of Natasha, but I don't know how to break it to her. After she told me about what she did to her last man, I don't want her to go acting crazy on me."

"Man, you sound like a chump," he laughed. "Out of all the girls you left hanging, how many came back on you for some revenge? That's movie shit."

"None," Then, I quickly retaliated with an event from his past. "What about that chick, Shannon, you broke up with that time? She tried to slice your ass up like a grapefruit when you broke up with her."

"I almost killed that trick, too, didn't I? Those are fighting words when you come at me with a blade, buddy."

"Look, I'm not even trying to go through all of that. I'm just gonna break it to her as nice as I can. I can't continue to pretend that I'm interested in her when all she is to me is sex."

"There go my Darrel, the heartbreaker is back in action."

"Man, I don't want to hurt nobody's feelings. I shouldn't have ever got involved with her in the first place."

"Ahhh, and why don't you take her some tissue so she can dry her eyes when you give her the boot," he said sarcastically. "Man, tell that chick to hit the road and be out."

I couldn't believe Rex could be so cruel. Even

more so, I couldn't believe I used to be just like him. "One day you're gonna get what's coming to you if you keep on doing women like that."

"Did that shit with your uncle and his wife scare you or something, D?"

"No, but it made me think. I don't want to hurt nobody that bad that they wanna come wreck my stuff."

"Man, you can buy new stuff. Damn those chicks. They can get mad at Rex all they want, but none of 'em better ever put a dent in my Lex."

"So you're back to driving the Lex?" I asked.

"Yeah, I'm rolling with the Lex again. I was getting too gas happy with that damn bike and got a ticket."

"You got a ticket? How fast were you going?"

"Man, they tried to say I was going ninety in a forty-five, but I think I was going around eighty."

"Well, gee, Rex, what's the big difference? You were still speeding."

"The *big difference* is the person that gave me that fucking ticket!"

"Who was it?"

"Remember that dude everybody use to pick on back in high school?" He paused, while snapping his fingers trying to recall the person he was speaking of. "Spooky... Spooky Collins."

"Dexter Collins," I corrected it him with a frown. Rex had practically made the guy's life a living hell back in high school.

"Yeah, that's that bastard," Rex said with a mean look on his face. "His punk ass. I call him Spooky Collins. His ass used to be scared of everything."

"Dexter gave you a ticket. How ironic." I giggled. I thought it was so amusing that the guy Rex used to pick on all the time finally got his revenge on him.

"Yeah, it's ironic alright. He thinks he's bad now, with his big swollen arms, looking like a big, black

Incredible Hulk. That used to be your little buddy. I never could figure out why you used to be so nice to that little scrub."

"Because you guys used to pick on him all the time. It was so messed up. He couldn't stand up for himself, so I decided I would help him out. Y'all know y'all were wrong for picking on him, too. That's why you got what you got."

"Yeah, well, if he didn't lift so many weights, and he wasn't a cop now, I would've gave him one right across his lips."

"You never quit, do you?"

"No, he thinks he's bad, now. He done put away those big bifocals he used to wear, and gonna tell me to get off *my* bike. Boy, you just don't know."

"That's what you get. You should've left him alone back then."

"Whatever. He's not a cop twenty-four hours a day. I'll catch him off duty. I'm not scared of him because he got muscles. My shit's kinda cut, too, you know," He held his arm out and made a muscle.

"You better leave that dude alone," I warned him.

"Whatever. I know I bet not see him again."

As Rex continued to ramble on about his misfortunes with Dexter Collins, my mind drifted off into thinking about Veronica. I couldn't help but wonder what she was doing at that moment. I wondered about what she was wearing, and if she was thinking about me in any shape or fashion. I didn't know why, but I just couldn't help but think about her. "Rex, you ever thought about getting with someone you were really close with once?"

"What?"

"You know… a homegirl."

"I never got that close to a chick. I just sex 'em, D."

I shook my head. I was more upset with myself

than at him for even asking him that question. "Never mind."

"No," he laughed. "What? Are you trying to get with someone from way back?"

"No, not get with 'em. It's just that I'm kinda diggin' this girl I was really cool with back in college. We were so tight, man. I could tell her anything."

"Who? I don't recall you being down with a chick like that."

"Rex, you know you dropped out and barely came around back then. You never met her…" I stopped myself and quickly remembered that he did see her before. "Well, do you remember that girl that almost ran me over at the gas station last week?"

Rex laughed, "*That chick*! She almost splattered your ass. Then she was piping mad at you. What do you wanna mess with her for?"

"I don't know. I'm just suddenly attracted to her or something. I don't know what it is."

"You didn't hit it back in school?" he asked.

"No, we were strictly plutonic."

"So, you're telling me that you got a crush on someone you could've had back in college, but you never made a move on her? Am I right?"

"To tell you the truth, Rex, she was too smart for my games back in school. I never even tried anything. I didn't even look at her that way."

"Then why do you wanna run game on her now?"

"I don't. I just want to spend time with her. It doesn't even have to be about sex."

"Spend time? You sure can pick 'em," he gripped.

"I sure can," I answered as I almost forgot to mention she was involved. "She's engaged."

"She's engaged! Man, leave that alone. Don't get caught up in the mix like that."

"But she's about to marry a dude that's not even

right for her, man. He's a jerk."

"I don't care. Leave that alone."

"She's suppose to be marrying Terrance Friday."

"What?" He let out a harsh grunt and rolled his eyes. "You mean to tell me you're thinking about getting with somebody that Terrance Friday is about to marry? The million-dollar basketball star! Nigga, have you lost your damn mind?"

"No," I frowned. "I wasn't talking about getting with her in a relationship. I just like being with her. I'm so different around her, Rex. I like how I am around her. It's always been that way."

"D, man, I love you, but something's wrong with ya'," he declared. "You got game, but you're talking about messing with the property of a multi-million dollar professional basketball player. You have charm, but this nigga got game. Real game! Have you ever seen this nigga's crib?"

"Yeah, I was just there the other day, remember?"

"Oh boy, how are you gonna look in that man's face and be thinking about scoring with his lady?"

"Hey, for one, I didn't say I wanted to have sex with her," I corrected him. "It's not that it's out of the question, but something's just different about her."

"It's called the rebound," he yelled. "Friday grabs them, and you're on one. And that's about the only thing you and him have in common."

"He doesn't know her like I do."

"He's got money, though. Lots of money, D."

"She's not with him for the money."

"Then what the hell else could she be with him for?"

"She's not like that. She's just looking for love."

"Why is everybody looking for love these days? Is anyone out there just looking for sex, anymore?" He shook his head. "So you think you can give it to her?"

I stared into his eyes and thought about his question for a few seconds. I nodded my head. "If I had the chance, I know I could."

"D, I'm telling you this for your own good. Leave it alone. Cats like Friday don't lose. They get and keep what they want until *they* decide to let it go."

"Hey, all is fair in love in war, right?"

"That nigga got about one hundred million reasons to why it won't be a fair fight. And all of those reasons are green. And another thing, you have to get rid of that fireball you got now before you can even consider chasing down somebody else's chick. It's hard as hell to juggle too many women at the same time, dude. You know I know all about that. The shit's rough."

"I wasn't thinking about pursuing, Friday's girl. I was just entertaining the thought, kinda."

"Well, you need to put your sights on somebody that isn't engaged to a freakin' millionaire. You can't win, D. Listen to your boy on this one."

"It was just a thought."

"Make sure that's all it stays as," he said as he jumped out of his seat. "I'm gonna get a beer. You want one?"

"No thanks."

"Alright, I'll be back." He said walking away. "Get ready to set that pool table back up, too."

"Okay," I answered. My mind was still transfixed on Veronica. I didn't know why, but I just couldn't stop thinking about her. I knew Rex wouldn't be any help. But just talking about Veronica got me excited about seeing her again somehow.

I sat on my bed, staring at the tube, watching an episode of Good Times. I looked over to the piece of paper that Veronica had written her number on, on top of the coffee table alongside my bed while James Evans explained to Florida why he had lost another job. I wasn't too much into watching another rerun of my favorite show. I was more inclined by my urge to call my good friend from college to strike up a conversation before it got too late into the night. She did ask me to call her some time. I could just visualize myself calling her up, but my only problem was that I didn't have any idea as to what I could say. Despite my lack of subject matter, I finally mustered enough bravery to pick up the phone and just dial. I dialed her quickly since I had remembered the phone number by heart. I had been staring at it for over an hour. The phone rang. With each ring, my heart pounded faster. I wanted her to answer quickly, yet at the same time, I was so nervous that I didn't want her to answer at all. At least I tried to talk to her, I thought.

Right on the brink of hanging up after the fourth ring, she answered, "Hello."

My throat went dry and made it a struggle for me to get even one word out. "Veronica," my voice cracked.

"Darrel?"

"Yeah," I said timidly, as my heart rate began to settle down. "It's me."

"Darrel," she giggled, "What's up?"

"Oh, nothing. I was just calling to see how you were." I couldn't believe how on edge I was.

"I'm fine. You're not in the bed yet?"

"No, I'm watching Good Times."

"Really? I was watching it too."

"Yeah," I laughed. "It's the one where James throws the chair into the wall."

"I know," she said. "That's one of my favorite episodes."

"Yeah, that was a good one." I said, as I realized that I really had nothing to say. I was just excited she was on the other end. A few moments of silence consumed the phone.

"Sooo," she said, "Do you go to work tomorrow?"

"Work? Yeah, I'm going to work tomorrow."

"What time do you have to be there?"

"Do you wanna go to church with me on Sunday?" I blurted out.

"Church?" she paused. "Sure, I'll go to church with you."

"Really?" I asked. "That would be great. I told my mother that I was coming, and I thought that I may as well bring someone else along with me. So I was like, let me see if Veronica wanted to go."

"That's fine with me, Darrel."

"Yeah, yeah," I fumbled. "You'll like my mom's church. That choir of theirs can throw down!"

"Darrel, are you alright?"

"Yeah," I answered. "Why'd you ask that?" But I wasn't alright. I didn't know what to say next. It was as if I was Superman and she was kryptonite, weakening my brain.

"You just sound a little different, that's all. You actually sound a little nervous about something."

"No, no, I'm fine. It's just late, you know. A brotha' sounds a little different when it gets late."

"Uh-huh," she uttered. "Well, what church does your mother go to? I'm suppose to go somewhere with Terrance later that day, so I'm going to have to meet you there."

"First Baptist," I answered.

"Oh, I know where that is. What time does service start?"

"Eleven."

"Well, I'll be there. Is that all you wanted to ask me?"

"Yeah."

"Okay. Well, you have a nice night, Darrel."

"You too," I answered. "Veronica!" I yelled, just

144

as she was about to hang up.

"Yes."

I knew I wanted to say something else, but I still didn't know what. "Thanks," I said as I just gave up trying to strike up any real conversation.

"No problem, Darrel. Thanks for inviting me. I'll talk to you later." She hung up.

Frustrated, I threw the phone onto the edge of the bed. I flopped on my side as I felt I had made a total fool out of myself. I knew I should've thought about what I wanted to say before I called her, but I was way too anxious. At least the call wasn't a total waste. I did get her to come to church with me, so that was definitely something for me to look forward too. My main concern was if I would act normal when she arrived to church with me. Ever since I discovered my little crush on her, I could hardly talk to her. I didn't want to come at her like I would with any other female because she knew me like a book. And on top of that, she was no ordinary female to me. She was much more. I still didn't know exactly what I wanted with her, but I was sure glad I was guaranteed another day of her company.

Chapter Nine

Some people love their jobs, while others walk into their place of employment, yearning for the end of the day as soon as they step foot in. I guess I did a little bit of both. I loved my job, but I despised some of the knuckleheads my job forced me to be around. And yet, on the latest episode of Darrel Walker and the Knuckleheads, today was the day we finally reviewed the finished product for Terrance Friday's documentary. I sat at a huge round table along with Dale Summers and my boss, Perry Putnam, as we wrapped up our screening of the video. As the final credits rolled, Putnam looked at me with a gigantic smile.

"You guys have outdone yourselves," Putnam stated.

"We did it all for you, Perry," Summers chuckled as he flicked the remote towards the television, shutting it off. "It's ready for it's premier Monday night."

"Monday night! I want that piece to be broadcasted every night next week. It's excellent."

"That's what I'm talking about," Dale turned to me. "Isn't that great, Walker?"

"Sure," I answered as I folded my arms, feeling a bit chilly in the frigid room. Putnam always had it feeling like the South Pole in that room.

"You guys didn't let me down." Putnam rose from the table. "Believe me when I tell you that you guys hooked me up–you hooked me up! And you two will definitely be rewarded for your good works."

"We're just looking forward to the next special project, sir," Dale added. "It's a pleasure to be your go-to man when you want something of this caliber completed."

"And you two surely know how to get me what I ask for. This won't be the last time I pair you men together. I have to make a few calls to set everything in motion," Putnam proclaimed as he walked to the door. "Good job, men. Peace, now."

"Thanks," I replied as I cringed to the thought of working with Dale again.

"Anytime, sir. Anytime at all." Dale quickly replied, sucking up. "We'll be waiting on that next assignment."

Putnam left the room as I gazed at Dale with a disgusted look on my face. He could never do anything without sucking up to people, and I despised it. But what I hated even more was when he was done kissing butt, and he'd rapidly revert back to his annoying cockiness, acting as if he didn't do anything wrong.

"That's what the hell I'm talking about, Walker. I can just feel myself moving up in the ranks of the company as we speak. Pretty soon, I'll have Putnam's job." he declared.

"It's a video that no one in their right mind will watch," I told him.

"Are you crazy? Friday is a living legend. Everyone in Atlanta is gonna tune into my production."

"He's overrated." I disregarded his comment of sole claim to the production. I could care less if my name was attached to it at all. I was just happy it was over.

"Whatever, chief," he said as he jumped up and headed for the door. "You did a good job on this project, Walker. Just don't let your negativity hold you back in the future. The way my career is going right now, you just may need something from me one day."

"Thanks for the advice. When I really need some, I'll let you know."

He turned away from the door while I gathered all of my paperwork and put it into one pile as I prepared to leave.

"What's the deal with you, Walker? You never have anything good to say to me."

"Maybe I don't like you, Dale."

"Why wouldn't you like me?"

"Because you make it so easy to do." I could've came up with over a million reasons, but that one was probably number one.

"Walker, I have you know that everybody I know likes me. You're just jealous of me, that's all."

"You know what?"

"What?"

"You're right, Summers. I *am* jealous of you. It just kills me when I see how effectively you make folks wanna gag when you come around. How in the hell did you get so good at doing that, man?"

He pointed his finger at me with a small grin on his face. "You know, I'm going home now. I'm just gonna let that one slide. I was going to cut you in on a piece of that fat check I'm getting for my scoop on Friday's wedding, but things aren't looking too good for you right now, buddy."

"Well, don't do me no favors," I said shrugging my shoulders.

"Good bye, Walker," he said as he slammed the door behind himself.

I felt a little bad after I told him off, but it was only the truth. I knew he would get over it and return Monday to aggravate me all over again. Feeling pleased that I'd finally gotten under his skin for once, I sat back and peacefully reclined in my chair. I had a lot on my mind. I spent the majority of my week dodging calls from Natasha while I weighed my options on how to break up with her. Back in the day, I could let a dame go at the blink of an eye. But now, I was trying to be gentle. I didn't want to hurt the girl, but I needed to let her go. And I'd decided once I got Natasha out of the way, I could then get to the bottom of my situation with Brandi and her mind games. My plan was to find her, and tell her what she could do with her pathetic sense of humor.

Ruth knocked on the door and stuck her head in. "Darrel, could you please answer line three, immediately? There's a woman on that line that has been calling in all morning, demanding to speak with you as soon as your meeting was over. This is her sixth call. She's been waiting on hold now for twenty-seven minutes and she refuses to hang up. Can you please talk to her?"

I looked towards the phone in the corner of the room, "Sure, I'll see what she wants."

"Thank you very much," she replied closing the door.

I walked to the phone knowing exactly who it was. It was Natasha, and she was beginning to tick me off by calling me at my job the way she was doing. No man likes to be hunted down, especially by a woman he's not diggin'.

"Yes," I calmly answered the phone.

"Darrel," she replied, almost sounding like she was out of breath. "Where have you been? I've been calling you all week, boo."

"Working. I've just been working."

"Well, why haven't you called?" she asked. "Did I do something wrong? I'm sorry if I did. I've been calling you for days trying to find out what's up."

"Nothing's up. I've just been working extra hard this week. I've been working on this project about Terrance Friday that's suppose to air next week." My mind was constantly debating on ending it all right there over the phone.

"Oh, I can understand it if you were just busy. I just got worried, that's all. I had to make sure my boo was okay," she giggled.

"I do need to talk to you, today—in person." I opted to do my business face-to-face and not like some chump over the phone.

"Well, we can talk. I'm off today, so you can pick

me up from home. Is it really important?"

Well… we'll discuss it when I get to your place later. Is six okay?"

"Sure," she replied anxiously. "That's fine."

"Okay, then I'll see you…"

"Darrel," she interrupted.

"Yes?"

"I love you," she replied slowly.

It was as if somebody had punched me in the stomach. She said the "L" word, and it caught me completely off guard. "I'll see you at six," I replied as I slammed the phone down, acting as if I didn't even hear the statement at all. I shook my head as I came to the ultimate conclusion–the girl was sprung! Now how in the hell was I gonna get out of that?

I had no idea how I was going to tell Natasha that I wanted to part ways. All I did know was that it was going to be said in some form or fashion. If she was falling in love, it was time for me to snap her out. I arrived at her house exactly at six sharp, just like I advised her. I pulled into the driveway and parked beside a green Impala with a set of glossy rims that could just about blind a person standing too close.

I hopped out of my ride and noticed Chester and another guy standing on the porch, each holding leashes to two very vicious looking pit-bulls. I took precise caution as I approached the two because I've never been fond of any kind of dogs.

Chester immediately saw me coming. "D, what's going on, dawg?"

"C-Dawg," I said, as I looked towards his pet that had just began to ferociously bark at me.

"*Shut the hell up, dog!*" he yelled as he angrily yanked the dog back with the leash. The animal's noise quickly ceased. "It's cool, D. He ain't gonna bite."

"What's up, cuz?" said the other guy as he shook my hand. His dog was much calmer, and just sniffed my leg. "The name's Brick."

"Mine's Darrel. What's going on?" I replied. He wore a white tee-shirt just like Chester, but his was much tighter around his stomach since he was a bit out of shape. The brotha' was high yellow, but his lips were black as coal. Obviously the brotha' had been choking up on too many of those funny cigarettes because I smelled the scent on both of 'em.

"You come to see Natasha, right?" Chester asked.

"Yeah. She in there?" I replied.

"Nah, she went off with Brick's sister to pick up something from the store. She'll be back in a minute, though. You can wait in the house. We're about to slide down the road to let these niggas know whose dogs bark the loudest."

"Yeah," Brick added. "I lost about five hundred down there last week. Son of a bitch almost ripped my dog's throat off. I got Luther this week. He's quiet, but lethal. That's for damn sho'."

"Well, I wish you guys luck," I replied with a puzzled look.

"We don't need no luck, D. With Brick's dog, and my little Bitch right here, them niggas gonna leave broke as hell with some messed up pups." He bent down and stroked his dog on the back of it's neck. "Ain't that right, Bitch?" His dog stuck his tongue out, relishing all of his owner's attention. Chester looked up at me. "The door's open, dawg. Ain't nobody but Ma in there. Just make yourself at home. You ain't no stranger."

"Okay," I said as I walked towards the door and entered the house.

I walked in, and the sounds of Marvin Gaye's 'Let's Get It On' filled the air. The house wasn't as neat this time around. It was a bit messy and there was a lot of smoke consuming the place. As I walked towards the den, I noticed a heavy-set, medium complexion woman, sitting on the sofa with a cigarette burning in one hand, flipping through a magazine that was hanging off her lap with the other. She wore a pink robe that revealed a good portion of her sagging cleavage and a scarf on her head with rollers bulging out from under it.

"Hi," I said.

"Hello there," the woman answered. "You must be Tasha's man. Come on in here. I finally get a chance to meet you."

"It's nice to meet you, also."

"Natasha got her a good looking man, too," she said.

I walked in slowly, a little surprised by her kindness. She sounded a lot nicer than she looked. I walked towards the chair that was across from her. "Uh-uh, baby, sit over here," she said as she pointed to the area next to her on the couch. "I won't bite."

"That's fine," I said, feeling a bit uncomfortable. I sat right next to her. I tried not to look towards her for too long because I didn't want her to think I was trying to look down at her breasts. The view I was getting wasn't pleasant at all because all I could see were huge stretch-marks running down the opening of her outfit.

"There you go," she said as she closed the magazine and slung it onto the coffee table. "Let me put this cigarette out," she said as she closed the opening of her robe and put her hand over her chest area to keep her breasts from rolling out while she smashed the cigarette into the ashtray on the table. "It done got so smoky in here now. Can you breath alright? I don't want you to croak in here on the account of my second hand smoke. You know they're starting to say that's just as bad for you now."

"Yeah, I'm fine," I answered.

"That's good. I don't want to be rude, now.

Normally I keep the place straight, but I just got off work and you know how it is to just be getting off. You don't feel like doing nothin' at all," she advised me. "And that damn boy out there is more concerned about his dog fighting than picking up one single thing in this house. He don't do nothin' around here to help me out. What we gonna do about this generation… You know, I didn't even catch your name, son. What is it, again?"

"Darrel, Darrel Walker, mam."

"Oh, okay, now I remember your name," amazingly she was able to tilt her body towards me on the small sofa. "You're the one that got my daughter on cloud nine. She's been doing *some* talking about you, I tell ya'. Now I can see why."

"Really?"

"Yeah. She talks about you all day and all night. I almost feel like I already know you, and this is the first time I'm meeting you. And I'm so impressed by all the good things I'm hearing about you."

"Gee, I don't know what to say," The last thing I wanted to do was meet the girl's mother, and break up with her on the same day. I wasn't going to let that stop me, though.

"She said you work at the TV station–the public one."

"Yeah, Atlanta Public Access." Our close proximity made me extremely hot as I began to feel more and more uncomfortable by the second. I was hoping Natasha would just burst in at any minute to relieve me from my impromptu meeting with her mother.

"She said you could lay the rod down pretty good there, too."

"Huh?"

"Don't act surprised, Darrel. We're in the new millennium, now. I talk with my daughter. How do you think she learned all those moves with her hips when she's

153

on top? She learned that from me, chile."

"Excuse me, mam."

"Oh, Darrel, don't even act like that. I know she rides you." she laughed. "That used to be my specialty before I put on all this weight. Boy, I could ride a man to sleep."

"Uh, Mrs. Stanley…"

"It's Ms. Williams. Stanley is Natasha's no good daddy's last name," she moved closer to me with her right breast about to roll on out. "But you can feel free to call me Rose."

She placed her hand on my thigh, and I immediately jolted off of the couch. "Okay, now, I think I'm gonna go outside and wait for Natasha in my car."

"There's no fun out in the car, Darrel," she said as she jumped up and reached at me.

"Whoa, there," I pushed her hands away. "Now, mam, I'm seeing your daughter right now. And truthfully, I don't get down like this."

"What's the matter, Darrel? You don't like big women or something? I may not be able to ride it like I used to, but there's a ton of other stuff I can do. All you gotta do is try it out, baby."

"I can't help you with that, mam. I told you I was seeing your daughter right now," I repeated myself. I was wrecking my brain trying to figure out what was wrong with this nutty woman.

"Well, break up with her then," she said as she wrapped her arms around my neck. She was certainly quick for her size. "I don't mind having my daughter's sloppy seconds. I kinda like the idea."

"Well I don't!" I pushed her back. "Now lady, you're gonna have to back up, now. You've got me all wrong."

"No, honey, come on and get some of this. Don't you know that the older the berry the sweeter the juice? I'll have you begging for more of this, baby" she said as she started grabbing for my manhood.

"No thank you," I continued to push her away. I felt as if I was defending myself from the likes of death.

"Come on, just give mama a little piece."

"*No!*" I yelled.

Suddenly, the thumping sound of music could be heard in the driveway. We both froze and looked towards the window. Through the thin white curtains we could see Natasha jumping out of a white Navigator. The crazed woman sucked her teeth and retreated to the sofa.

"Too late now," she said as she picked up her cigarette and relit it. "You could've had some of this and climaxed in less than five minutes. You just don't know how good this stuff is."

I didn't even look her way. I just straightened myself up so when Natasha walked in, she wouldn't expect anything had just happened. And I didn't dare get anywhere closer to that crazy woman she called her mother. She opened her magazine and started looking through it again as if I wasn't even there. I had already made a mental note to myself not to ever step foot in her house again. Not even if my life depended on it.

Natasha walked in. "Darrel," she said as she looked towards me. "I'm sorry, boo. I had to pick up some relaxer for my mom. The first store we went to was out of the kind she uses."

"That's okay," I said, still a little shaken up.

She gave me a strange stare. "Why are you standing by the door? Did you get a chance to meet my mother?"

I looked back towards the den and gave her mother a brief glance. "Yeah, we've met."

"Just leave the relaxer on the stool beside the door, baby," her mother yelled out.

"Okay, Ma," she said as she placed the bag on the

stool.

"You ready?" I quickly grabbed the doorknob.

"Sure. Ma, I'll be back later," Natasha advised her mother.

"Okay. Tell Darrel he can come by anytime he wants to, baby. That's a fine young man you got there." the woman yelled.

I was already through the door and totally ignoring any comments made after I left the house. The woman's attack almost ruined the idea of intimacy for me permanently. She had severely traumatized me. I rapidly marched to my car, not waiting on Natasha at all.

"Darrel, are you okay?" she asked attempting to catch up with me. "I'm sorry for keeping you waiting like that. I thought it was only gonna take a few minutes."

"I'm fine," I said not looking back. At this point, I was quite sure that everyone that lived in her house was missing a couple of marbles.

"You seem a little bothered," she said as she trotted to the passenger side of the car.

"I'm good." At this point I didn't care how I broke it to her, as long as it was finally over. We hopped into the car simultaneously.

"Here you go, boo," she said as she pulled my face to hers and gave me a kiss. I didn't kiss her back. She pulled away and looked at me strangely. "Are you sure you okay, boo? You didn't kiss me back."

"Natasha…"

"I'll be more than happy to make it up to you when we get over to your place, baby," she promised as she began caressing my inner thigh.

I took a deep breath and looked towards my window. I couldn't hold it in any longer. "No, everything's not okay, Natasha."

"Well, what is it? Did I do something wrong? I can change it, whatever it is."

I shook my head while examining the fear in her eyes. "You didn't do anything wrong. It's me."

"What? Do you need some space? I know we're moving kinda fast. I can understand it if you need some space. I'll be glad to give it to you, really. I don't wanna pressure you or anything."

"Natasha, it's not space. I…I'm just not ready for all of this."

"Well, Darrel, we can chill out for a while. I don't mind."

I placed my hand on top of hers. "I'm afraid that we're not gonna be able to see each other at all, anymore. I'm sorry, Natasha."

I could literally see the wells of her eyes begin to water. "Did I do something wrong?"

"No, no, no," I advised her as I gently squeezed her hand. "It's me. I'm just not ready for the relationship thing, that's all. You're great, Natasha."

She quickly wiped a tear away that had found it's way down her cheek. "Well, we can still see each other, right? This doesn't have to be goodbye, does it?"

I nodded my head. "I'm afraid so. Natasha, you're a great woman. I'm quite sure there are lots of guys trying to get with you on a daily basis. I just don't feel that it's fair to you, for me to be feeling the way that I feel inside, consciously knowing that there's not any real future for us. I just can't do that to you. I will not do that to you."

She turned away from me and bowed her head. "I can do anything you want me to do, Darrel. All you have to do is ask."

"Then walk away, Natasha. Find a man that's going to love you the way that you deserve to be loved. You need more than just a sex partner."

"I thought we were more than just sex, Darrel. I… I have feelings for you. Don't you feel the same way, too?"

I turned away from her not wanting her to see the

cold truth from my face. There wasn't a word that I could say. The saddest revelation that crossed my mind was the fact that to me, we were just sex. Simple, loveless sex.

There was a silence in the car. I came to the conclusion that her heart was going to be broken no matter what I said, and it saddened me. All I could say was that at least I didn't let it go any further.

"Well, I guess you've made up your mind," she said as she burst into tears.

"Natasha," I said as I reached at her for a hug.

She pushed me away and dashed out of the car. All I could do was look as she retreated into the house. I felt like the dirtiest man on earth. I wanted to run out on that porch of hers, break the door down and tell her that I was sorry, but I knew it wouldn't change anything. So I started my car, backed out of her driveway and headed for home.

Chapter Ten

Now if there's one thing that made my mother happy, it was me going with her to church. Yet, if there was anything that made her even happier it would be for me to be tentative during the whole service while I was with her. You see, it was hard for a brotha' to party all night at the clubs and then try to stay awake during the whole church service the next morning. And being that I wasn't a child anymore, my mother didn't smack me on the back of my neck like she used to. She just grabbed my hand and squeezed it. The more I dozed off, the tighter she would squeeze.

With those party days being long behind me, and Veronica accompanying us to service, I was well rested and ready for the good Word. I wanted to be fresh and alert for everybody because my mother always liked to show me off to her church family and Pastor Frye. Pastor Frye was sort of a surrogate father to me after my father passed away when I was fourteen. He'd occasionally stop by the house and take me places and explain different parts of the Bible to me. I think I disappointed him a bit because I became an adult that knew and understood the Word he preached, but I could never resist that one thing he tried so hard to drill into my head the most—fornication. He always thought I could do so much better with my life if I just found that one special woman and settled down. And I must admit, I tried it, but I just didn't get too far with it. However, I don't think my situation with Brandi would've received his full blessing.

As I checked myself out in the mirror one last time, I heard the deafening sound of the horn to my mother's '78 Cutlass Supreme. She wanted to pick me up because she said it was a special occasion for me to stray away from all those demons that had been keeping me away from the church for so long. Maybe that was one of her reasons, but I was quite sure it was to pick me up to make certain that I brought my black tail along.

I gave myself one last stare, and I was pleased by what I saw. I was wearing my black designer suit and my favorite tie, wanting to look as fine as I could for Veronica. I also wanted to look good for anyone in the church that knew about my flawed marriage–just to let them know that I was still going strong and that crap didn't break me.

I hurried out of the house and jumped into my mom's jet black automobile. "Hi, Ma," I greeted her.

A big smile sprang onto her face. "You sure look good, son."

"Thanks, Ma. You don't look too shabby yourself." Ma always looked good on her favorite day of the week. She wore her stunning light blue dress with her sparkling pearl earrings pop gave her the year before he passed. She wore them every Sunday since he gave them to her.

"Now tell me, are you looking that good for the Lord or for this young lady you took it upon yourself to invite, Mr. Walker?"
I chuckled, "Of course you know I'm looking good for the Lord… and a little for that nice young lady I invited.

She laughed, "Well, Darrel, the Lord don't care how you look as long as you come. And if this young lady is as nice as you told me, she wouldn't mind neither."

"I know, Ma. But you raised me to look good everywhere I go, and this is just a continuance of your good teachings."

"Boy, anyway." She began backing out of the driveway. "Gone head and put on that seatbelt. I don't want you to go busting your brains out if we get in a wreck. You know these people 'round here can't drive."

"Okay, Ma." I strapped the seatbelt across my chest.

"So tell me a little more about this lady friend of yours," she requested as she streaked down the street.

"There's really not a lot to tell. I met her in college, and she's a good friend."

"A good friend, huh? Well, out of all the friendly females you've had over the years, son, you ain't never invited any of 'em to church. Now, I may be old, but I'm not stupid. You're sweet on this girl, aren't you?"

"Ma... she's engaged. I thought I told you that yesterday. I just invited her because I wanted her to come. And then meet you of course. I wanted to show you that I wasn't after every female back in school."

"Hogwash, Darrel Walker! Are you forgetting that I raised you, and I can smell a lie coming outta' your mouth a mile away?"

I rolled my eyes. "Okay, Ma, I may have a little crush on the woman. But honest–she's engaged."

"Hmmm, engaged is not married, Darrel Walker."

"Now, Ma, how are you gonna say that? Aren't you suppose to be pro-marriage? The advocate of settling down and having kids."

"And you're right, son. I am an advocate of marriage, and I just can't wait for some grandchildren. But this friend of yours ain't married yet. And you'd be a fool if you think that she could be the one and you let somebody else take her from you," she advised. "You better make sure you know what you're doing, Darrel. You may not get too many more chances for Miss Right. I done told ya'."

"Ma, I know. But I'm not even trying get involved like that. We're just friends. Nothing more, nothing less."

"Well, wait until I meet her. I'll let you know if she's the one for my baby. A mother knows these things, you know?"

"That's fine, Ma," I replied, "But just try not to call me your baby around her. That's kind of embarrassing at my age."

She chuckled, "I'll try…. my baby!"

"Real funny, Ma."

I decided to wait out on the church steps for Veronica's arrival while my mother was inside doing her habitual Sunday greetings. I continuously traded smiles with the folks who stared at me trying to figure out who I was, and the other people who tried to familiarize themselves with me since they hadn't seen me for so long. As the early morning temperature began to rise from the sun breaking through the vanishing clouds, I realized I really needed to come to church more often.

"Brother Walker," a deep voice from behind me called out. I turned around, and it was Pastor Frye.

"Pastor Frye…" I uttered. He looked much different than the last time I saw him. He had stopped dyeing his hair black and was now showing off his glittery gray.

"It's good to see you made it," he said as he greeted me with a firm handshake.

I smiled, "I guess Mom told you I was coming."

"Yes, she did, son. So how have you been?"

"I've been doing fine. Mostly working and what not."

"That's good. It's good for a man to stay busy. An idle mind is the devil's playground."

"Yes sir, it is." I said as I shoved my hands into my pockets attempting to hide my nervousness. They had began to shake as I knew he was going to begin interrogating me with more specific questions about how I was living. It was a habit that haunted me throughout my childhood with him. Ma always said it was just the devil trying to find a snug place to hide inside me.

"The church hasn't seen you in a while, Darrel."

"Well, you know, like I said, I've been working and what not."

"Well, you're not too busy for the Lord, are you?"

"No, no, no…. I'm never too busy for the Lord."

"Then why haven't you been around, son?"

My mouth was wide open, but nothing was coming out of it. I didn't know how to answer, so I decided not to even attempt to be creative about explaining myself. "I don't even know, Pastor Frye."

"Well, that's not good, Darrel. You need to find your way down here more often and get your head stuck into the good book. You know we don't have forever to find out what we're gonna do about our relationship with the Lord."

"Well, I'm working on it, Pastor Frye."

"Maybe you need to work a little bit harder, son." he placed his hand on my shoulder and examined me from head to toe. "My, you've grown up to be a fine young man, Darrel. The spitting image of your father."

"Thank you," I replied, surprised that he had unexpectedly changed gears on me at the blink of an eye. Maybe he wasn't going to be too hard on me after all, I suddenly thought.

"I heard that you were married for a spell," he said.

Maybe not. "Well, yeah, I got married. It really didn't work out."

"Did you get to know that woman through all the four seasons, son?"

I couldn't believe he was grilling me the way that he was. And there wasn't anything I could do about it but break down in front of him like a big ole' oaf. "I think we spent most of the spring together, sir."

"The spring! Son, you're suppose to get to know your partner from winter to fall. That's probably why things didn't work out like they should've. Darrel, you know better than that."

Goodness, I hated when he made me feel like a heathen. "I guess it was spur of the moment. I honestly thought it would work."

He nodded his head with a frown. "You did, huh. Well, we live to make mistakes, Darrel. It's only when we learn from them that we really excel. That's why our God is a forgiving God. He knows we're gonna mess up, but we can't get no closer to him unless we make changes on how we do things."

"Well, I am trying to make changes, sir."

"That's good, Darrel," he said. "I'm glad that you're striving to do what's right. You've grown to become a fine young man. Wisdom will come soon enough. Just remember that you don't have forever to steer in the right path."

"I know, Pastor Frye. I'm working on it." I felt like a total moron. He broke me down like a car on four flat tires.

"It was good talking to you, son," he said as he patted me on my shoulder. "Now, I'm expecting to see you here more often, alright?"

"You will."

"That's good. That's real good," he said. "Well, let me go get ready. I look forward to seeing you inside, Darrel."

"And I'm looking forward to hearing you speak."

"The Lord," he corrected me, swinging his index finger in the air. "The Lord speaks through me, son. I'm just his messenger."

"Well, you know what I'm saying, sir." He sure had a lot of messages of his own to give me about my marriage.

He smiled, "See you inside."

When he walked into the church, my stress level dwindled by fifty percent. I was still tense because Veronica had yet to arrive. What kind of girl would stand a guy up at church, I thought. Then I caught a glance of Veronica's truck speeding down the highway and briskly pulling in at the end of the church parking lot. She made it.

"Darrel, has she come yet?" my mother asked as she strolled up behind me. "Service is about to start in a few minutes. Pastor Frye just walked in."

I looked back at my mom, attempting to keep in the huge smile that I was trying so hard to contain. "She just pulled in, Ma."

"Where she at, child? Let me see her," she demanded as she put her hand over her eyes to block the blinding sunlight to gaze down the parking lot.

"She's coming, Ma. Just be patient."

"Don't tell me to be patient," she replied. "I wanna see the girl that's got my baby head over heels."

"Ma…" I rolled my eyes and decided not to even go there with her.

Veronica rushed through the parking lot with a light brown dress and her hair fixed up. She didn't have on too much make-up, but just enough to make her beautiful face flare.

"Darrel," she called my name out.

"We weren't going nowhere," I replied. I looked over to my mother. She had a huge smile on her face. I could tell she was impressed by Veronica's class.

"We sure weren't, baby." Mom replied.

Veronica approached my mother with her hand out for a handshake. "You must be Darrel's mom. It's a pleasure to meet you."

My mom bypassed the handshake and engulfed Veronica with a captivating hug "It's nice to meet you, suga."

Veronica glanced at me with a grin while being taken hostage by my mother's greeting. I shrugged my shoulders, knowing that my mother wasn't going to settle just for a handshake.

"You are a nice looking young woman. Just nice looking, yes you are," my mother advised her. "You're as every bit of beautiful as Darrel told me."

Veronica looked over to me and blushed as my mother finally freed her. "I'm glad Darrel thinks so highly of me."

"Oh yes he does," Ma replied. "Come on in this church before we miss something." Ma grabbed her by her hand and led her into the church. "Come on in here and follow us, Darrel. Don't act like you're scared now."

"I'm coming, I'm coming," I replied.

My mother was acting as if we were about to get married. I walked in and followed them to ma's selected spot for us to sit. Ma sat between the both of us and held each one of our hands. While the church announcements were going on, Veronica and my eyes would randomly catch a glimpse of each other. I'd dare not say anything because my mom always felt that church was a time for listening and praise, even through the announcements.

"Oh, Darrel, I got to go to the restroom. I knew I should've went before they even got started up there," Mom whispered into my ear.

"You can go ahead and go. Pastor Frye's not even up there yet."

"I know. I know." She looked towards the back of the church, frustrated she had to leave to go to the restroom now of all times. My mother was a settler. She hated making any extra movements from wherever she was whenever she had gotten comfortable. I think I could count on one hand the few times she had to run off after she finally claimed her spot during service.

"I'll be back," she said as she jumped up and hastily made way to the back of the church.

I decided I would use that moment to slide over and talk with Veronica. It appeared she was highly focused on Sister Fleming who was standing at the front of the church announcing all of the upcoming church events.

"And how are you this morning? I really didn't get to say anything to you earlier," I said in a low voice.

"Darrel, you know your mother is gonna kill you for talking," she said, not even looking at me.

"My mom ain't gonna do nothing. I'm just being a gentleman and speaking to my guest."

"Well, don't get into any trouble, Darrel. You know we can talk after church." She looked at me and smiled. "I'm sorry for being late, too. Something came up at the last minute."

"Everything's fine, right?"

"It's nothing really."

"You sure?"

"We'll talk about it after church."

"Okay," I caught my mom returning out of the corner of my eye, and I wasted no time with sliding back over. I surely didn't want to hear her mouth.

Ma slid her way down the aisle, forcing everyone in her path to make harsh adjustments to move out of her way. She was never the slimmest chick, but you could never advise her against sitting in the middle of the pew, no matter how many legs she would smash if she had to move in or out.

"Did I miss anything," she asked me as she reclaimed her spot between us.

"No, I think they said something about bingo on Thursday night, though." I answered.

"You see, if you were listening, you would know what she said and you wouldn't have to think."

"I just blacked out for a second, Ma."

"Well make sure you don't black out when Pastor Frye gets up there to speak the Word," she said. "You need to hear everything he gotta say."

"I know, Ma," I replied with a sigh.

After Sister Fleming finished with her announcements, First Baptist's very own crowd moving choir came out and tore the house down with a few of their holy songs. All the magnificent singing got momma in full throttle with her clapping and praising. Every time she got up and clapped, she made sure she kicked my leg for me to join in. She only had to do it once because I was too smart to sit my butt down in that pew while my momma was about to catch the Holy Ghost. Either I was gonna have to catch it with her or at least look like it. Sitting down while the praising of the Lord was going on was a definite no-no. I was sure to get my behind up when momma did, just like dad did when he was living. Anything else would be a whole lot of trouble.

Pastor Frye finally got on the altar and began his preaching of the Word. He had on his purple robe and his glasses that always made him look more sophisticated but a lot older than what he really was. As he began, he looked over to me with a smile. I smiled right back at him with a sense of paranoia running through my mind. There was no doubt in my mind he and my mother had a good long talk about good ole' Darrel Walker.

"...and I know I'm gonna make some of the people in here feel a little uncomfortable up in here this morning, but I wanna make sure a lot of you folk don't get content with where you are. You see, a lot of you folk ain't living right."

"Uhm, hum," my mother mumbled as she nudged me on the elbow. I sat there acting like I didn't feel it, setting my full focus on the pastor.

"You see, a lot of y'all wanna live like you're married but ain't."

Oh Lord, he was giving his sermon about relationships. I knew it was blatantly inspired by my arrival.

"You wanna wake up and fix your man or your woman coffee in the morning with some eggs and some grits after you laid up all night doing things you know you ain't got no business doing."

"Tell 'em 'bout it Pastor Frye," my mother yelled

out.

"Oh, I come to bring it this morning," Pastor Frye spoke.

Brandi looked over at me and smiled. I didn't even smile back. I just sat there emotionless. My mother knew she had me when I agreed to come. With Pastor Frye's help, she made certain I got something out of the visit.

"And neither one of you got a ring, ain't been before the Lord, just sinning your lives away. Talking about you thinking about getting married. Or we ain't ready for no commitment. Or, or, my personal favorite, I'm too young to be tied down. Now correct me if I'm wrong, but you ain't never too young to go to hell."

A whole slew of 'that's rights' and 'amen's' followed behind Pastor Frye's words. His message was simple, if you're not married, then you don't have any business sleeping around. I heard it many times before with our one-on-one sessions during my youth. As he continued to speak I looked over to Veronica and fell into a brief trance. I thought, now that's a real woman. Her hair, her eyes, her smile, that was everything I wanted in a woman. I thought, if I could find a woman that just had half of the qualities she possessed, that would be alright. But if I could have the original, that would be even better. Then I thought about how I didn't want to mess up her life with all of my foolishness, knowing good and dern well I wasn't totally over Brandi. But I knew one thing, I would treat her a whole lot better than Terrance Friday could.

"Boy, your pastor know he can speak the truth," Veronica said as we walked down the steps, exiting the church.

"He's good now," I added. We stood on the curb, as I looked back for my mother who was busy yapping off to all of her friends inside the building.

"That's exactly what I needed this morning, I tell

ya'."

"Has something been bothering you?" I asked.

She shook her head. "I'm alright now."

"You sure? It sounded like something was bothering you earlier."

"Well that's before I heard that wonderful sermon. I'm alright now, Darrel."

"Okay, I'm just checking." My attention shifted towards the church entrance. "Now I wonder where that woman is up in there. It's getting hot out here *quick*!"

"Oh let your momma mingle with her friends. Besides, you know that you're a momma's boy."

"A momma's boy? How you gonna call me a momma's boy?"

"Because you are. Ain't nothing wrong with being a momma's boy, though. I was always my daddy's little girl."

"Ain't nothing wrong with being a momma's boy? Girl, I'm not a momma's boy. Have you bumped that pretty little head of yours?"

"Nope, but I can tell a momma's boy when I see one. And you're one Darrel Walker. I bet she still calls you her baby," she laughed.

"Woman, stop the nonsense. My momma knows what's up. She doesn't try to play me like I'm some child."

"You can tell me anything, Darrel, but I know you... and you are a momma's boy, just face it."

I sucked my teeth, not wanting to admit that she was actually right. The last thing any man wants to admit is that he's a momma's boy, no matter how much he loves his mother. "I'm not even gonna argue with you."

"Don't worry, you can't."

"Why'd y'all run off," my mother cried out as she approached us. "I had some folks that I wanted you two to meet."

"Now, Ma, you know I'm not gonna let you have

us talking to all your friends up in there. They'll have us up in church 'till midnight."

"The more time you spend in church, the better, Darrel Walker," my mother said firmly. "And how did you like the service, Veronica? Did you enjoy it?"

"I loved it, Mrs. Walker," she answered.

"That's good. I'm glad you enjoyed it." My mother grabbed her by the hands and caressed them. "You know, the church is open every Sunday, and we're always looking for new members."

"Well, Mrs. Walker, this definitely won't be the last time I'm gonna visit."

"I hear that. Now if I can only get this one right here to come more often, I'll be alright." Ma said pointing at me.

Veronica giggled. I guess she thought it was amusing. "Now, Ma, why you wanna be so hard on me today?" I asked.

"Because that's how I should've been a long time ago. I hope you were in there listening, too."

"I was, Ma."

"Can you guys excuse me for a moment? I need to check my messages," Veronica requested.

"Sure, go right on ahead," my mother advised her.

"Thanks," she said as she pulled out her cell phone and walked off.

As soon as she moved far enough away, my mother grabbed a chunk of my arm and pinched me.

"Ouch... what was that for, Ma?"

She whispered, "You mean to tell me that you're willing to let that nice young lady escape from you?"

"Ma, she's engaged."

"I don't care. That's the future Mrs. Walker standing over there, Darrel. Don't let her pass you by. She's exactly what you need."

I whispered right back at her, "She's already gone,

Ma. She's about to marry Terrance Friday in a month or so."

"Who?"

"Terrance Friday. You know, that basketball player that calls himself 'TGIF'?"

"Child, I don't know nothing about no Friday afternoon. What I do know is you better not let that woman slip out of your hands, Darrel."

I looked towards Veronica, and couldn't help but notice something was bothering her on the other end of her phone. It was written all over her face, although she was doing her best to hide it. "Ma, I'm not letting her pass me by. She has other plans with her life. And they're all with someone else."

"Well, you need to see to it that you get yourself in some of those plans of hers. That's a fine woman there. One that I've always imagined you'd bring home to see me."

"It's not gonna happen, Ma." I advised her as I noticed Veronica approaching us. Her call had ended.

"Hi." Her expression didn't have any of the traces of life it had in it earlier. Whatever news she received on her cell sure didn't look like it was good from her expression.

"Hey, you okay," I asked.

"I'm fine," she answered, doing her best to hide her frustrations. "Ms. Walker, thanks again for welcoming me this morning."

"It's no problem, dear. I'm just happy that I had a chance to meet you. Darrel never lets me meet any of his friends. He must be ashamed of me or something."

"No, I'm not, Ma," I interjected.

"Besides, baby, what are you doing for the rest of the day, anyway?"

"Ma," I interrupted, trying to put an end to her interrogation.

"Darrel, it's okay," Veronica said. "I was supposed to be spending some time with my fiancé at Stone Mountain. But I guess something came up for him."

Mamma quickly nudged me on my arm. I looked at her like she was crazy. She was stuck on the idea of Veronica and me hooking up more than I was. I finally decided that I may as well try and get into something for the day with her if possible anyway. I really didn't have anything else to do.

"Stone Mountain, huh? If it's okay, I'll go out there with you. I haven't been out there in a while."

She smiled, "No, Darrel, it's okay. I don't need your sympathy. I know you have plenty to do today."

"He ain't got a thang to do, Veronica," my mother intervened.

"Thanks a lot, Ma." I shook my head. There wasn't any shame in my mother's game. "But really, I don't have anything to do today. I would love to go out there with you and climb that mountain."

"So you've taken the trail up the mountain before?" she asked.

"Nope, but it ain't nothing to it. What's a mountain?"

She laughed, "Okay, okay, Mr. Mountain Climber. We'll see what's up when we get out there."

"Hey bring it on," I said with an over abundance of arrogance. I had only been to that park once when I was younger, and I was scared to take the airlift up then. I looked over at my mother who was making tremendous strides to keep her laughter in. She knew how terrified I was to go up that mountain.

"I'll pick you up in an hour," she said.

"I'll be waiting with a fresh pair of Timberlands on my feet. You know the address." I said.

"Okay, see you then." She looked towards my mom. "It was nice meeting you, Mrs. Walker."

"You too, Veronica," my mother answered.

"See you in an hour, Darrel. Now don't try to chicken out," she said as she made her way down the row of cars.

"I'll be ready. Ain't no chumps over here."

"Ain't no chumps, but a whole lot of chicken," my mother said out the side of her mouth.

"Ma, why'd you say that?" I turned to her, frowning.

"Have you forgotten when me and your father took you out there when you were younger and you were crying like a baby when we were going up that mountain?"

"Come on, Ma, that was years ago."

She shook her head. "I wanted you to go out with the girl for her to see how good of a man you are, and you're letting her take you up that mountain where I ain't never heard you cry louder." She looked up at the sky, "Lord please help this, boy."

"Ma, you're a trip."

"Come on here and let me get you home," she said as she began wobbling down the parking lot. "And you gonna start coming to church with me more often, too. Your first day back in church and the Lord done gave you a date with a nice woman."

I followed her. "Ma, it's not a date."

"That's what you think," she said as she continued to ramble on through the automobiles.

I waited for Veronica on my couch, nervous like a kid anticipating a report card at the end of the school day. As soon as my mom dropped me off, I threw on some jeans and a polo shirt. I knew a plain ole' tee-shirt would've been much lighter since the day was beginning to feel like it was going to be a scorcher, but I didn't want to look too laid back. I didn't want her to see me too much as her *good ole' friend Darrel*, but much more as *Darrel's not a bad*

174

looking friend. If Friday did manage to do something to make her mad, I wanted to assure my spot as the next man waiting in line.

I heard her car pull into the driveway, and I dashed to the door. I paused for a moment, not wanting to seem too anxious. After I assessed my composure, I stepped out of my house and strolled to her truck. She had a wide smile on her face as her eyes followed me all the way around to her passenger side door. I slid into her ride, nice and smooth.

"What's up, lady?" I asked.

"Hello, Darrel," she said. She had her hair tied back in a pony-tail with a pair of shades fixed on top of her forehead.

"You know I can drive if you want me to."

"No, I'll drive, Mr. Walker," she said as she backed out of my driveway and began easing down the road.

"I don't know why nobody wants to ride in the Maxima no more. It's not as flashy as these big trucks, but it still has it going on, especially mine. My baby's sparkling clean."

"Trust me, Darrel, no one's hating on your ride. I just feel like driving, that's all."

"I know. I just want it to be known that the Maxima is still hot," I announced playfully.

"I know, Darrel," she chuckled.

"So how are you feeling?" I quickly put away my pro-Sedan speech, and jumped right into my questioning. I wanted to get the latest update about her and Friday.

"I'm great. Is something supposed to be wrong with me?"

"I don't know. You tell me. From my understanding, somebody else was suppose to be taking this field trip with you. Am I right?"

She laughed, "Have I told you about how nosey you've gotten over these past few years, Darrel?"

"In Lenox Square, but I don't care. You know me well enough to know that if I got a question, I'm gonna ask it."

"I see that. But for your information, Terrance had to fly out to Los Angeles last night."

"Really?" I asked abruptly.

She looked at me with her mouth wide open. "Yes, and why did you respond like that?"

"No reason. No reason at all."

"Oh, Darrel, you're so full of it," she stated rattled. "Come on, why'd you respond like that? I just know you have something to say."

I wanted to tell her, but I wasn't sure how to. I didn't want to overstep my boundaries with her relationship. "I just did, that's all. I didn't mean anything by it."

She looked at me with that you've-got-a-lot-of-nerve frown that all women have on their faces when they're confident a man is lying to them. After she gave me her look, she focused on just driving. Silence overcame the vehicle. Through my window, I observed the scenery, as the buildings of Metro Atlanta were beginning to become buried amongst the long standing trees along the highway. I knew darn well my not answering her was eating her up inside, and she was contemplating blessing me out about it.

"Tell me!" she demanded.

A grin surfaced upon my face. Women are so predictable when they know information is being withheld from them. They just can't stand it, and Veronica Bethel was no exception.

What I wanted to say was right on the tip of my tongue, but I had to release it carefully. The last thing I wanted to do was piss her off with my opinion. "It just didn't seem like you expected Mr. TGIF to be out of town today, that's all. It looked kinda like he stood you up."

"Darrel, I told you what happened at church. Something came up for him."

"Well, it looked as if the whole ordeal with Friday ticked you off. Now I may be wrong, but that's how I saw it. If something's going wrong, don't hesitate telling me, because I'm just here to help"

She didn't reply. Her face was calm without any expression. Suddenly she let out a harsh sigh. "Darrel, what's it to you? Why has my relationship with Terrance gotten your undivided attention all of the sudden? None of my relationships even concerned you back in college."

"College? You didn't do nothing but study and listen to my problems in college. You didn't date."

Her mouth dropped. "I know you didn't. I did so date. I went on a date with that guy Rodney Malone one time."

"Woman, that wasn't no date. That was Burger King. And I rode there with y'all."

"Well, it was suppose to be a date. You were the one that asked for a ride."

"But if it was suppose to be a date, why'd you let me come? You didn't have to take me along."

"I don't know, Darrel. Because you asked, I guess. That's not even the issue. My question is why are you so concerned about me and Terrance?"

"Veronica, believe me, I'm not," I answered quickly, wanting to change gears.

"Okay, Darrel. You don't have to get nasty about it."

"I'm not getting nasty. I just don't want you to think I'm sweating you two. You're my girl, and I was just looking out for you, that's all. No harm intended."

"Alright, Darrel. I am a grown woman, you know?"

"Nobody said that you weren't."

"I know. I'm just letting *you know*, Mr.

Protective."

I glanced at her for a moment and smiled. She didn't have to worry much about me noticing that she was now a grown woman, because I already knew that. She was all woman. She was far from that little bookworm I would crash in on after a date back in school. Yes, indeed. She had dropped the bifocals and over-sized clothes and developed into one hell of a knock-out.

Now as I stated before, I knew the day was gonna be a scorcher. After a few minutes of waiting in line for admission at the resort's entrance building, we were making our way up the walking trail of the mountain. Being a woman, she was well prepared with a squirt-bottle of water hanging off her arm. Myself, being a typical male and well unprepared, didn't have anything to keep my throat wet. I was just happy I wasn't one of those folks that dehydrated too quickly. We were halfway up the mountain, and it was already kicking my tail.

She stopped walking and took a swig from her water bottle. I looked at her, envying every gulp. "You want some?" she asked.

"No, no I'm fine." I said, lying. Boy, I wanted some of that water. Being a man that was just too proud was keeping me from getting any. I guess one fatal flaw for most men is that we never know when to stop playing the macho role.

"Alright, don't go dehydrating on me out here. I don't wanna have to roll you back down the mountain," she said, twisting the top back on her container.

"Hey, I'm a real man. I ain't no chump," I said as I continued hiking up the mountain.

"It's not about being a man. It's about being smart enough to know that you're just a man. We got about a mile more to go upwards, and the sun isn't being too kind to us right now. If you're thirsty…"

"Woman, what I say?" I playfully interrupted.

"Alright, Darrel, don't say I didn't warn you?"

"You just keep enough for you because I know you're gonna be worn out by the time we reach the top."

"We'll see," she added.

It was just a little bit over an hour and we had reached the top of the mountain. I was thrilled to find out that my minor fear of heights was gone. We shared a spot beside each other at the edge of the mountain. All we could see were the trees far and wide. The view made the hike worth all the while as the gentle breeze raced across our faces. To me, the mountain felt like the entire world, and we were just sitting on top of it like king and queen.

"What are you thinking about?" Veronica asked.

I looked towards the far end of the sky and watched the birds glide carelessly through the air. "Nothing. It's just so peaceful up here."

"It is, isn't it? I remember every summer my parents used to take us camping out here for a week. It was always my favorite part of the summer. I used to walk the trail with my father twice a day back then. Every time was just as exciting as the last."

"You're a real nature buff, huh?"

"No, I just like quiet places. You can't get any better than this. Away from all the chaos of the city and all the stress from the real world. It's not up here. We're free from all aggravation."

"I know that's right. I like to go to places like this to clear my mind, too. I remember when Brandi and I split up, I used to just sit in the park for hours, just staring at the pigeons until sunset. I just had to get away from it all. I was there so much, most of the bums offered me change."

She turned towards me. "What really happened between you two?"

I looked into her eyes and harshly debated on revealing my story. It was so embarrassing to me, the player, that had finally got played. And on top of that, giving the scoop to the one person that always warned me that I was gonna get what was coming to me. Revealing myself to her would give me a pain that I wasn't certain I could handle, but I wanted to.

"Everything you told me that was going to happen, happened. What came around, went around. I caught her cheating on me."

"Oh." She nodded her head.

It was clearly not what I expected. I anticipated an outburst of *I told you so's* from her, but she didn't give me that. "Oh? Is that all you're gonna say?"

"What else is there to say, Darrel? Your wife was unfaithful to you. I'm sorry to hear that."

"You're sorry. You're not gonna boast about all the warnings you gave me in the past? All the constant nagging for me to quit."

"No. I wouldn't do that to you."

"Really?" I was at a loss for words.

"Darrel, if you of all people found it in your heart to make a real commitment to someone, well, that person must've been very special. I wouldn't intentionally rag on you about something that I warned you about in college. As far as I'm concerned, I wish I was wrong. I don't want to see you hurting. I want to see you happy."

The sincerity in her voice brought chills down my spine. "Well, thank you. I just thought you were gonna give me an *I told you so* since you always warned me that I was gonna get mine someday."

"Back in college, Darrel, come on. We're grown now."

"You're right, we are." I said, thinking about how I led a majority of my adult life playing the field. I thought about my uncle, and how he led his life. He was in his early fifties without any known children, something he always wanted. At him and his wife's age, the idea of children on the horizon was a far cry. Unless one of his mistresses from way back revealed that he had fathered one of their's, unc was going to live the rest of his life childless. That's exactly how I didn't want my life to wrap up.

I stared at Veronica thinking damn I know I could have some pretty kids with her. I almost burst out into laughter because the thought caught me off guard so quickly. I never really took the time to think about having kids of my own. I was always too busy acting like one.

"What are you smiling about, Darrel?" she asked.

"Nothing, just thinking. Are you and Friday planning on having any kids?"

"Well, I want to, but Terrance says that kids will make him feel old. I told him we aren't gonna be young forever. He just laughed and told me that he was." She paused for a moment. "But yeah, I want some."

"Two, that's how many I want," I declared.

"Hmm, it's really easy for a man to point out he wants two of something on a menu when he's not cooking the product."

"Don't even start. You women have it going on with that threshold of pain."

"We have to. Especially with brothers like you talking about he wants two."

"Well, that's what I want. Two boys."

"And what's wrong with a girl?"

"I can't deal with 'em. As soon as she wanna start dating, I'd be sitting right on my front porch with my shotgun, scoping out the first guy that just reminds me a fragment of how I used to be. I can't deal with that, Veronica."

"Stop being silly. If you raise 'em right, you won't have to worry about it, big head."

I chuckled, "I haven't heard you call me that since college."

"What? Big head?"

"Yeah."

"Your head is big, big head," she laughed.

"Whatever. My head is well proportioned to my body. Now that cat, Rodney Malone, that boy had a big head. You better be glad you took me to Burger King that night. I could see y'all now, all married up and stuff, with about four little bobble-head kids trying to walk and stay balanced at the same time."

"You know you're wrong for that, Darrel."

"I know," I giggled.

We stared into each other's eyes for a moment. We said nothing, but the energy was obvious between us. Nervous, to admit anything, we both turned away and looked straight ahead.

"I thought I was gonna be nervous, coming up this mountain. I thought I was still gonna be afraid of heights" I said trying to spark another conversation.

"He stood me up."

"What?" I asked as I turned to her. She looked down, as I saw sadness suddenly overcome her face.

"He didn't even bother telling me he was going out there. His maid left the message on my phone."

"I'm sorry."

"It's okay," she advised me. I could look at her and easily tell that it wasn't okay. "You know, he's a professional basketball player. He's constantly on the road. And then he's a free agent this season, trying to negotiate the right deal…"

"Are you making excuses for him?"

She handed me a puzzled look. "I know he loves me."

"I knew Brandi loved me, but it didn't stop her from breaking my heart."

"What comes around goes around, right? I never played the field."

"I'm sure half the ladies I slept with never played

the field, but I still slept with them."

"So what are you trying to say, Darrel?"

"Nothing. You're the one getting married. That says it all. You love him enough to commit the rest of your life with him, right?"

She nodded, "I do."

"Then there shouldn't be anything for you to worry about. I'm sure he loves you just as much." Initially, I wanted to just bash Friday for just being the jerk that he was. But looking into her eyes, I could tell she really had feelings for him. I didn't want to rain on her parade just because I wanted her exclusively in my life. I had my chance a long time ago, and I missed it. Just like Uncle Jim always told me, I was young, dumb and just trying to get some. I didn't want to hate on Friday just because I missed my chance, even if he was a jerk. Nobody likes a hater.

"So are you ready to get back down to reality," she blurted out as she jumped to her feet.

I got up, also. "Man, that's gonna be a long walk down."

"Who said anything about walking? We're taking the lift down."

"The lift?" I didn't know why, but a flash of fear ran through my body when she mentioned the airlift.

"Yeap, come on," she said as she began walking towards the lift station.

I stood there in total disbelief. I had suddenly rediscovered my fear of heights. I couldn't stand that darn airlift.

She pulled into my driveway as we got down to some old school hip-hop that was blasting on the radio. It was The Fat Boys, singing 'Don't You Dog me'. We were in rhythm with the music, bee-boppin' and dancing all in our seats.

"This was the joint, Darrel!"

"It sure was. Man, they don't make music like they used to."

"The Fat Boys, Doug-E-Fresh, Slick Rick, those guys are legends."

"No, no, but guess what I got in the crib, right now."

"What?"

"Krush Groove on DVD!"

Her eyes lit up like a lighthouse. "Darrel, don't play with me."

"I got Krush Groove in the crib… right now."

"You don't." She shook her head.

"Yes, I do."

She squinted her eyes and poked her lips out, "Darrel, I'ma kill you for this." She shut the engine off and jumped out of the car. "Come on."

I exited the car. "What?"

"Come on and open this door," she said as she made her way to my front porch. "We're about to watch Krush Groove."

"Alright now. Don't be calling me in the morning talking about you missed work because of Kurtis Blow and Sheila-E," I stated as I took the lead to open the door. Maybe I was wrong for not wanting our time to end, while at the same time, coming to terms with myself not trying to make an effort to sway her heart in my direction. And yeah, I knew Krush Groove would reel her in, but I just wanted the night to last just a little while longer.

Chapter Eleven

My eyes cracked open to the ceiling fan as it slowly twirled it's circle of cool air throughout the den. I angled my head down towards Veronica who was peacefully snoozing on my shoulder. My arm sat idle alongside her waist. A smile erupted on my face because it felt so good to be in the position that I was in. I looked towards the television, and my DVD player had turned itself off, as the clock on the display revealed that it was fifteen minutes after three. We had both dozed off in the middle of the movie.

I gently tapped her arm. "Veronica, wake up."

Her eyes opened. "What is it?"

"It's after three."

"It is?" She sat up and stretched out. "Uhm, we fell asleep."

"Yeap."

"You have to get to work it the morning. I'm sorry," she patted her hair to make sure it was kept in tact.

"I'm fine. Are you gonna be alright driving home?"

"Uhm, hmm. I'm only fifteen minutes away."

"Because if you want, I can take the couch and you can have the bedroom."

She grinned, "No, I'll be alright, Darrel. But thanks for the offer."

She stood up and walked towards the door. I followed.

"Thanks for the movie. Too bad we fell asleep on it." She stopped in front of the door and turned around.

"We can watch it again some other time."

She nodded her head with a smile. "Good, I think I'd like that."

"Then it's a date."

"Good," she gave me a hug. "I would give you a kiss on the cheek, but I know my breath is crucial right about now."

"Mine, too," I said as I grabbed the door knob and opened the door. "But I'll take a rain check."

"I bet you would."

We walked out together. She eased into her ride and rolled the window down. As she was about to start her car, she paused while smiling at me.

"What is it?" I asked her.

"I don't know what it is, but something's different about you, Darrel. At first, I thought it was too funny when you told me that you had changed. But you have. I feel sorry for your ex-wife because she really missed out on something special."

"Well, thanks."

"No, thank you." She started her car. "Goodnight, Darrel."

"Drive safely," I advised her as she backed out of the driveway. I watched her streak down the street until her taillights were no longer visible. Then, I strolled into my castle with a feeling better than sex, and I hadn't taken one article of clothing off. Just being in the presence of that woman made me have a feeling inside that I couldn't attempt to explain.

I turned off my television and all the lights in the house, knowing darn well I was gonna sleep good. I sat on my bed, grinning ear to ear as I replayed the whole day in my head one final time. It was a long time since I had so much fun.

Unexpectedly, a loud clashing noise pierced throughout the house. It sounded as if it came from the den. I rushed into that room, and after I turned on the lights, my eyes zoomed towards a brick on the floor that had just been thrown through my window. I grabbed the brick and anxiously made my way out of the house. I soon heard the screeching sound of tires as I ran outside. All I managed to see was the taillights of a white Navigator speeding down the street. The same white Navigator I saw at Natasha's house a few days ago.

Pissed off, I ran into the middle of the street. "What the fuck is wrong with you?" I yelled. I wasn't the brightest person in the world, but there was no doubt in my mind who was behind it all… Natasha Stanley–a woman scorned.

Now I can deal with a woman being upset with me because I broke things off with her. That's only natural for anyone since nobody likes to feel abandoned. But what I can't tolerate is a female out for revenge. Even though I had doubts Natasha would strike again, I still felt on edge about what she could do. I made it my business throughout the day to call her to seek answers as to why she felt the need to do what she did. And even though I didn't see her actually throw the brick, I knew it was her handy work. Unsurprisingly, nobody at her house was picking up the phone. With that crazy bunch, they all probably had in on it.

"What's going on?" Rex asked as he scooted into the booth where I was sitting. I had been waiting on him for over an hour at the sports bar. He was late, but that wasn't anything new. The only reason I didn't leave was because I knew him so well. The word 'prompt' wasn't a part of his vocabulary.

"About thirty minutes earlier and you would've really shocked me," I advised him.

"What? Is this a job interview or something?"

"No, but it doesn't hurt to be a little courteous sometimes."

He picked up a menu as he sported his infamous grin that symbolized he really didn't care. "Whatever, D. You sound like one of my chicks now."

"I'm gonna act like I didn't even hear that comment."

"You know I'm just playing," he laughed. "I got tied up with ole' girl I had on my bike that day. She just won't take *no* for an answer."

"What does she want?"

"Me," he said sternly. "Now, Darrel, you know me. Once you've been ran through for a couple of times, it's over. But ole' girl ain't feeling it. She done started calling me at all times of the night, poppin' up all unannounced, begging me to keep kicking it with her. And then she keeps complaining about that tattoo she got on her ass, talking about she did that out of love for me. I asked her if she had lost her damn mind? That shit don't mean nothing to me. You know what I mean, D?"

"Yeah, I know you."

"She keeps suffocating me, man. I can't breathe with that chick. I think I might have to put a restraining order on the chick, man. She's stressing me out."

"Well, I can relate to that," I agreed.

"What? What's going on with you and the fireball?"

"Nothing," I shook my head. "I had to let her go."

"What? You kicked her to the curb, too."

"I just told her we needed to part ways."

"Shit… you kicked her to the curb. Did she start crying? My chick didn't cry. She's just beginning to act crazy as hell. If it wasn't for that, I'd probably let her come over one more time so I can break her off again. That stuff sure was good to me."

"I don't know about all of that, but Natasha did let it be known that she didn't like me breaking things off with her."

"What she do?"

"She threw a brick through the window in my den last night."

"Why in the hell would she do that?"

"I don't know. She didn't stick around long enough for me to ask her," I replied. "She probably was stalking me and got mad when she saw Veronica leaving the crib."

"Veronica…" he took a moment to put a face with the name. "You talking about Friday's chick?"

"And I know what you're gonna say, but you're wrong. We fell asleep on a movie, and she ended up leaving a little bit after three."

"Three in the morning? Man, I thought I told you to leave that chick alone. And why in the hell is she leaving your place at that time? You're still trying to hit it, aren't you?"

"No, we'd just spent the day together at Stone Mountain, and she decided to stay over to watch Krush Groove with me afterwards. I didn't have any bad intentions in mind."

He frowned, "Negro, please! That's about the oldest trick in the book. Talking about some damn Krush Groove. That's your freakin' secret weapon, tricking them girls to stay over with a movie. Did you hit it?"

"Hell no. Didn't I just tell you that I didn't have any bad intentions?"

"Oh please, D. You telling me that you aren't plotting on a female is like a woman saying she ain't gonna shop no damn more. That shit's just impossible."

"Well, I wasn't plotting for your information. I was just enjoying her company. And that psycho had to try and mess it up."

"She did it after the chick left, right?"

"Yeah. Less than five minutes after."

"Well, that's what you get," he said pointing his finger at me. "I told you to leave Friday's chick alone because she ain't nothing but trouble. That whole situation ain't nothing but trouble."

"And you're supposed to be the one to talk with your problems."

"My problems ain't like yours. You got a psycho stalking you, and you're trying to get into the pants of a chick that's almost married. My problems are nothing like yours."

"See, Rex, you don't even understand what's going on. My mom likes Veronica."

"How does your mom even know her?"

"She came to church with us."

"You took her to church with you? What in the hell did you do that for?"

"I don't know. I had to see her, Rex. When I called her, that was the first thing that came up."

"Church... and you know Mama Walker is gonna like any girl you bring with you to church. Man, you're crazy. You're just playing with fire. Hell, I thought you were back, but you're not back. The Darrel Walker I know would never do some crazy shit like that. I can't believe you took that girl to church. I mean, you take chicks that you're serious about to church with you."

"She's only a friend, Rex. I'm not even trying to pursue anything with her. I promised myself that I wouldn't."

"So you promised yourself that you're not gonna try to score with this Veronica chick?"

"I sure did?"

"And you're sticking by that?"

"I sure am," I answered, solemnly final with my answer.

"Why?"

"Why? Because I said so."

"No, D, you're gonna keep it real with me. Now tell me why you're trying to be so fragile with this chick? What is it about her?"

I took a moment to think about his question,

knowing he wasn't going to settle for some cheesy excuse about me caring about her feelings, in which was indeed the truth. Nah, Rex would never settle for that. He didn't believe that there was a caring side to me. I was better off by just not answering his question at all. "I'm just not interested in her like that."

He burst into laughter.

"What?"

"Darrel, do you realize how long we've been friends?"

"Yeah," I answered, "Since elementary school."

"If we've been friends for that long, then why in the hell are you trying to feed me that bullshit?"

"What?"

"You got a chick at your crib at three in the morning and you're not interested–that's bullshit, Darrel, and you know it."

"I don't know what you're talking about, but I can have a plutonic relationship with a woman."

"Plutonic? Alright, you don't have to know what I'm talking about. But I'm telling you one last time, that situation ain't nothing but trouble. Leave it alone before it gets out of hand, man."

"Whatever you say, Rex," I said looking around for our waitress.

"Take what I say for a joke. You're gonna be the one that's sorry," he said. "Man, where the hell is the help around here?"

"Well, she came around a couple of times when you were suppose to be here."

"We got a chick?"

"Yeah."

"She cute?"

"She looks alright," I answered as I saw those wheels inside his head beginning to churn.

"Well, let me go into the restroom to check myself

out before she comes over." He hurried out of the booth. "I might be able to get us some free food up in this piece."

"Well, go for it," I advised him.

He ran into the restroom as I held my chuckle in. Our waitress wasn't cute at all. I knew that would only piss him off when he got back, but my little white lie would give me a chance to be by myself for a moment. If it wasn't one thing, it was another. If Brandi Brown wasn't sending me flowers and love letters, Natasha was throwing bricks through my windows. Yet none of it even mattered because I had thoughts of being with Veronica running through my mind. Just the mere idea of her name brought on this strange feeling inside of me that tickled my entire body. I couldn't believe I was tripping over her the way that I was. At a blink of an eye, I had fallen for one of my closest and dearest friends, but I knew she could never be mine. There was certainly too much standing in the way of us. But the idea, just the idea, was giving me a hint of happiness throughout it all.

There ain't nothing like getting lost in a good movie. After my outing with Rex, I lounged peacefully across my sofa as I snacked on some hot, buttered popcorn. With just a tee-shirt and sweatpants, I reclined in front of my favorite flick, *Out Of Sight*. By far, this was my favorite movie, watching George Clooney's cool ass flip Jennifer Lopez head-over-heals in love with him as he plotted his smooth getaway from the authorities. That movie always had a way of relaxing my nerves.

I had my television blasting to the max, not just to be engulfed into the realms of the movie, but to drown out all of the loud thunder that was violently rumbling outside. The night was a stormy one.

Unexpectedly, my phone rang. I glanced at it across the room, debating if I should answer it or not. I hated to be interrupted when my flick was on, but being that it was about a quarter till eleven, I figured whomever was calling must've had something on their mind that was really important.

"Hello," I answered the phone.

"Darrel?"

"Hello." I repeated, straining to hear through the deafening tantrum of my home theatre.

"Darrel, why do you have your television turned up so loud?"

It took me a few moments to recognize the voice, "Veronica?" I scrambled to find the remote to turn my television down. "What's up, lady?"

"Nothing. Have you gotten hard of hearing all of the sudden, though?"

"No, you know I love that surround sound when I'm watching my movies."

"Don't make yourself deaf by all of that ruckus," she laughed.

"I won't."

"So what are you watching anyway?"

"*Out Of Sight.*"

"With George Clooney as the bank robber?"

"Now don't act like you know something about my movie."

"I don't know what *you're* talking about, but that's one of my favorite movies."

"Stop lying."

"No, for real. I think it's so romantic how Jennifer Lopez saw pass him being a criminal even though she was a Federal Marshall. That's what I call a love story."

"It was more of an action flick to me."

"It was a little bit of all of that, but it was more of a love story," she advised me.

"Well, I'll go along with that," I said as I returned to my spot on the sofa. "So, you must be bored."

"Why do I have to be bored, Darrel?"

"Well, calling me at this time of the night."

"Is there a law against calling you at this time?"

"No, I just thought you'd be talking over your wedding plans with Friday around this time." Yeah, it was a trick a lot of females used to check a guy's relationship status, but I'm sure the women of the world wouldn't mind me borrowing it once for my own means of resource. I had to get information somehow.

"Well, if I was bothering you I can let you get back to your movie."

"No, no, no... I was only playing."

"Are you sure? Because I don't want to cramp your style."

"Nah, you're not cramping my style. So what's up?"

"Nothing, what's up with you?"

"I told you what I was doing, about to watch George tap that ass one good time."

"You're at that part already?"

"I just paused it for you."

"How sweet."

"Anything for you."

"Anything for me, huh?"

"Yeah," I answered without hesitation. If she only knew how much I meant it.

"Why couldn't it be that way a long time ago?"

"I don't know. Maybe I wasn't ready." I thought back to my conversation with my mom a few weeks ago, about her and my dad hooking up.

"Timing is a crucial thing, isn't it?"

"It sure seems that way, don't it?"

"Yeap." she answered.

It was like we were both skating on some thin ice that could break at any moment. Our entire conversation seemed to have a hint of another meaning to it. Something that led into an area that it seemed we both were afraid to cross into. It was all too foreign to me. I had always prided myself on being straight to the point by being confident in what I wanted. But with her I didn't know what I wanted, and I wasn't quite sure on how to get it if I did.

Suddenly there was a silence between the both of us. A calm silence. A silence that said more than any words could. "Have you heard from your fiancé?" I asked, finally breaking the peace.

"He called."

"I saw him on the news tonight. He finally signed with Los Angeles, huh?"

"That's what I heard."

"Good ole' LA." The last thing I wanted to talk about was her future hubby, but that's all I could think of.

"Were you really tipsy that night?"

"What night?" I asked.

"That night–never mind!"

"No… what night are you talking about?"

There was another brief silence, "You know, that night back in college."

"College?" I said, trying to recall the event. "You mean the night we kissed?"

"Yeah, that night," she answered reluctantly.

"Well…" I never really sat down and thought about the events of that night as a whole." But I did remember that night. We both had a few drinks, but not enough to do any real damage. To be honest, I really wanted to kiss her that night. A part of me wanted to be down with her way back then. "Yeah, I was a little wasted." I answered, lying.

"Oh." A hint of disappointment was in her voice.

"Well, I mean, I really don't remember," I said, trying to reverse my original reply somewhat. I couldn't understand why I just didn't tell her the truth–that I was fully aware of what I was doing when we kissed. That even back then, something inside of me was attracted to her, but I was just too stupid and immature to take the time to figure it out.

"Well, I barely even remember that night," she laughed. "I don't know why I was even thinking about it."

"I'm surprised you remembered it at all. We did a pretty good job of acting as if it never happened."

"I really hadn't thought about it since it happened. College was something else, wasn't it?"

"It sure was," Damn it. I hated not telling her the truth.

"Do you have any regrets?"

"Here and there. I guess we all do. I'd probably pay more attention to the things around me if I could do it all over again."

"Why?"

"A lot of things were there, and I just didn't pay any attention to them. I was too busy doing my own thing. Whatever that accomplished."

"Well, life is full of choices, Darrel. You never know what the right one is until after you choose."

"You're right about that."

"I regret not being more outgoing."

"You were outgoing, girl."

"*To you!*" she laughed. "I confined myself to my room every night of the week, with my nose glued to those books. I should've done more, Darrel. I should've gotten to know more people."

"It's all about choices, right? You just chose to get your studies while everybody else did the partying. And believe me, you really didn't miss a thing."

"Yeah, I guess you're right," she paused. "Do you wanna go out to dinner tomorrow?"

"Are you asking me out, Veronica Bethel?"

"No, I was hoping that you'd ask me."

"What about TGIF?"

"What about him? He's out in LA making deals. I can go out to dinner with a friend, or is there a law against that, too?"

"No, there isn't a law against going out to dinner with an old friend. Not yet, anyway," I chuckled. "So you wanna go out tomorrow night?"

"Yeah, but I swear you were much smoother back in college."

"Very funny. Is seven a good time for you?"

"Seven's great."

"Good."

"Now can the Maxima handle this little date?"

"*All the time!* You better act like you know that the Maxima is still the bomb."

"Okay then, Darrel. We'll see."

"Well, I'll see you at seven."

"Darrel," she called out as I was about to hang up.

"Yeah," I answered.

"Thanks, okay?"

"I'll see you at seven. Have a good night."

"You, too."

I hung up the phone happier than a runaway slave that had just arrived to the North. I was going out on a date with someone I could actually get into for a change. All of a sudden there was daylight in the situation. I wasn't sure how far we were going to go, but I was ready for the ride.

I fell asleep on the couch. The night's wind whistled as it rode along my chimney at a steady rate, and the light tapping of rain rattled against my window. At first I thought my imagination was deceiving me, but there appeared to be someone knocking at my door. I looked towards the clock and it was well after four in the morning. Just to make sure I wasn't going completely crazy, I scurried to the front door, squirmed my eye through the peephole, and my heart almost jumped out of my body as I discovered someone was actually standing on the other side of my door.

"Who is it?" I asked, immediately feeling threatened. I reached over to a stool next to the door and picked up a statuette I had on it. "What do you want?"

"Open up, Darrel," the faint voice requested.

"Veronica?" I said to myself. It sounded like her voice, but not quite. It definitely was a woman, though.

"Identify yourself," I demanded. I could barely see anything out of the hole. All I could see was the baseball cap on the figure's head.

"Open up or I'm leaving," the person demanded.

I unlocked the door, but I didn't slip up the chain lock. I cracked the door open. "Who are you?"

"It's me, love," said the woman attempting peak through the crack. "Your wife, Brandi, love."

"Brandi! What in the hell? Wait a minute." My heart rate tripled as I pushed the door closed, took the chain off and opened the door. It was her indeed.

"Hello, Darrel," she smiled. She stood in the doorway wearing a black trench coat and a baseball cap on her head.

"What in the hell do you want?" I asked her, attempting to stay as calm as I could.

"Can I come in?" she asked.

I took two steps back and cleared the way for her to enter. She was drenched from head to toe, and I was trying my best not to care.

"Thank you, love," she said as she pranced inside. She looked around the place as if it was her first time inside. "It still looks quite nice in here."

"I've been doing a good job of keeping out all of the trash," I advised her as I slammed the door. "What do you want, Brandi? I was just getting ready to hit the sack."

"Is that anyway to talk to your ex, love?"

"It could be worse."

"But why, love? Life is too short to be holding grudges," she said as she roamed to my sofa. "Why don't you have a seat beside me?" She took her cap off and her silky black hair rolled down her shoulders.

"I'd rather stay standing. You do have to be leaving soon. You really should go home and dry off."

"You used to like me wet, love," she grinned, but it disappeared as quickly as it spawned. She saw my face, and there wasn't a smile to be found. "I take it that you're still upset with me."

"What in the hell would give you that idea, Brandi?" I yelled. "Could it be that most people tend to flip out when they find their spouses in bed with someone else?"

"I suppose that was a bit rude of me. I'm sorry, love. I came over here just to apologize to you."

"Oh really? It's been almost a year, and now you're coming over to apologize. Not only that, but you just had to come rushing out in the middle of the night to do it. I take it that it couldn't wait 'til sunrise."

"No, love, it couldn't wait," she said as she approached me. I quickly backed away. "But you're not going to accept my apology, are you?"

"Why in the hell should I? You hurt the hell out of me."

She hung her head down, frowning. "Ely told me he bumped into you at the mall. He said you weren't very happy."

"Yeah, and as a matter of fact, I don't appreciate being toyed around with the way you've been doing me the past few weeks."

"You didn't like the flowers?"

"No, I didn't like the flowers! You don't play with people like that. Are you crazy or something?"

She frowned and nodded her head, "Yes, love. I am crazy."

"Well, you need to take that shit elsewhere because I can't fix it."

"I'm crazy in love with you, Darrel."

"Well, I don't feel the same way about you. As a matter of fact, you need to be getting off on your way, right now." I returned to the door and opened it.

"I beg to differ, Darrel."

"This here ain't an option, honey. Now if you don't mind, you need to be getting the hell up out of here."

"I'm not going anywhere."

"Like hell you aren't," I approached her, fully ready to throw her out.

"I told you that I wasn't going anywhere, love," she said as she slid her coat off. She wasn't wearing a thing underneath it. I froze like a farmer walking up on a snake. "Now are you gonna make me leave?"

"What in the hell are you trying to prove?" I said as my eyes surveyed her beautiful physique. It had been so long since I last saw her beautiful flesh, and all of it still looked remarkable.

She approached me. "That you can't resist this."

"I can," I advised her. I was trying more to convince myself.

"You can't, love. You need me, just as I need you." She placed her soft hands along my face and blessed me with a soft kiss. She smelled so sweet. Her hands were so soft and warm. My manhood was now standing at full guard. "Don't you need me, love. Don't fight it. Just say it."

I closed my eyes, while shaking my head. My mind was saying no, but my body was having the toughest time agreeing. I kept replaying the words her lover advised me of a few days ago, about her games. I didn't want to become her pawn, but she was standing right before me, tempting me with all she had. She slid her hands down my shoulders, and further down my back. She pulled her body into me with her perky breast jelling against my chest. I was trying so hard to resist.

"You need to be leaving, Brandi."

"Then make me, love. I promise that I won't ever come back if you tell me not to," she said as she began kissing on my neck. She licked up and around my ear lobe as my weakened knees were about to buckle. Her presence was weakening me. It would've been so easy to pick her up and lay her across my bed and make love to her throughout the night. I tried so hard to resist the temptation. As she worked her lips along my chest and neck, her hands were busy at work, untying the strings to my sweatpants. I stood frozen. My pride was so unbalanced. I wanted so hard not to give in.

"You can take it, whenever you decide you want it," she said.

My pants hit the floor. My rate of breathing insanely increased. My heart pounded faster. Sweat began to roll down my face. The back of my throat ran dry. And I gave up. Great goodness, I just couldn't take it anymore. I grabbed her by her buttocks and pulled her up off of the floor. She pinned her elbows on my shoulders and overwhelmed me with kisses from her juicy, wet lips.

"Take it, daddy."

"I hate you," I mumbled softly.

"Obviously not enough."

I stumbled across the den and into my bedroom, my hands still gripping her soft rump. I laid her along my bed as I rolled out of my underwear, and entered her warm, wet walls.

Chapter Twelve

It was a bright, sunny day. There wasn't a cloud in the sky as a gentle breeze governed the atmosphere. I was peacefully lounging on a park bench all by my lonesome. Before me, the birds were chirping, children were laughing and playing, and couples deep in love scattered the terrain with their arms around one another. It was such a beautiful sight, but something just didn't feel right with it all. As I observed all the happiness that was surrounding me, I soon realized that I was the only one alone. I didn't want to be alone. I needed someone with me.

Then something urged me to turn my head towards a different direction. There was something on the horizon. There was someone on the horizon. I looked towards that other direction and someone was coming. That someone was approaching me. As my eyes focused in on this person, I soon realized this was the one person that I was waiting for all along. It was Veronica. She walked closer and closer, as my heart pounded to each step she made. She was wearing a beautiful white dress as her long, black hair softly blew with the kind breeze. Her eyes laid on me as a miniature smirk surfaced onto her face. An expression that I believed told me, yes. Yes, Darrel, it is you. It is you that I too have been waiting on.

"Hey," she said

"Hi," I smiled.

"Someone sitting here?"

"No," I answered.

She settled into the spot next to me. Now feeling relaxed, I slouched back and placed my arm behind her back. She looked at me with a subtle smile and rested her head on my shoulder. You couldn't offer me any dollar amount in the world to be anywhere else.

"It's such a beautiful day."

"It is now. I wish it could be like this forever," I declared.

"It could be," she said. "But you need to fix one thing."

I leaned my head back, admiring the different shapes of the floating clouds that had just emerged. "And what's that?"

"You gotta fix you."

"Huh?" I uttered as I rapidly looked down at her.

"You didn't really think I could commit to you with you being the way that you are right now, did you?" she asked as she lifted her head and faced me.

"What's wrong with me?"

"Well... you're a liar."

"What? Veronica, where's this coming from?"

"Come on, Darrel, you know that you're a liar. You told me that you had changed, but you didn't. You slept with her again."

My jaw dropped. "How did you find out about that?"

"It's obvious, Darrel. I know dogs." She stood up. "And you're one. I guess it's true about not being able to teach an old dog new tricks."

"No... I didn't mean to sleep with her. She just came over, and..."

"And you acted off impulse." She shook her head. "When are you gonna learn, Darrel Walker? No matter what you do or what you say, it's always gonna be the same thing. Once a dog, always a dog."

"Veronica, don't say that. I want to be different. I want to be different with you. I know I can do better."

"Goodbye, Darrel. To think, I was really gonna give you a chance. I'm so glad I didn't make that mistake."

"But you don't understand. I love you," I cried. "I'm in love with you."

"Nice gesture, Darrel, but you don't love no one

but yourself and that thing hanging between your legs. I'm through with you, Darrel." She turned her back on me and began walking away.

"Veronica, that's not true. That's not true," I proclaimed as she kept on walking, neglecting my plea. "*Veronica... Veronica... Veronica!*"

"Darrel!" A voice called.

"Huh?" I bolted from under the sheets in a cold sweat. I was sleeping. It was all just a dream. A horrible, horrible dream.

"You had a nightmare, love."

I looked to the side of me, and Brandi was curled up against the headboard, feasting on a bowl of strawberry ice cream. I couldn't help but notice she had managed to find one of my favorite tee-shirts and slipped it on. "I see that you're just making yourself right at home, eh?" Instantly, I became upset with myself as flashes of having scorching hot sex with her ran through my mind. As I visualized her on top of me, screaming out my name from the bare bottom of her lungs, I fell backwards, sinking into my pillow. My lower brain had struck again.

"'Ben and Jerry's' really do make the best ice cream, love," she said.

"What did I do?" I groaned.

"Well, for one, you need to stop talking in your sleep. Maybe you'd sleep a lot better if you did. And who is this Veronica you kept mentioning? She seemed to upset you while you were snoozing."

"She doesn't concern you."

"Hmm… is she someone you met recently?"

Realizing the damage was already done and there wasn't anything I could do to change that fact, I pulled myself up against the headboard and sat up beside her. "She's a friend, and that's all you need to know."

She giggled, "Oh my, I do believe my Darrel has a crush on someone else. Say it's not true, love. I know there's only enough room in your heart for me. You certainly did a good job of proving that last night."

I turned to her, not yet bold enough to tell her to get her stuff together and get the hell out, "Why are you even here? I mean, what possessed you to come over here last night?"

"Why you act as if you don't appreciate my company anymore. It didn't feel that way a few hours ago, though. Do you feel guilty now, love?"

"Wait a minute. I'm the one asking the questions here, so you need to start coming up with the answers. Why'd you come over, Brandi?"

"Because I felt that you needed me. Didn't you need me, love?"

Frustrated, I took in a deep breath. I didn't know how to answer her. At this point, I didn't know what I wanted. I stared at her for a moment, wishing that I could pick out just one flaw that could make me give her up with ease. She was just so damn beautiful. All I could do was pretend that I didn't want her around. "No, I don't need you. I was doing just fine by myself. I didn't have to deal with anymore of that turmoil you brought into my life."

"Do you really think of it as turmoil? I like to think of it as excitement. I still remember the first time we met. You walked into the club thinking that you were the ultimate man. You were all cocky and what not. And then our eyes crossed each other…"

"And it was all downhill ever since! Brandi, why did you come back? Haven't you messed me up enough?"

"Okay." She slammed her bowl down on the nightstand next to the bed and rolled her arms up like an angry, little kid. "I needed you, love. I missed you. That's why I came over."

"Really?" I said knowing undoubtedly she had an ulterior motive. I looked over to the clock, and it was almost seven. I had to cut my question and answer game short or risk being late to work. "You know what? I gotta get ready for work. So you can keep your little secrets all to yourself. I got bills to pay."

"Are you trying to tell me something, Darrel?"

I rolled out of the bed and slipped on my boxers. "Well, you're not staying here today, that's for sure."

"Are you trying to kick me out, love?"

"Not formally, but yes. You need to be getting ready for your departure–love!"

"Well, I've never felt so used in my life."

"Really, Brandi," I frowned. "Who really got used here?"

"You're so silly. Does anyone ever get used in love?"

"We had sex. So maybe the next time I make love, I'll think about the answer to that question and get back to you on it."

"I take giving you some was not enough to make you forgive me." She grabbed her clothing from the side of the bed. "Well, that's just fine, love. One day you will forgive me. Just let me take a shower, and I'll scurry out of your way."

"Fine," I grunted. I sat right back on the bed as she stomped out of the room. I could tell I hurt her feelings, but I was determined not to let her in. I had come too far in my efforts of trying to get over her to let her trip me up. It was bad enough that I slept with her again.

I looked up, and she had returned, gazing at me from the doorway. "I know you still love me, Darrel. You've already proven that, love." With a devious smile on her face, she left the room.

I didn't hurt her at all. She was on a power trip at my expense. I slammed my fists against my forehead and fell backwards onto the bed. Me and my penis! If I only made my decisions from my upper-brain instead of my lower, much smaller brain, I'd probably be a whole lot better off. With the dream that I had and the fact that I had spent a majority of my night having sex with public enemy number one, that eerie, edgy feeling of things beginning to fall apart began to overwhelm my spirit. I prayed that it wasn't a sign of things to come. I wanted desperately for things to go right when it was time for me to pick up Veronica later, but I knew if I wanted to survive the night I would have to put Brandi Brown in the back of my mind and leave her there. That was easier said than done.

I spent a majority of my life taking actions first and asking questions later. For the longest time I believed that was how things were suppose to be done. Most people would probably call it a habit. I always thought of it as a ritual. It was just how I did things. Yet, it was the one part of my personality that I knew I would definitely have to change if I wanted to become a better Darrel Walker. I thought I was really making some serious progress, but sleeping with Brandi was definitely a huge step backwards. All throughout the day, our night replayed itself in my mind. It felt so good while it was happening, but having what we did in the back of mind was driving me crazy. All I could hear was her saying "love, this", and "love, that." I couldn't believe how I let her come in and manipulate me the way that she did. She came there for one reason, and she got exactly what she wanted. She used me like a dirty sock. The last thing I wanted to think about was Brandi Brown while I was on my outing with Veronica.

I arrived at Veronica's apartment complex at about a quarter til' seven. I took a quick shower after work to freshen up and ran my ride to the carwash for a clean wash and some vacuuming. On a normal date, I wouldn't go through so many changes with so little time, but this was Veronica. Impressing her was worth all the trouble.

As I stood in front of her door, I could feel the butterflies squirming down in the depths of my stomach. I couldn't have been any more nervous if I had done something wrong as a child, and my father was approaching me with his big, black belt, aiming to tear the skin off me. I wanted to knock on the door the right way, look the right way, and even smell the right way. I knew there were going to be limits to the date, but I wanted to enjoy my time with her before she became Mrs. Veronica Friday. That was a thought that made me cringe every time it skipped through my mind. I balled my fist and raised it, strenuously debating if I should knock hard or soft.

"Darrel," Veronica said as she opened the door.

"Veronica?" I nervously answered. Her stunning beauty had just about knocked me off of my feet. In the matter of seconds, I zeroed in on every inch of her beautiful body. She wore her silky, black hair down, some small gold loop earrings graced her ears, and a classy black dress hung on her body like a bee to some honey.

"I thought I heard someone. Have you been out here long?"

"Uh... no. I just got here." I don't know what caught me off guard the most... her pulling the door open or how good she looked.

"Great," she answered as she walked away from the door while running her comb through her hair. "Come on in. I'll be ready in a minute."

"Okay," I said as I eased into her cozy little pad. Her place was nice. Always a lover of art, she had her walls decorated with paintings of black people participating in an variety of activities. Her den was decked out with some classy leather furniture, and a state of the art entertainment system. It was all straight. Now beyond all the nice stuff she had my eyes taking in, one thing that grabbed my attention the most and on top of that, made me want to gag, was the numerous pictures she had scattered throughout the apartment of her and Friday together. I guess it was just that feeling people have when they want to believe a relationship that someone they're interested in isn't that serious, and they try and continue to pretend that it isn't, even though it is. That was exactly how I was feeling. I just didn't want to believe she was going to marry him.

"We took that picture in Mexico City," she advised me.

She stood in the doorway of her bedroom. I didn't realize I was gawking so hard at the picture. "Really, I didn't know you made a trip south of the border. How was it?"

"Hot! Too hot! A sister left that place two shades darker. And you know I don't need to get any darker."

"Girl, hush up. You're about as red as an apple. A little tint won't do you any harm."

"Whatever, Darrel. Where are we going anyway?"

"I was thinking about this little place right outside of Buckhead where we could do a little dancing after we eat."

"Dancing? When did you have corrective surgery on your two left feet?"

I frowned and raised my eyebrow, "Lady, I don't know who you think you're talking to, but I got some moves."

"Darrel, you can't dance a lick, and you know it."

"Woman, please. I used to be Mr. Soul Train back in school," I suggested as I claimed a spot on her sofa.

"Whatever you say, two left feet," she chuckled. "You know you can't dance."

"Anyway," I replied. I surveyed the coffee table, and there was another annoying picture of Friday posing by himself in a heart-shaped frame. I picked it up with a grin. He's just as arrogant away than he is in person. "So how much longer is Mr. Friday gonna be in L.A.?"

"I don't know. I think he said for another three weeks. He's doing the training camp thing and looking into some real estate."

"Real estate. Isn't that something he should be doing with the future Mrs. Friday?"

She moved in front of me, appearing to be ready to go. "Hey, that's his money. I'm not entitled to any of it right now, and don't care much about it when I am. All a sista' knows is that if I don't like where he puts us after the wedding, then that's when I gotta speak out. So for now, he can do whatever he wants to. You ready?"

"Sure," I answered as I jumped up and headed towards the door. "Well, at least he called."

"Well, we're gonna have to talk about that issue when he gets back."

"Really?" I replied, intrigued by the statement.

"Leave it alone, Darrel. I don't need your input on the situation again."

"I wasn't gonna say anything. Actually, I was just wondering when the big day was."

"It's three months away."

"Wow, just three months and I didn't get an invitation yet?"

"You don't send out wedding invitations this early, Darrel."

"Just making sure you're not trying to buy time."

"Buy time for what?"

"Cold feet."

"Sorry, Darrel, no cold feet here. It's now or never. I can't wait forever."

"Really?" I walked through the door. "Well, as long as you know what you're doing."

"Here you go again," she laughed. "I know exactly what I'm doing, Darrel. Now move it."

We strolled into the exquisite restaurant laughing about our college days. Our professors and former classmates always had a way of tickling our hearts.

"…and remember Dr. Hodges?" she asked.

"How could I forget? Him and his trifocals. His glasses were so thick, I swear he could see two months into the future if he wanted to."

She was almost into tears laughing, as we followed the host to our table. The people in the upscale outing immediately recognized black folks were on the way into the hub as they began to whisper and point amongst one another.

"You are too crazy, Darrel," she advised me as I pulled her chair out and she sat down. I walked around to my chair and quickly planted myself down.

"What will you be drinking?" the pointy nose host asked.

"Water," Veronica answered.

"Me, too," I agreed.

"Your server will be with you briefly," he said as he retreated from our table.

I leaned over and whispered, "These white folks are gonna have us kicked out of here if we keep showing out."

"That's you," she jokingly warned me.

"I ain't gonna worry about it. They need a little soul up in here anyhow." I picked up a menu and looked through it. The prices were astronomical, but that was the price I was gonna have to pay for a good night with my precious date. I was just fortunate that I spent so many months in solitude. Not going out for that stretch sure did wonders for my bank account. My eyes eclipsed over my menu, and I noticed Veronica staring at me with a smile.

"And what are you looking at?"

"You," she answered.

"Oh, so you like what you see, huh?" Without me really noticing it, my nervousness had disappeared, and I was just myself around her. Just like in the good ole' days. It felt good, too.

"Yes, I do. I almost forgot how much fun we had with each other."

"Yeah, we did have some fun."

She opened her menu. "Alrighty, these prices are up there. You know we could've went somewhere else that was a little less expensive."

"It's straight," I advised her. "Besides, I know you're accustomed to going out to places like this with Mr. TGIF."

"Please! Terrance? His favorite spots are Checkers, McDonalds, and Pizza-Hut. You wouldn't believe he's a professional athlete with all the junk food he shoves down his throat. And spending more than ten dollars on a meal… well, let's say he means well."

"Not Mr. Friday's tight with the funds."

"Only with going out to eat. He loves spending money. At times, I wonder if he's gonna have anything left by the time he gets old, with all the spending he does. That's why I told him that if we're gonna be together, we're getting a financial advisor."

"I hear ya'. So I guess you and Friday have pretty much everything planned out," I asked, gently trying to pry into their relationship a little further.

"Not really, Darrel. But there's only so much a woman can take."

"Good evening. My name is Ivan, and I'll be your server for tonight." The Russian accented waiter placed our drinks on the table and whipped out his pad as he prepared to take down our order.

"Hi, Ivan," Veronica greeted him.

"How are you, mam. Might I say that you look stunning," he said.

She blushed, "Thank you."

As our waiter requested her order, I just sat there and admired her beauty. She was indeed stunning, smiling with those luscious, round lips and light brown eyes. She was never the one to wear too much make-up, simply because she didn't need it. As she recited her order, I thought to myself, I could marry this woman. This is the woman I could spend the rest of my life with.

"And you, sir?"

"Y'all sell hamburgers, Ivan?"

"Darrel, stop playing."

"Yes sir, we sell some of the finest gourmet burgers in Atlanta."

"Are those burgers made out of real angus beef, like Hardees."

"You are so silly," she giggled.

"I'm not sure about that, sir, but I can confirm it with our chef."

"No, no, you're fine, Ivan." I took another look at the menu, not wanting my humor to grow stale too fast. "I think I'll have the royal shrimp casserole."

"Would you like an appetizer for the table, sir?"

"Would you like something, Veronica," I asked her.

"No thanks."

He took our menus. "Your orders will be ready shortly."

"Darrel," she asked as soon as the server was out of sight, "Angus beef?"

"It was a joke."

"Okay, now I think you're really trying to get us thrown out, for real."

"We're not going anywhere. We're the life of the party."

"Why are you in such a good mood tonight?"

"Why shouldn't I be? I'm in a classy restaurant, sitting across from a fine black woman, waiting to be served some royal shrimp casserole. It can't get no better than this."

"No better, huh?"

"Absolutely, not?"

"So is everything going fine with you and your friend?"

"Friend? What friend?"

"The girl that almost snatched your arm off when she thought I was trying to get with you in the club that night."

"Oh, now look who's trying to be nosey. Talking about me."

"I was just inquiring, that's all."

"Oh, but when I start inquiring, I'm trying to be nosey."

"But, you are. I'm just asking a simple question. You don't have to answer it, if you don't want to. But the Darrel Walker I used to know couldn't wait to tell me all of his business."

"This isn't the same, Darrel Walker."

"I see that now."

"Anyway, she wasn't nobody. We kicked it a couple of times, and that was it."

"Oh, so you're still kicking it with people."

All of the sudden the previous night with Brandi started rumbling within the walls of my brain. "No, I told you I'm looking for more."

"More, huh?"

"Yes, more. I'm not the same person anymore, Veronica. All those games I used to play–done! I'm looking for Miss Right."

"Well, you sound serious. I hope you find her," she said.

"I will. I think I know right where she is." She was sitting right in front of me, yet I felt so helpless. I wanted to tell her to forget about Friday and to jump into my arms, but I couldn't.

"Well, don't let her get away, Darrel."

"I'm trying not to."

"Knowing you, you won't."

"So how did you come to the conclusion that you

and the basketball star were made for each other?"

"I don't know, I guess it just happened. I told you that I had found another side to him, and I guess I fell in love with that."

"You guess? You're suppose to know."

"Really?" she blushed. "Well, how did you know Miss Brandi Brown was the one for you?"

She stopped me in my tracks. It was a damn good question. One, a few months ago, I thought I could answer. I liked the way she looked, but as I thought more about it, I didn't know what I loved so much about Brandi. The sex was good, but I couldn't come up with anything else.

"Did I stomp you?"

"No, you didn't stomp me."

She laughed, "Nah, I think I stomped you. How about this, here's an easier question for you, Mr. Reformed. What is love?"

"Love?"

"Yeah, what's your definition of love? You say that you're searching for it, so tell me what it is. You can't be looking for something and not know what it is, can you, Darrel?"

Damn, she stomped me again. I knew what I wanted in a woman, which was her. But was it love? Was what I had with Brandi considered love? When I caught her cheating on me, it hurt like hell, I knew that much. To dodge looking like a total moron, I decided to chicken out of answering the question completely. "Well, what's your definition of love?"

"That's not fair, Darrel. I just asked you."

"Well, like you said just now, how can you ask a question and not know what kind of an answer you're looking for?"

"Boy, you know you're tripping, trying to flip stuff around. But I'll answer it. I'm not scared."

"Well, go ahead and tell me then."

She shook her head, while revealing her big, pretty smile. "Love, Darrel, is spontaneous. To me, it's just saying something to that special person that is so off the wall, and no one at all understands it except you two. That's love, Darrel. It's trying to say it, and show it in a way that's never been done before. It's faceless. It's felt right here," she said as she placed her hands over her heart.

"That's deep." I was amazed by her description. "No matter what answer that could've came out of my mouth, there's no way it would've been as deep as what you just said."

"It's not deep, Darrel. It's real."

Suddenly, a vision of her and Friday popped up in my mind again. "Is that what you felt when you discovered yourself in love with Friday?" The anticipation for her answer hung over my ears like a student waiting for the last bell of the day to ring.

"Somewhat, Darrel," she answered. "It's kind of chilly in here, isn't it?"

Saying that her answer disappointed me was an understatement. Trying to pry into her relationship with Friday anymore would've been a waste of a perfectly good date. So with all good intentions in mind, I didn't pursue it any further. I decided to go on with the night. "Well, why don't we warm up with a little dancing," I proposed, holding my hand out. It wasn't my type of music that echoed throughout the fancy diner, but it was nice and slow and easy to groove to.

"You want to dance right now?"

"Why not?"

She blushed, "Okay, I see you're trying to show another side. We can dance." She put her hand into mine as we joined the folks already on the floor. We took a spot in the center of the floor, and I gently pulled her body into mine as we danced.

"This is nice, Darrel."

"It is, isn't it?"

"It really is. I didn't expect to have this much fun. It's strange."

"What's strange about it?"

She rested her head against my shoulder. Her sweet smell brought a crisp vibe throughout my body. "I don't know. Just being here feels… right. I know I sound crazy."

"No, you don't." I smiled. "You're having a good time. There's nothing wrong with that."

"He didn't call me. I called him," she sighed. "He gave me this story about his cell phone not working and that he was trying to call me."

I quickly sensed the trouble in paradise, but I didn't want to infringe upon it. "Maybe he did call." I couldn't believe my mouth.

"Yeah, maybe. I just feel so scared sometimes, Darrel."

"Cold feet," I responded.

"No cold feet," she gave me a soft pinch on my arm.

"Alright, you know I don't like to be pinched."

"Stop trying to be funny, then," she advised me. "I just don't won't to be making a mistake. I mean, I want the married life, but I want it to last forever. I want it all to be with the right person."

"My momma always told me that there's no doubting in true love."

"You think I'm doubting things?"

"No, you said it's now or never, right?"

"Yeah."

"Alright, then. You gotta follow your heart. That's as if, this is what you want."

She giggled.

"What's so funny?" I asked.

"I just remember when I used to give you all the

advice. It feels funny the other way around."

"Well, I had to grow up someday, right? I bet you didn't expect that to happen."

"Yes I did." She stopped dancing and grasped me with a hug. "Thanks for coming back into my life, Darrel."

"Thank you for letting me," I said as I hugged her back. The mellow music played on as we danced in each other's arms.

I don't know what it was, but the drive back to her place was pretty quiet. We had so much fun and laughed so much, I guess we were both drained. The ride wasn't long, but I was soaking in every minute of it. I just didn't want our night to end. I walked with her upstairs and stopped at her door.

"So I guess this is goodnight," she said as she unlocked the door and turned around to me.

"I guess it is. I hope that you had a good time."

"I did. I had a wonderful time. How about you?"

"Yeah, oh yeah."

A sudden hush overcame the both of us. All we could do was look at each other with blank faces because neither of us knew what to say next.

"Look, Darrel, I know I've already apologized for that day that I almost ran you over, but…"

"No, don't even go there. In some strange twist of fate that incident brought us here. There's no need for an apology."

"A twist of fate," she smiled.

"Yeah, so you know, if you ever have a chance, maybe we could get together again. Stir up the white folks again."

"I'd like that. We can both get burgers this time."

"Angus beef, right?" I blurted out with a chuckle.

Staring into her eyes and trying to think clearly was an obstacle in itself. I just wanted to kiss her. To delve into her world. To make her mine. To make sweet love to her.

"Give me a hug," she requested.

"No problem."

In an instance, I embraced her. I was overwhelmed by her sweet, savory scent, while enjoying the positioning of her soft body within the realms of my arms. She looked up at me. "Twist of fate, huh?"

"Twist of fate," I replied as my eyes gazed into hers. As I admired the exuberant sparkle that labored in her eyes, I felt a force draw my head closer to hers. My lips had found their way against hers. A small peck had suddenly erupted into much more. Something more intense. Not just a kiss, but a heated entanglement. A sultry engagement that finally brought our wandering hearts together. Nothing around us even existed any longer.

She pulled away. "Darrel, we can't be doing this."

Reality.

"Right, you're right. We shouldn't be doing this. I'm sorry. I don't even know what I was thinking."

"No, I'm sorry," she stated. "I guess I started it. Darrel, I didn't…"

I placed my finger against her lips. "You don't have to say anything. I understand. Just go inside and get yourself some rest. We'll just act like it didn't even happen. "

She softly nodded, "Okay."

I backed away, not believing what had just happened. I wanted her, but not under the circumstances where she could regret it. I turned away from her with my head down. Sure, I could've pressed a little harder, but for what? I wanted much more than a one night stand this time.

"Darrel," she called.

I stopped and turned around. "Yeah." I looked at

her, uncertain about what was going to happen next.

"I… I don't wanna act like it didn't happen again." She slowly walked towards me. The closer she got, the faster my heart pounded. She had me open, and I just didn't know how to handle it. "Was what just happened an accident or was it on purpose?" she asked.

I took a moment to think about it. If I told her the truth, that it was on purpose, she may not respond the way I wanted her to. But if I told her it was an accident, she could think I didn't want her and that would've been exactly what I didn't want. Not only that, but it would be a blatant lie. One that I wasn't sure I could tell. Honesty sure works out to be a double-edge sword sometimes.

"It was all on purpose," I said. Not only did I decide to be honest about it, but I decided to go all or nothing. "I've been wanting to do that for a while now."

She didn't say anything. She just stared into my eyes. My heart pounded fiercely as my mind rambled a thousand thoughts a second. I couldn't read anything from her face. I just awaited her response.

"I was just checking," she said as she wrapped her arms around my neck and gave me a gentle peck on my lips. She leaned away for a moment and said, "Don't let this be a mistake by letting you in."

I shook my head, nervous, yet overjoyed. "You'll never have to worry about that."

We kissed again. This time more passionate, more intense than ever before. My hands, they picked her up as I found myself inside of her abode, lost in her affection, yet conscious enough to navigate into her bedroom.

On top of her, my body rested. Her neck, her breasts, her thighs, all victim to the exploration of my lips. I wanted to taste every portion of her body. I tasted every portion of her body. Our souls intertwined. Inside her, it was like dancing on clouds. Her skin against mine. Her lips against mine. Her moans, all in sync with mine. One word–heaven.

Chapter Thirteen

Time flies when you're having fun. So does it when you're in love. I must say that it's a great feeling to have. Every minute you spend with that special person just doesn't feel like it's enough. Sure, Rex would say I was slipping again, but I didn't care. He didn't know what I knew about love, and he was too scared to find out. Unlike him, I was willing to learn all that there was to know.

"I would sit on that bench for hours." I pointed out my designated bench to Veronica as we strolled through the park.

Our hands were joined together as we walked in perfect harmony. It had been a while since I made my last visit to the old park, and this time, I returned feeling the exact opposite of what I had felt during my gloomy visits over that past year. I was happy this time around. Very happy.

"So that was your spot, huh?" she asked.

"Yeah," I stopped and stared at the bench for a second. At that moment, I saw an image of myself sitting there, heartbroken with my head hung down. It brought chills down my spine to reminisce the coldness and loneliness I had felt on those days I chose to spend my time on that park bench. Feelings that I never wanted to experience again.

"You okay?" Veronica asked.

"I'm straight," I replied as she slipped in front of me and slid her arms around my waist.

"You don't have to worry about sitting there by yourself anymore. I don't plan on breaking your heart."

I gave her a kiss on her cheek. "I can't express how happy I am with you. These last few weeks have been amazing."

"I feel the same way too. Who would've thought

222

five years ago we'd be in each other's arms today? I must admit, Walker, it feels good to be here."

I gave her another kiss. "It's good having you here. My only concern is…"

"Don't even go there," she said pulling away. Our hands were still joined together as we continued our park journey. "I know what you're concerned about, and I'm just gonna have to handle it when he gets back."

"Have you even talked to him?"

"No, we've been playing a lot of phone tag back and forth. When I did get to talk to him, it was only for a minute."

"You couldn't extend the conversation long enough to let him know what's up?"

She rolled her eyes. "No, Darrel. I am engaged to the man."

"But now you're with me."

"Darrel, I'm not the heartbreaker that you are. I can't be all cold about it. I still care about his feelings."

"Heartbreaker. Me? I'm no heartbreaker."

She gave me a soft punch on my arm. "You better not be anymore."

I chuckled, "I'm not." I stopped and swung her into my arms. "Nah, baby, I'm here to stay. I told you that. I just want you to let my man know that it's over, that's all."

"I will in due time, but on my terms, Darrel. I gotta do this my way."

"Hey, that's cool with me. I'll wait as long as I have to for my lady."

She laughed, "That sounds so weird coming from you."

"What's weird about it?"

"I don't know. I guess all the times I hid my secret crush on you back in school, it just feels funny hearing things like that coming from you now."

"Secret crush? Back in school?"

"Yeah," she blushed. "I don't have to keep it a secret anymore, Darrel. So yeah, it's true, I had a crush on you."

"For real? Why didn't you say anything?"

"Because you weren't ready. You were out having your fun, doing things that I just didn't want to put up with."

"But maybe if you had…"

"Don't even say it. You just weren't ready, and we'll have to live with that. Besides, the portion of you that I did get, I was satisfied with it. I never imagined I would've ever gotten anything more."

"Portion? What portion?"

"The nights we talked, the studying, all of that. You didn't really think I was interested in your chatter about all of those girls of yours, did you?"

"But, I thought…"

"You thought wrong, Darrel. Women know how far to go with a man. We know what to expect."

"So what did you expect from me?"

"Nothing."

"Nothing?"

"If I didn't expect anything from you, Darrel, I couldn't get my feelings hurt."

"Well, what do you expect from me now?"

She laughed, "Well, let's just say it's a little bit more than nothing."

"I don't know if that's a good thing or a bad thing."

"We'll leave it as a good thing."

"You women and your way of thinking," I said as we started walking again.

"That's why you men can't figure us out."

"I got a well kept secret to tell ya'. We ain't trying to figure y'all out. Mess around and get a migraine."

"Shut up, boy!" She bumped me.

I must say, things with Veronica and I were going

good. The only dark cloud lingering over our relationship was the Terrance Friday factor. It was like looking at a twister from afar. You see it coming, but you don't know how it's going to hit. I don't think neither one of us was prepared for that confrontation, and it worried me so. It brought a little fear to my heart, with a bit of skepticism. I didn't want to lose her, but things were just going too good, too fast. It was almost like I was dreaming, everything was so perfect. And if it was all a dream, I sure as hell didn't want to wake up.

"And when his daddy went to snap the picture, I looked down and there go Darrel with a chunk of dog pooh in his hand, chewing," my mother said bursting into laughter.

"I know he didn't," Veronica laughed. "Darrel, you ate dog pooh? That is so disgusting."

"Ma, why you gotta tell her that story? You know that didn't happen." My mother was in the midst of telling Veronica item number one on my life's most embarrassing moments list.

"Boy, you better not call me a lie. You know you ate that dog's stuff. Don't be embarrassed, son, you were only five years old."

"Do you have to tell everybody that story, though?"

"Boy, hush up," my mother said.

Veronica was beside me, still in tears from her laughter. We were out in my mother's backyard at one of her infamous summer cookouts. We sat at the table under the old pine tree. In my younger years, it was my top secret base while playing spy games with the neighborhood kids. In my older years, it was just a spot to get out of the blazing sunlight.

The Temptations played in the background as my Uncle Jim and his friends stood at the grill with their hands loaded with brews, joking about old times and things they never got a chance to do. Their wives huddled opposite of them, just as animated, gossiping and trading information about the latest soap drama. It was a great day for all of it.

As my mother rambled on with even more of my moments of privacy, my mind wandered. Every day since the night Veronica and I made love, we couldn't be pulled apart from one another. I called her in the morning before work and spent heavy time with her afterwards. It was beautiful, but as with every good thing, I was awaiting the bad stuff to make its rounds. Everything seemed too good to be true. She hadn't heard from Friday, and I didn't hear a peep from Brandi. My hopes were maybe the both of them had vanished off of the face of the earth and would never return. It was only a wish, and I knew the odds of any of it happening was basically nil.

"Mrs. Walker, I'm gonna have to excuse myself for a few moments. I gotta go to the ladies room and freshen up," Veronica announced.

"Go right ahead, child. You know where it is," my mother responded.

"Thanks," she replied. "I'll be back, Darrel."

"Cool," I said, staring at her as she left.

"You got love in your eyes, Darrel Walker," Ma whispered.

"And what are you talking about now, Ma?"

"My son's in love. I told you she was the one for you."

"Ma, she's still engaged to Terrance Friday, so nothing between us is really official, yet."

"What are you talking about? She's here with you, isn't she?"

"Yeah, but, Ma…"

"Don't *but* me, child. Be thankful you got time to work some magic. It doesn't matter if she's engaged to this other guy. She's here with you right now. You got a chance, son. Take advantage of it, and stop worrying about what could happen wrong."

"I've been trying to, Ma, but this thing is bugging me."

"Well don't let it. Do what you have to do to keep this woman in your life and don't blow it. When I see you two together, it reminds me of your father and me when we were young. We were so happy together. Just don't take your time for granted, son. The Lord isn't putting her here with you for nothing, believe that."

"I know, Ma."

"Well, shut up then. Overwhelm this girl with so much happiness she won't even remember she was thinking about marrying somebody else. Whoever this character is, he sure ain't worried about her too much. Especially if she's able to spend all her time with you."

"Tell me about it."

"Have some fun for a change, son. 'Cause I ain't gonna lie, I really like this girl."

"I can tell. You've told her every terrible experience of my childhood."

"Not all, but I'll wait until you two tie the knot before I tell her the real good stuff."

"And here you go, already got us married. The girl hasn't even left her first fiancé yet."

"Well, at your age, if you're not thinking about spending the rest of your life with a person you're in a relationship with, what are you wasting your time with 'em for?"

"I'm not wasting time with Veronica."

"You are if all you can think about is negative things."

"I'm not being negative, Ma. I'm being real."

"Real? Is that what you young folk call it these days? We'll let me be *real* with you for a moment, son." She started pointing her infamous finger at me. "You can lose this woman if you want to, but there may never be

227

another good one like her to come around again. Don't take this time for granted. I done told ya'."

"I hear ya', Ma."

"Is that *real* enough for you, son?"

"Yeah, Ma. I hear what you're saying."

"Alright then. Enjoy this woman and treat her right. I'm not playing when I say I like this girl. She's pretty, too. She can have me some nice looking grandchildren."

"You and your grandchildren."

"What else do I have to look forward to at my age?"

"Rex." His name slipped off of the tip of my tongue as I saw him and his mother walking in from the front of the house.

My mother turned her head with a slight frown. "Stella and her devil child," she whispered as she turned to me again.

"Oh, you know Stella is your girl. That's your gossip buddy."

"Darrel, you know your mother doesn't even take part in any of that foolishness," she replied.

"Darrel, hey baby," Rex's mother greeted me.

"How are you today, Mrs. Tyson?" I asked.

"I'm just fine, baby. My back ain't hurting me today, so I guess I can't complain." She looked towards my mother. "Mabel, now that hairstyle sure looks good on you. When did you get it done?"

"Thank you, Stella. I just got it done yesterday," Ma said softly patting her hair with a proud smile.

"What's going on, Momma Walker?" Rex asked as he tapped me on my shoulder.

"I'm fine, Rex," she answered.

"Mabel, I got some news for you, chile," Stella said, getting started with her gossip column.

"Well, tell me while I go fix me some of that chicken before Jim burn it all up. Those heathens are good for leaving all the burnt pieces sitting there," my mother said as she grabbed Stella by her arm and headed towards the grill with her.

Rex stood in front of me, staring at me as if I had done something wrong. "What's wrong with you?" I asked.

He grinned as he took a seat. "You know what's wrong."

"No, I don't."

"You ain't call a nigga in two weeks. What's up with that? Did I piss you off or something?"

"Nah, I've had a lot of work to do. I just needed some time to myself to get it all done."

"You must've been doing some heavy shit, you can't call nobody. I was like, this nigga must be hung up on that Brandi chick, again. What she do now, D.?"

"Nothing. I haven't even heard anything from her. I've just been taking care of business, that's all. It was nothing to do with her." I didn't even want to mention Veronica to him because his lecturing would soon follow. But I knew it was inevitable since she was coming back at any moment.

"Shoot, I can understand that. So what else have you been up to?"

"Nothing, just chillin' and working, that's all."

"Well, hell, all work and no play, that's no fun. Do you wanna hit the Hot Spot tonight? We can bag a few honeys and hit the Waffle House afterwards. Just like the old days."

"Nah, I don't think that would be a good idea."

"Why not? You're a free man, just like I am. Ain't no rings on these fingers, right?"

"Well, because…"

"Darrel, where'd your mother go?" Veronica interrupted.

Rex looked towards her with his mouth shot open.

Her appearance stunned him just as much as it did me.

"Hey, Veronica, this is my best friend, Rex," I jumped up and angled her towards him.

"Oh, so you're Rex. I'm sorry, I didn't even see you sitting there. I've heard so much about you," she said extending her hand.

His grin surfaced while shaking her hand. "That's funny, I haven't heard anything at all about you."

"Well you know your friend as well as anybody," she winked at me. "He's always keeping something under wraps."

"You can sure say that again." He gave me a brief frown.

She turned to me. "Look, I'll let you guys do your little men thing. I'll go hang out with the ladies."

"That's cool, baby," I replied.

"Nice to finally meet you, Rex," she said.

"Oh, the pleasure was all mine," he advised her.

She walked towards the grill. When she got far enough, Rex directed all of his focus on me. "Taking care of business, huh? What the hell are you thinking about?" he asked. "I know who she is. That's Terrance Friday's chick."

"I know what you're gonna say, Rex, and everything's cool, believe me."

"Everything's not cool. You're messing around with a chick that ain't nothing but trouble, and then you kicked me to the curb for her. That's some real bullshit right there, dude. Apparently you like trouble."

"Rex, come on, man. The last thing I need in my life right now is some drama. And ain't nobody kicked you to the curb, so stop playing. Things just happened, that's all."

"Just happened, huh?" He shook his head. "How in the hell did this just happen? What, some more late night movies? Bible study? What was it this time?"

"One thing led to another. That's all I can really say about the situation. Actually that's all that I'm gonna say about it."

"So how does the celebrity fiancé feel about all of this?"

I sighed, "He doesn't know yet."

"Boy, I tell you what. You just move from drama to more drama."

"It's no drama, Rex. This is love, man. I love this woman."

"Just like you loved Brandi Brown, right?"

I paused for a moment. When he said Brandi's name it ticked me off a bit. "Man, why'd you have to bring Brandi's name into this. This doesn't have anything to do with her. You should be happy for me, anyway. I think I've found the right one for me this time."

"Is she really yours, D? What I'm getting from you is that her man don't know nothing about you two. So what do you think he's gonna do when he finds out?"

"He can't do nothing. If she wants to be with me, he can't stop her."

"Negro, do you really think she's gonna drop a million dollar cat like Terrance Friday to be with you? Don't take it personal, but he's loaded with dough and you're not. There's no way in hell she's turning all that cash down."

"It's not even like that. She's not with him for the money, and she's with me because she loves me. You don't know what you're talking about."

"Alright, we'll see. Because after she's done playing with you, she's gonna go right back where the money is."

"I actually expected you to respond like this. You don't know nothing about love, man. If you did, you would feel me on this one."

"Please, I don't even wanna hear that nonsense.

Since you have all of these expectations, I'm gonna tell you what's gonna happen. He's gonna kick your ass, and she's gonna leave with him. That's exactly what's gonna happen?"

I stared at him, trying to stay as calm as I could. He was my boy, but he was beginning to strike some serious nerves. Nerves that could bring fighting words into any long standing friendship. "Well, that'll be something that I'll have to deal with if it happens."

"Gonna happen!"

"I'll deal with it I said."

"You can deal with it all you want to, but don't expect me to get involved. I've always had your back, but this is too big this time."

"Who said I was getting you involved? You're not involved now. I'm a grown man, and I can handle my own problems."

"All I'm saying is that people like Friday run deep with a caravan of fools that are specialized in taking care of their dirty work. If you're gonna be messing around with ole' girl, you need to watch your back. Because like I said before, she ain't nothing but trouble."

"Well, I'll worry about all of that. Terrance Friday doesn't bring any fear into my heart, nor do any of his goons."

"Well, I hope she's worth it because this whole situation stinks."

"Oh she's worth it," I said as I turned and glanced towards her at the grill talking with my mother. "She's worth every bit of it."

He laughed, "I don't know what I'm gonna do with you, D. You're always getting into something new."

"Well, brotha', that's just me. But trust me, I got this."

"Okay, if you say so. Just be cautious about the shit."

"I got it, k?" he responded with a nod of his head. The smile on his face was phony and only told me that he didn't want to let it go. But he had no other choice. "Now, the last time I checked this was one of my momma's famous cookouts. Now we can sit here and chat or we can get some of Jim's barbequed chicken before it all gets snatched up."

"That's cool with me," he said as we both got up and headed towards the grill.

"Let's go see what Jim's talking about over here on this grill."

I always felt that Rex took a little too much to do with my private life at times. I never said anything because I knew he was only trying to be a good friend. Besides that, most of my private life has always included him to some extent. But my business with Veronica was none of his business whatsoever. And I liked it that way. My intention from jump were to make it stay that way, too.

Chapter Fourteen

Rainy days. I don't know what it is about them, but they make you just want to find that person you're really close to and just settle in. Now rainy days combined with Atlanta traffic makes you want to find that person really quick, settle in and not come back out for a very long time. Be that as it may, I was in route to Veronica's place. We had made plans to go out for dinner and catch a movie, but with the weather being how it was, I was hoping that we could simply stay in and catch a flick on the tube. After a long day of meetings with Dale and Putnam, I needed a break. And even though being with Veronica soothed my soul, I just wanted to take it easy for the night.

As I stood in front of her door armed with a bouquet of roses I'd picked up on the way over, I wondered if she had a chance to talk to Friday. I just couldn't relax until I knew for sure all ties to him were severed. I guess it really had a lot to do with what happened between Brandi and I. I wanted our relationship to be secure, that's all. I guess that's what some women mean when they say they're waiting to exhale. I discovered what it felt like, and I wanted to exhale my damn self.

"Darrel," she said opening the door. Her face lit up like a Christmas tree. "I was waiting for you."

"What's going on, babe?" I gave her a peck on her cheek. "These are for you."

Her smile became even bigger when I revealed the flowers to her. She grabbed them and sniffed them with her eyes focused on me. I eased inside and closed the door. She sat the roses on the sofa and jumped into my arms, kissing me repeatedly.

"Thank you, Darrel."

"No problem."

She pulled me by my arm. "Come on, I got

something to show you."

"I'm coming, I'm coming," I playfully advised her.

She guided me into her dining room, and we both stopped to observe the feast she had prepared. On the table she had some buttery rolls, sultry ham, yellow rice and a slew of other home-cooked items. It all looked too delicious in the candle-lit room.

"I know we had plans, but I was hoping we could dine in tonight. That's only if you don't mind."

I walked towards the table amazed by all of her hard work on the dinner. "Girl, I didn't know you could throw down like this. You sure you don't have my momma hiding up in here somewhere?"

"There's a lot of things you don't know about a sista', but hopefully you'll stick around long enough to find out everything. And no, I don't have Mrs. Walker hiding in here nowhere. I got skills."

"You certainly do. And you surely don't have to worry about me going anywhere. With cooking like this, I'm definitely here to stay."

"I hope that you'll stay for more besides the cooking," she said as she graced me with another kiss.

I slid my arms around her waist, pulled her close to me and kissed her right back. "Don't worry, the pretty face helps out a lot also."

"Watch yourself," she said as she pulled away and took a spot at the table. "Let's eat."

"You got it," I said anxious to get my grub on.

We sat down and began digging into the food. While feasting, I often caught myself gazing at her, thinking about how lucky I was to have her. She was a woman. I mean a real woman. One of those women that just had everything right about her. Her look, her smell, her personality, everything was so perfect.

"What are you thinking about?" she asked.

"Why I gotta be thinking about something? I'm

just enjoying the supper, that's all."

"Yeah, well you look like you're thinking about something. How was work?"

"It was straight. Nothing but the same old stuff. Putnam is considering airing that piece on Fri..."

"Why'd you stop?"

"No reason."

"You were about to say something about Terrance, weren't you?"

"Yeah well, Putnam's thinking about airing his piece again since he's suppose to be getting married in a month or so."

"So that made your talking cease?"

"Hey, I just didn't want to go there. You said you were handling it, so the ball's in your park now. My hands are tied."

"That's right, Darrel. I am going to handle it. You can still say his name. It's not taboo or anything."

"I know I can say his name. I just prefer not to. I don't even want to think about him to tell you the truth."

"And you don't have to."

"Well, did you talk to him today?"

"No, I didn't speak with him today, Darrel."

"What kind of relationship do you two have? Nobody calls each other. What's up with that?"

"He's a ball player, Darrel. He's always busy. I understood before I even got involved with him the type of schedule he keeps with this lifestyle."

"I'm gonna be honest. I don't think his time is all ball playing and contract negotiations. You and I both know that, so let's stop pretending that it is."

"And what's that suppose to mean, Darrel?"

"Once a player, always a player, that's all."

"Sounds like the pot calling the kettle black to me."

At the blink of an eye she broke me down. I couldn't say anything about Friday because I had just got off the same road he was traveling. "Well, I'm different," I proclaimed without thought.

"Really," she wiped her mouth with a napkin, then folded her arms up. "Tell me how, Darrel."

"What do you mean, tell you how?"

"If you're so different, you should know what differentiates yourself from Terrance."

"Well for one, I know what love is now. I'm not all about the games anymore. All that stuff is old."

"Love? Darrel, you couldn't even explain to me what the word meant to you when I asked you about it."

"I could. I just couldn't put my words together how I wanted them."

"Really?"

"Yes, really."

"Then put them together now. You've had more than enough time to think about it. What is your meaning of love, Darrel?"

I paused, more nervous than an stripper in church. All I could do was dodge the question completely. "I don't feel like it."

She shook her head. "Unbelievable."

"What? I just don't feel like it."

"But you're so different," she mocked me.

"That's what I said."

"You know what? I've lost my appetite." She jumped up and headed towards the den.

"Veronica," I said as I pushed away from the table and jumped up to catch her. I grabbed her arm to prevent her from leaving.

"What do you want, Darrel?" She snatched her arm away from me and faced me.

"Don't be mad. That's why I didn't even want to bring his name up."

"But you were thinking about him."

"How can I not be thinking about him? You're

engaged to this guy, but all your feelings are with me."

"And how do you think I feel, Darrel? What about me? Think about someone else besides yourself for a change. I didn't plan for things to turn out like this. I never cheated on nobody before. I just want to do the right thing."

"I know."

"No, you don't know. All you see is the black and white. What about the gray area, Darrel? He has feelings, too, and he deserves an explanation."

"I didn't say that he didn't deserve one."

"You didn't have to. Your actions did."

We stood silent, staring at each other. I didn't know what to say. I was still fuming on the inside, but I didn't want her to be mad at me. I just didn't like seeing that irritated look on her face.

"Look, I'm sorry..."

"Don't be sorry, Darrel," she interrupted. "I need you to be understanding."

"I'm trying to Veronica, but this..."

"Whatever!"

I couldn't even get the rest of the words out of my mouth before she left me standing high and dry all by my lonesome. It's the 'but' that always seemed to get me in trouble.

I walked into the den where she was sitting on the edge of the sofa with her head resting on her fist. I could look at her and tell I pissed her off good. I eased in and took a seat on the opposite end of the couch. If silence could kill, at this point, it would be a mass murderer. I glanced at her for a moment, reneged on making any comment and looked away. I knew I had to say something, I was just scared of setting her off again.

"I understand," I said. More silence followed. I didn't know what I expected to happen after the comment, I just said it. I assumed that was what she wanted to hear.

She turned to me. "I love you, Darrel. I really do. There's nothing in this world that I would like more than to give you my complete and undivided affection. And I will. But please don't pressure me into doing this. I don't know how I'm going to do it, but I will. I just have to do it my way."

Her words came straight from the heart. They were so real it brought a brief chill down my spine. I slid over to her and placed my arm around her shoulders. "I'm sorry, baby."

She relaxed herself along my chest and wrapped her arm around my waist. "I'm sorry, too."

I guess I was so impatient about her breaking up with him, I failed to realize the stress she was up against of having to break things off. I guess it was my insecurity. I just didn't want to be alone again. I leaned my head back and stared at the ceiling. I thought about how crazy this world was. In college, I didn't give Veronica a second look, and Terrance Friday was just some dumb jock we both couldn't stand. Flash forward five years, and I'm head over heels in love with her, and she's engaged with the world's most obnoxious jerk. A crazy world indeed.

Her phone rang. We both jolted straight up and stared at the phone across the room. Deep down inside we both knew it was something that wasn't good. It rang again and neither one of us moved an inch.

"You gonna answer it?" I asked.

"Yeah," she said. She walked towards the phone. My eyes were still glued to it. "Hello," she answered.

My eyes were on her like an eagle to a worm. I just knew it was Terrance Friday.

"Terrance," she sounded surprised.

My heart started thumping something awful. I wanted to hear her break it off right then and there. My ears hung to every word released from her lips.

"I haven't been doing much. I've just been waiting

for you to come home, that's all. We have a lot to talk about."

I could tell from her nervous tone, she wasn't going to address the matter with him. And despite our previous conversation, I got hot. Red hot. Within seconds the conversation ended. No break up. No change in relationship status. I immediately started considering the things Rex advised me. Maybe she wasn't going to give up the lavish lifestyle Friday could provide for her.

She hung up the phone, took a deep breath and stared at me. I looked away because I couldn't look into her face. I was disappointed in her although I probably shouldn't have been.

She sat beside me. I wanted to move instantly. "He's coming back this weekend," she said.

"Then I guess I'll talk to you then." I got up and walked towards the door.

"Darrel," she yelled. The frustration was evident in her voice. "Why are you leaving?"

My hand was on the doorknob, and I didn't want to respond to the question. My feelings for her was the only thing that made me turn around, but my anger was all that I could display. "I don't want to get in the way of you doing the right thing."

"So that's how it is? You're just gonna pout and leave. Are you really gonna leave me like this?" Tears began developing in the wells of her eyes.

Staring at her, all I wanted to do was hold her. I couldn't bare the sight of seeing her cry, but there just wasn't going to be any peace between us until it was completely over with her and Terrance Friday.

"Thanks for the dinner." I walked out before I even had a chance to think about what I was doing. As I stomped down the hall, I could faintly hear her voice begging me to come back. My ego wasn't about to let me feel it. I had to keep moving.

As I streaked down the highway, my destination was home. The weather had cleared up, but my future was all cloudy. I knew I shouldn't have left, and I regretted doing so, but I'd rather leave than to stay and say something I would regret later. I knew the night was just too good to be true when it all started.

I was stuck so deep in thought, I didn't realize I was pulling into my driveway. My intentions were to take a shower and hit the sack with the ringer to my phone turned off. I didn't want any connections to the outside world whatsoever. I walked to my front door and just when I was about to insert my key, I noticed the door was cracked open. I cautiously pushed it on open. I walked in and looked around. Everything looked normal, but I knew I didn't leave the door that way when I left for work. I eased into my bedroom and what laid before me almost knocked me off of my feet.

"Hi, love!" It was Brandi, all spread out across my bed, garnishing some kinky lace lingerie.

"What in the hell do you think you're doing?" I yelled.

"I'm trying to surprise you, love. Aren't you surprised?"

"Why are you here? How in the hell did you even get in?"

"Silly, I still have a key. I used to live here, you know."

"Not anymore."

A puzzled look consumed her face. "Why, love, I don't think you want me here."

"Brandi, you have never been so right."

"You don't want me here?"

"Here's a clue. No!"

"Darrel, you're so callous." She jumped off of the bed and walked towards me. "Let me help you get out of those rags of yours. I'll make it alright, just like I used to."

I swiped her hankering hands away. "Look, you need to put on some clothes."

"But these are all that I have, love."

"Well you have yourself a very serious problem. It's time to go, and I'm not playing with you." I grabbed her arm and pulled her into the living room so she could make her exit.

"But, Darrel, we haven't made love yet."

I stopped walking and released her. "You just don't get it, do you?"

"Get what, love?"

"I don't want you anymore."

For a moment, it appeared that I'd made a dent in that thick skull of hers. She stood before me with the strangest look on her face. "You're serious."

"I am *so* serious. I am as serious as a heart attack."

"You don't love me anymore?"

"No!" I said shaking my head like a toddler with a final answer.

"I don't believe you."

"What?" I stood astonished by her diligence.

"I think you've forgotten how good it feels to make love to me," she said grabbing for me. "Let me show you how it feels, love. You won't have to do a thing at all. Just enjoy me."

"Get away from me." I pushed her back.

"What is it?"

"Woman, look…," I paused before any word could escape my mouth. For a brief moment, I flashed back to how I left Veronica by herself without reason. I realized that I had messed up and the mere thought of it all crippled my spirit. "I'm gonna take a shower. I expect you to be gone by the time I get out."

"Darrel," she grabbed my hand.

"No," I snatched my hand back. "Go home, Brandi. I can't deal with you right now."

"But, love…"

I didn't look back as I stomped into my bedroom and slammed the door close. I couldn't believe how I left Veronica. All I could think about was how she must've felt when I left. I left with such haste. I let my ignorance drive me away from her. It was a huge mistake. I was gonna have to call her and beg for her forgiveness. I wasn't about to lose her over some bull.

I stood in the shower with my head down and my hands against the wall. With the steamy water rolling down my back, my mind incubated. Brandi should've been well on her way home and Veronica… I just didn't know what Veronica was doing. I yearned to turn back the hands of time and take back everything that was done. But I knew time travel wasn't a reality, and when I got out of the shower, I was gonna have to make right what went wrong.

As I turned the shower off, I heard what appeared to be a knock at the front door. "I'll get it, love," Brandi screamed.

A sharp jolt of nervousness overcame my body as I realized that nutcase hadn't left yet and she was about to open my door to someone. "Brandi, no!" I yelled as I almost broke my neck to get out of the tub. I quickly whipped a towel around my waist. The water had me freezing as I rushed through the house to stop her from answering the door.

"Brandi," I called out as I made way into the den. She had already opened the door, lingerie and all. She backed away from the door with a petite smile on her face. She cleared the path for my view, and standing on the other side of the door was Veronica. With her mouth wide open, she was just as surprised as I was.

"Veronica, I can explain," I immediately tried to plea my case.

"Darrel," her lips trembled, "Same old, Darrel."

"Veronica, no," I yelled as she turned around and

headed towards her truck. I brushed pass Brandi and hurried outside. I didn't care if I was half naked. "Baby, let me explain."

"She's naked. You're naked. You don't have to explain anything to me." She opened the door to her vehicle. "I'm fully capable of interpreting what's going on."

"Nothing happened. I swear."

"It certainly looked like nothing was going on, Darrel," she said as she jumped into the truck.

"Will you please let me explain?"

"There's nothing to explain. You left me to be with your ex-wife. I understand."

"No. It didn't go down like that. She was already here when I came through the door."

"How'd she get in, Darrel?"

I paused as I took a moment to think about how ludicrous it all sounded to myself. "She had a key."

She shook her head and laughed, "How convenient. You know, I can't believe I even gave you the time of day. But with as much as I already knew about you, I guess I don't have anyone else to blame but myself." She slammed her door shut and started the engine.

"Veronica," I mumbled, realizing that there was no use. It was all over. I stood frozen as I watched her back out and drive away, taking my heart along with her. It all happened so fast, I didn't believe it. With my head hung down and my pride wrecked, I headed towards the front door.

I walked in and Brandi was sitting on the couch eating a bowl of ice cream. All I could see was red. She cost me so much this time around.

"Now that that's over, would you like to take me up on my offer, love? I promise you won't regret how good I'll make you feel."

I wanted to cry. "Why do you exist? Did I do

something so horrible that I'm now sentenced to be tortured by you for the rest of my life?"

"Love, you don't sound like yourself." She sat her bowl on the coffee table and approached me. "I'll make everything alright. I promise."

"Don't... don't touch me," I shunned her away. "Believe me when I say, you can't make anything okay for me."

"Don't be upset because your friend left you. I'll keep you company."

I began to laugh hysterically, "Do you really think I want your company? Is that what you think?"

"Well... yes."

"You just cost me something so important that I can't even stand the very sight of you right now."

"What was that?"

"Love... you, you psycho."

"Darrel, you're beginning to hurt my feelings."

"They need to be hurt. Get out of my house, too."

"You don't mean that," she paused, "Do you?"

"I mean it from the very bottom of my heart. I want you out."

"But don't you love me anymore?"

I laughed again and looked up at the ceiling while shaking my head in disbelief. "Brandi, the woman that I love just left me. You see, today, for the first time in my life, I learned something. I learned the difference between love and lust. From the first day I met you, I lusted for you. I wanted to have sex with you. I wanted to hear you scream out my name while I was on top of you. I wanted to rip your clothes off every time I laid eyes on you. But that was all lust, Brandi."

"Darrel, you're wrong. If that's the case, then neither one of us know what love means. And we probably don't. That's what's so beautiful about us."

"No, no, no. That's where you're wrong. That

person that just left from here, I love her. Being with her is like breathing in fresh air. It's so much more than just sex. So much, you wouldn't understand it. But that's okay, because now I've lost her."

"But… you still have me." She walked towards me. "It's fate. Just like the night we met."

"*I don't want you!*" My words stopped her in her tracks. The truth was finally revealed.

"So, I guess you're serious, love," she said softly. "You've never been this way towards me before."

A tear slid down my face as I nodded. I didn't want to put things out there like that, but it was the only way. "I'm sorry, Brandi."

She placed her hand on my face and gave me a kiss on my cheek. "Maybe you're right, love. Maybe it was lust. Whatever it is, it surely hurts." She grabbed her keys and walked toward the kitchen.

"Brandi… where are you going?"

She smiled, valiantly attempting to hold in her own tears. "Oh… I parked my car in the back to surprise you."

"Oh, okay."

"Oh well, it was fun, lo…," she stopped herself. "It was fun, Darrel."

When she walked out, it was like a part of me left with her. A part of me that I didn't know anymore. A part that I didn't want to know anymore. I took a seat on my sofa feeling like my world had just ended. Bad had just turned to worse and through this spiral I called my life, I was in very familiar territory once again. There wasn't a peep to be heard in my vacant abode as I sat on my couch and remained single again.

Chapter Fifteen

The week blew by, and every day in it, my soul suffered. Every night, I would hover near Veronica's place before going home. At times, I would make it into the parking lot of her apartment complex and attempt to muster up enough nerve to make it to her front door, but to no avail. All I wanted was to reclaim my place in her life again, but the whole thing seemed hopeless. I hadn't heard anything from her all week and deep down inside I knew that I wouldn't. When I called her, she didn't answer. I left messages and got no replies. At night, I would sleep with the phone against my chest, praying she would call, but it never happened. My only assumption was that her plans to marry Terrance Friday were ongoing.

I pulled into my driveway and as I was about to turn my engine off, I paused. Something stopped me. I sat and thought about my life before Veronica had reentered it, and it all depressed me. I was so empty. I didn't want to go back to that. I wanted to infringe upon a future with her. I wanted to hold her, kiss her, and make love to her every day for the rest of my life. I wanted to have kids and grow old with her. I just wanted her. That same force that stopped me from turning my car off and calling it a day, guided me straight out of my driveway and back onto the highway. For whatever it was worth, I was determined not to give up that easy.

As I moved through traffic, reality began to sink in. It had my stomach turning in knots. The closer I got to her place, the more my stomach aggravated me. I was hung up on what to do, but I was determined to do something. I at least wanted to provide an explanation as to what really happened when she caught me with Brandi.

I zoomed up the stairs and found myself at her front door. As I waited for her to answer my knock, I couldn't help but notice the sounds of music and a lot of laughter coming from the other side of the door.

"Hello," a short-haired, dark-skinned chick answered. My eyes crawled to the numbers above the door to verify I was at the right place. "Can I help you?" she asked hastily.

I was indeed at the right place. "Yeah, is Veronica in?"

"Yeah, who are you?" she snapped.

"A friend," I snapped back.

She gave me a brief stare down. It was hate at first sight, no doubt. "Hold on a minute," she said closing the door.

I stood there with a sinking tolerance for the bald chick's attitude. If she came back out with more of it, I was well prepared to put her in her place.

"What is it?" Veronica asked as she opened the door.

"Veronica," I mumbled. Even though I came to see her, I wasn't quite ready to actually see her.

"You needed something?" she asked coldly as she exited the apartment and closed the door.

"Yeah, uh, I want to talk to you about some things."

"If this is about last week, I don't want to hear it. I know what I saw, and I don't need any explanation.

"I think you do need an explanation because you don't know what you saw."

She chuckled, "I think the lack of clothing clued me in well enough. But if you feel the need to waste my time and yours, enlighten me on your take." She leaned against the door with her arms folded. From the way she looked, I could tell she wanted our meeting to be brief.

"Look, I know things looked bad, but nothing happened. I got home, she was in my bed, I told her off and to be gone by the time I got out of the shower. That's the honest to God truth."

She shook her head. "Don't blame me for not believing your story. I mean, it probably would be believable if I had a brain the size of a flea."

"I admit it looked real bad. And I know I'm asking a lot from you to believe it, but it's the truth. It's all the truth. I'm not trying to play you for a fool, Veronica."

"Then why does it feel that way, Darrel?"

"Veronica just hear me out."

"No, you hear me out! Even if one percent of what you're saying is true, think about the way you left me here. You dogged me out over something that I needed time to handle. Time that I begged you for. You just abandoned me. You left me, Darrel."

"I'm sorry."

"Sorry ain't gonna cut it this time." She turned around and grabbed the doorknob.

"No," I yelled grabbing her hand.

"Let me go, Darrel."

"Not until you've heard me out.

She snatched her hand away. "Well, you got two minutes to say what you have to say."

"That's all I need. That's all I'm asking from you. Just a chance."

"Veronica, you okay?" The short-haired chick came out again and greeted me with another nasty stare.

"Yeah, girl, I'm okay. Tell everybody I'll be ready in a minute."

"Alright, girl, let me know if you need something," she said closing the door. She didn't fully close it until after she squinted her eyes at me one final time.

"Were you going somewhere?"

"I have plans."

"I'd give the world to be apart of your plans again."

"Well you're not. You said you have something to say, didn't you?"

I took a moment to gather my thoughts. "Well, I guess all I can say is that my life just doesn't feel right without you in it. I miss you, Veronica. There hasn't been a moment that has gone by that I haven't thought about you."

"Too bad you didn't think about me when it counted the most," she sighed. "You got one minute left."

"I know I deserve the attitude. I mean, with or without the situation with Brandi, I was wrong for leaving you, and I apologize for that. I'd give anything to change it all back."

"But you can't, can you? I told you on the night we kissed, Darrel, don't let me be making a mistake by letting you into my heart, but you did anyway. You treated me just like one of those girls of yours back in school. And I really thought I was more than that to you."

"You are, baby. You make me a better person. You give me this feeling inside that changes how I see the world."

"But it wasn't enough to keep you faithful to me."

"I didn't do anything with her, nor do I want to. I don't deserve you walking out on me like this."

"What about how you walked out on me, Darrel? What about that? And then I actually ran after you and caught you the way I did," she laughed. "I can't believe how stupid I was."

"You aren't stupid. You weren't stupid. Nothing happened, Veronica. Please believe me."

She shook her head as she quickly swiped a tear from her eye. "I can't, Darrel. No matter what you try to say, you can't change how I feel."

"Baby, you gotta believe me," I said as I moved closer to her.

"Don't. Don't get any closer, Darrel."

"You're trying to tell yourself you don't love me when you know you do. Deep down inside, you know that

I've changed, that I wouldn't do anything in this world to hurt you. You know that I love you."

"That's all fine, Darrel. Even if half of what you're saying is true, it doesn't even matter anymore.

"Well it should. It should count for something."

"Unfortunately, it doesn't, because Terrance is back."

"He's back. Well, that's great. Now we can lay everything out on the table.

"There's nothing to lay on the table, Darrel. All the calls you've made, the messages on my machine, and talking to you now, it means nothing anymore."

"No, it shouldn't be like this. I won't let it be this way."

"Well, you don't have much of a choice. The wedding date has been changed."

"What do you mean changed?" I awaited her lips to move with a response. She simply sighed and turned her head. Her hesitation was a clear indicator that her news wouldn't be to my favor. "What do you mean it was changed?"

"It's tomorrow, Darrel."

"What?" It was as if she ran me over with a garbage truck. "Tomorrow? It can't be tomorrow. This thing isn't even suppose to happen. You were gonna call it all off."

"Well, I've changed my mind, Darrel. Terrance thought it would be good to move it up, and I agreed. There wasn't any reason not to."

"What about us?"

"Like I said, there wasn't any reason not to move the date up."

"Nah," I shook my head. "This ain't even right. You love me. You don't love, Friday."

"Well, I'm marrying Terrance tomorrow, and there's nothing else to say about it. I need stability in my life."

"There's no stability with that, jerk. Come on, Veronica. What are you doing?"

"What I need to do."

"No… no, no. This ain't right. You can't do this."

"Can't do what?" a voice from down the hall asked. We both turned to it's direction, and it was Mr. T.G.I.F. himself, walking towards us with a big, black goliath in a snug black suit that appeared to be his bodyguard.

"Terrance," Veronica mumbled.

"What's up, baby?" he said as he kissed her on her forehead and slid his arm around her waist. "Walker."

"Terrance," I replied.

"So what can't be done?" he asked. I looked over to his shade wearing gladiator and opted not to act a fool. I wasn't scared of him, I just didn't feel like going through a scuffle that would no doubt pain one of us.

"Darrel isn't gonna be able to make it to the wedding tomorrow," Veronica answered.

"Oh," Friday frowned. "That's cool. I don't remember sending you out an invitation, Walker. But no hard feelings, right knocka'?"

"No, none at all," I replied staring at Veronica.

"Well, now that that's settled, I guess you can be off on your way," he so eloquently suggested.

I glanced at him and then at his overgrown bodyguard, who appeared ready for a brawl. He stood beside Friday gazing at me while cracking his knuckles. I decided not to even bother. I could take a hint.

"Well, I wish you two much happiness." I gave Veronica one final stare, hoping she would just have a change of heart. Instead, she looked away. "I couldn't dream up a more perfect couple."

"Thanks, Walker," Friday replied. "It ain't nothin' but another chapter in the TGIF experience. Know what I mean?" I looked at Friday, and I couldn't believe the huge mistake she was making by marrying that joke. "I can only imagine, Terrance." I walked away.

"Walker," Friday yelled.

I didn't want to stop, but I did anyway. "Yeah," I turned around.

"Hey, dawg, you did a real good job making me look good on that video. I appreciate it," he laughed.

Mad as hell, I looked over to his fiancé for one last stare. "Not as half as good as she makes you look." I kept walking.

I never lost anything before. I guess that's why it felt so awful to see my chance at happiness slip through my fingers when she told me she was still going to marry him. And even though it hurt me like crazy, a part of me felt like I deserved everything I got. All the crazy things I did in the past, all the lies and deceit. I guess it all finds a way to come back around somehow. Not the way you'd imagine if you've lived a life doing dirt, but in a fresh and unsuspecting way that just knocks the hell out of you. It sure knocked the hell out of me.

I didn't want to go home and be in the place where it all ended. If I so much as looked at my front door, I'd get sick. So somehow I found myself on the stairs to my mother's house. I stood in front of her door with my head down and my body feeling as if it didn't have any energy in it at all. It was the only place I could go.

"Darrel?" She opened he door, surprised to see me. "Darrel, what's wrong , baby?"

I looked into her eyes, trying everything in my soul to keep from bursting into tears. "I lost her, Ma."

"Who, baby?"

"Veronica, Ma. I messed up."

"Ah, Darrel, how'd you do that? Come on in here, son." I could hear the disappointment in her voice as I walked into the house and sat on the edge of the couch.

She sat beside me as she fastened her housecoat. "So go ahead and tell me. What'd you do this time?"

"I don't even know how to begin, Ma. I didn't intend for things to mess up. They just ended up that way."

"Child, with you, that just doesn't seem to surprise me," she said shaking her head. It was all covered up with pink rollers. "And she was such a nice girl. You must've really done something stupid for her to leave. So tell me what it was, Darrel."

"Brandi opened my door wearing some skimpy lingerie, and I was naked, too."

"Darrel," she huffed. "I thought you were serious about this girl. How'd you do something so stupid. Don't you have any self control?"

"I do, Ma. It really wasn't as bad as it looked."

"I don't know how it wasn't. If I had caught you that way, I would've left you too. There's not much explaining needed for that scenario."

"It's not like it sounds, Ma."

"Then what happened, Darrel? Because what you've told me so far doesn't sound too good. And it sounds just like you."

It was hard hearing that come from my mother, but it was the truth. I earned that reputation, and it did sound like me, even though this time around, it wasn't. "Ma, I came home, and Brandi was on my bed with nothing but a bra and some panties on. I didn't even argue with her. I just told her to be out by the time I got out of the shower."

She looked at me like I had lost my mind. "You didn't expect that child to believe that story, did you? Because Lord knows I don't."

"But it's the truth, Ma. That's the way it happened. It happened so fast I didn't even know what hit me."

She sucked her teeth and shook her head. "Chile, you get in more stuff than O.J. Simpson."

"I know, Ma. I just want everything to be like it

was. I don't want to lose her over this."

"So she went back to the other guy, huh?"

"The wedding's tomorrow."

"Uhm, why didn't you take your shower after that girl left? I mean, you should've been wiser than that, Darrel."

"Stupid, I guess."

"Well, you're making it hard to disagree with that, but my baby ain't stupid." She threw her arm around my back and pulled me into her. "Hard headed but never stupid."

"What am I gonna do, Ma?"

"I guess get her a gift."

I jolted away. "Ma, I'm serious."

"I'm serious too. You probably done messed up all of your chances with her. You may as well let her be happy with that other guy."

"But she's not gonna be happy with that jerk. He doesn't appreciate her like I do."

"How does she know if you never showed her?"

"What do you mean?"

"What I mean is that situation should've never happened, Darrel. No matter how many excuses you spit out, there was no excuse for letting that woman stay in your house when you found her in your bed. Not if you didn't want her there."

"But I didn't."

"Then why was she there?"

"I don't know, Ma."

"Well maybe that's something you need to think about, son. I know you say that you love Veronica, but what good is another chance if you're not ready for it?"

"But I am. I'm ready for her to be in my life. I want to spend the rest of my life with this woman."

"Then I think you're telling it to the wrong person."

"But it's too late, Ma. Her mind is made up."

"Is it? You told me the wedding was tomorrow," she advised me." "Remember when I told you about how your father and I got together?"

"Yeah, I remember."

"Well, Darrel, I wanted your father. And he was doing a lot of messing up. I mean a lot. I was willing to wait for him, but not forever, son. Don't expect her to wait forever for you to figure things out. Because while you're out here pussyfooting around, the world, it's still turning, child. And we can't wait our whole lives for the one we want to be with to finally get it right."

"She's gonna marry him, isn't she?"

"Only if you let her, son." She patted me on my knee. "I gotta wake up early in the morning. Stella and I are riding out to Augusta to visit her sister. Lord knows I don't wanna go, but I told her I would. So if you don't stay the night, make sure you lock up for me, suga'. I don't need no hoodlums coming in here talking about no home invasion mess."

"I will, Ma," I replied. "Thanks, too."

"No problem, baby." She kissed me on top of my forehead and waddled out of the room.

I fell back on the chair and placed my hands on my belly. For the first time in my life I didn't know what I was gonna do. Part of me wanted to get back to Veronica's place and demand her to take me back. The other part of me wanted to just let things be. Maybe she would be a lot better off without me meddling things up for her. Besides, Friday had money and he could give her things that I just couldn't give her.

As I laid stretched across my bed, fully dressed, I just stared at the ceiling. I couldn't get any sleep. I felt like a convict waiting to finally walk that green mile. As the night's hours passed, time was slowly catching up with me. Slowly I began to realize that this time I wasn't going to get what I wanted. The player had finally failed right after he had renounced his kingdom. A sad ending indeed.

I snapped out of my idle state when my ears picked up a screeching noise. It was faint to my ears and had probably been going off for about five minutes. Intrigued by the weird sound that appeared to be coming from outdoors, I got up and trampled into my living room. I peeked out through the peephole and there appeared to be a car outside

"What the…" I opened the door. "Hey," I yelled as the white Navigator skidded from the curb.

"Darrel!" Natasha uttered as she popped up from the other side of my car. She was wearing all black from head to toe, topped off with a black skully.

I quickly approached her. "Natasha, what the hell are you doing?"

"Nothing," she said as she dropped a switchblade.

"The hell you aren't." I was stunned as I looked at my car. She had flattened all four of my tires! She had also engraved the word 'Bastard' all along the door. "Girl, what's wrong with you? Why did you do this?"

She looked shaken. "Because I had to. You tried to sleep with your mother, you bastard!"

"Your mother?" I shook my head. For whatever reason, I wasn't even mad at her. I was too drained to be. "Girl, I didn't try to sleep your mother. She tried to come on to me."

"That's not what she said. She said you tried to put the moves on her."

"The moves? Look, I don't give a damn what she said. I didn't try to sleep with her."

"Well, my momma don't lie."

"She sure lied to you this time," I said shaking my head. "I can't believe you did this."

"You gonna call the cops?"

"No, but you're gonna pay for all of this. This was

real stupid, Natasha. You know good and well I wouldn't disrespect you by trying to get with your mother."

"How do I know that? I thought you liked me, but you dumped me. All you did was use me. All you wanted was my sex, and after you got tired, you dumped me. You bastard."

I took a deep breath, knowing undoubtedly the woman was right. "I was wrong Natasha. I admit that. But you can't keep going around damaging people's stuff, seeking out revenge like this. I work for this shit. Come on, do you really think I would sleep with your mother?"

She couldn't say anything. All she did was look towards the ground. "Well, maybe not. But that was messed up how you dumped me. You could've done me better than that."

"And I'm sorry, Natasha, but I had to do it. I couldn't continue to lead you on."

"I was just mad. I'm sorry," she mumbled.

"What?"

"I said I was sorry."

"You should be."

"Don't push it, Walker. I still think you tried to put the moves on my momma."

"Girl, get out of my yard," I advised her.

"I can go?" She almost looked as shocked as I felt.

"I should call the cops. But, yeah, you can go. Go ahead before your crew gets too far down the road."

"You sure I can go?"

"Go 'head before I change my mind."

She turned around and went walking towards the street. "Darrel." She suddenly stopped and turned around.

"Yeah," I answered.

"I'm sorry."

"Not as half as I am. Just do me a favor and chill out with the revenge tactics."

"I will, boo."

She turned around and continued her trek down the street. I picked up her blade, looked at my car and shook my head. "I'll be sending you a bill in a couple of days," I yelled.

"Okay," she yelled back.

I sat on the porch, staring at the blade while thanking the Lord she wasn't as psychotic as her potential showed. But she was just young and dumb. I couldn't believe she ransacked my car the way that she did. Even more, I couldn't believe I wasn't mad about it. I just sat there, listening to the crickets chirp as the swift breeze cooled my body. I was wondering what Veronica was doing.

Chapter Sixteen
And it ends like...

"D, wake up!"

My eyes cracked open as the piercing sound of a car horn went off. "Rex," his name stumbled off of my lips. I had fallen asleep on my front porch. I sat up and focused in on him jumping out of his car.

"Negro, do you realize that it's twelve noon and your crazy ass is out here sleeping on the porch? Have you lost your damn mind?" he asked approaching me.

"No," I answered with the most unforgiving ache in my neck. Somehow I drifted off shortly after Natasha left.

He glanced towards my severely damaged vehicle. "And what in the hell happened to the Maxima?"

"You don't even wanna know."

"I almost don't, but I guarantee it's got something to do with that Veronica chick, doesn't it?"

"In a weird way."

"So she did go back to Friday. I thought so."

"What makes you come to that conclusion?"

"Besides finding your dumb ass out here sleeping on the porch, it was all over the news this morning. Your boy's walking down that deadly plank at two o'clock."

"Two o'clock," I said stunned. Part of me still didn't believe she was going through with it.

"So are you gonna tell me what happened, or am I gonna have to beat it out of you?"

"I don't even wanna talk about it, man," I said as I jumped to my feet. Another sharp pain jolted down my spine. "Ooh, that hurt."

"Dumb ass shouldn't be sleeping outside," he joked as he followed me inside.

I flopped onto the couch as he took a seat on the chair across from me. "So what brings you over?"

"Well, for one, I haven't heard from you in a minute. And the other thing was seeing Friday on the news bragging about his wedding. I just came over here to make sure your ass didn't kill yourself or something."

"You don't have to worry about me. I'm good."

"But she left, though. Didn't she?"

"Yeah, she did," I answered reluctantly.

"See, don't say I didn't warn your ass. I told you she was gonna go with the loot. I told ya!"

"Hold up, man," I stopped him. "It didn't have anything to do with money. I screwed up."

"Whatever, man. I told you what that chick was all about."

"Will you just shut the hell up for a change?" I jumped in his face pointing my finger. I had reached my boiling point with him and his remarks about Veronica. "You don't know anything, you know that?"

"Chill out, D. You don't have to yell, dawg."

"I think I do need to yell right about now. All of this nonsense that comes out of your month is just noise. You're not saying anything at all. It's just noise, man." I took a deep breath in an attempt to calm my nerves but it didn't help. The only thing that could relax me was speaking my mind. "Do you realize that listening to your half ass theories caused me to loose her? That if I hadn't let you talk me into going out and meeting that psycho, Natasha, I would still have air in my tires. Listening to you."

"Dawg, you're a grown man. You don't have to take my advice about anything at all."

"And I shouldn't. But my dumb ass just keeps listening anyway.

"Look, D, if this is about the girl, I understand. I know you had feelings for that chick, but you gotta remember who you are. You gotta remember who *we* are. Easy come, easy go. It's as simple as that. You'll find another one."

I almost broke my neck trying to find a pillow to throw at him. Unfortunately I missed. "You see that—more stupid shit! Why do you think you know so much about relationships when you can't keep one going for a full week? All you do is talk, talk, talk."

"D, listen…"

"Shut up," I shouted. He didn't' dare say another word. "This playing the field stuff, Rex, is played out. We're too old for this shit. We're running through all of these women like we're sick or something. I mean, what does it really accomplish? We're missing our opportunities at real happiness."

"I'm happy."

"Really? What in the hell are you gonna do when you can't get it up no more? Huh?"

"Man, I'll always be able to get my stuff up. And if I can't, I'll just get some Viagra or something. Make me hard as a rock. I can just see myself now, putting the retirement home on lock."

I looked at him, completely lost for words. I couldn't believe he survived as long as he did with the brain that resided beneath his skull. "You're ignorant, Rex. You know that? Just plain ignorant."

"Darrel, man, what's the big deal? So you lost this one. At least you got your jimmy. We've been friends all our lives, and I know you almost better than I know myself. You'll bounce back."

"Not this time, Rex," I hopelessly dropped onto the sofa. Another revelation of her leaving flashed through my mind. "I love her. I can honestly say that I love this woman, and I don't want anybody else. She's my rib."

He chuckled, "Your rib, dawg? Come on, Darrel, listen to yourself."

"Rex, I'm serious. Maybe one day you'll find out how I'm feeling right now. That day when the Lord hits you upside that dome of yours, you'll discover this feeling called love. You will. And if you're not wise enough to respect it when it comes around, well then, you'll know how I'm feeling right now. It doesn't feel good, Rex. It doesn't feel good at all."

"D, come on, dawg. Don't act like this. You're strong. You can make it through this."

As he kept talking, my mind continued to wander. How did I screw up something so perfect I kept thinking. Finally Rex's talking ceased and he just stared at me. I looked back at him, not knowing what he wanted me to say. I was hurt, and he was lost.

"Do you really have love for her like that, D?"

I nodded my head. "I can't even explain how much. I just do."

He stood up and waived his car keys before me. "Well go get your woman then."

The thought barely grazed my mind, but it was there. I wanted to, but I was too scared to even conceive the notion. I looked up at him, thinking that was the best advice he ever gave me. I snatched his keys and jumped up. "That's not a bad idea."

"Hey, if it's like that, I'm your boy. I'm behind you on hundred percent. Just do what you gotta do."

"You serious?"

"Yeah, man. I ain't never saw you look that way in my life. Who am I to tell you how to live your life? Go get your woman, boy."

I was so happy, I gave him a hug.

"Hold up, now, save that for the lady."

"Yeah," I said as I let him go. "I'll do that."

He glanced at his watch. "It's almost one o'clock, dawg. You better get on some clothes and get there before she's gone."

"Yeah, you're right." My nervousness began to kick in, as I began to try to put in order what I needed to do next. "You wanna come?"

"Hell no! You're about to break up a wedding full of black folk. I'm not trying to get my ass kicked!"

"But you got my back," I laughed.

"I'll call somebody to come fix that car of yours, but I ain't messing around like that. You can go ahead and handle that. I'll be on standby with the paramedics."

"That's cool," I said, heading towards my bedroom. I stopped and turned around. "Rex."

"Yeah?"

"Thanks, man."

"Get your woman, dawg."

I was flying down the highway at eighty miles per hour. My heart was racing at the same rate of speed as the car. Rampant thoughts about time flooded my mind. Did I have enough of it? How far along was the ceremony? Will I make it there in time? It all made me a nervous wreck. The one thing that worried me most of all was the question of her taking me back. Would she?

Rex had left his radio on, and a song by Jagged Edge was playing. They were singing about having walked out of heaven. It was the exact feeling that I had, walking out of heaven. And in a way, I felt as if the tune was written just for me. I didn't like what I was feeling, and I was going to do my best to keep the whole thing from going down to reclaim my love. I didn't know what I was going to do, but I knew I had to do something.

I was cruising so fast, I didn't even notice the state trooper clocking speeders on the side of the road. I just blazed by him, and, unfortunately, I captured his attention. It was all like clockwork. His flashers lit up and he zipped behind me like a bee to honey. I was reluctant to take my foot off the gas, but I knew if I didn't, any hopes of stopping that wedding would be nil. So I pulled over.

The officer got out of his car and slowly

approached mine. Each step he took felt like it took an eternity. Even though he was a brother, I placed both of my hands on the steering wheel. I didn't want him to get anything twisted. I just wanted to get my ticket and be on my way.

He stopped at my window. He didn't have an ounce of expression on his face with his eyes hidden behind his dark black shades. He was a mountain of a man with muscles bulging out of his uniform. Any incident with him and a real criminal would almost certainly result in gunplay, because hand-to-hand combat would be undeniably to his advantage. I was just hoping he was nicer than he looked.

"Hi, officer," I said nervously. He didn't say anything. He just issued me a cold stare.

"Do you realize how fast you were going?" his deep voice spoke.

"Yeah, officer…"

"Shut up!" he demanded. He was going to be nasty at all costs, I discovered. "Do you realize how many accidents result from speeding the way that you were?"

"Yes sir, I…"

"I said shut up."

I closed my mouth as he gave me a stern look that was certainly a dare to say something else. On a different day, knowing my rights, I'd probably give him a few choice words, but that wasn't my battle for this day. I had to get where I was going and fast.

"Let me see your license and registration."

I quickly dug into my back pocket. "This is my friend's car, but I do have my license."

"We'll find out," he replied.

I handed him my information, and he gazed at it for a few moments. I could just smell trouble in the air when he pulled his shades off. "Get out of the car."

"Sir, is this really necessary?" I asked.

"Get out of the car, now!"

I bolted out of the car. At this point, I was getting severely aggravated with the whole ordeal. I didn't know what the trooper's gimmick was, but it was beginning to piss me off.

"Nice car," he said.

"It's not mine, sir. It belongs to a friend of mine."

"Really?" For whatever reason he circled me one good time, staring at me from head to toe.

"Is there a problem, sir?"

"No. No problem."

"I know I was speeding, so you can give me my ticket and I'll gladly pay it. I'm sorry about the whole thing."

He looked at me and then gazed back at the license. "Hit them with success, not your fist."

"Excuse me."

"Those are the words I live by."

"Am I missing something here, sir? Because I think you're gonna have to take me in. All I did was go a couple miles over the speed limit. Now either you're gonna arrest me or give me a ticket. All of this other stuff isn't necessary."

"You don't know who I am, do you?"

"Ah, five-o?" I replied, trying my hardest not to sound too sarcastic.

"Dexter Collins. I live by those words you told me so long ago."

"Spooky... I mean, Dexter... oh yeah, Rex said..."

He swallowed me with a big hug before I could finish my statement. "What's going on, Darrel?"

"Nothing, man..." I couldn't get a word out as I gasped for air from his strong arm apprehension.

"Boy, is it good to see you. Why are you in such a rush?" he asked as he released me.

"I got some personal things going on, that's all."

"Well you don't need to be speeding. These people drive like maniacs. It's too easy to get hurt out here on these roads. You gotta be careful out here."

"I know, and I'm sorry, Dexter. I'll pay the ticket, honest I will. I just gotta get going right now."

"Ticket? Don't worry about a ticket. We all make mistakes sometimes."

"Yeah, mistakes are what got me in the situation I'm in now. And to be honest, Dexter, if I don't get to where I was going, it may be too late to correct those mistakes."

"What's going on? Is somebody bothering you? Hey, let me know. I can take care of it for you, you know," he laughed. "Ain't no more skin and bones here."

"No, Dexter, it's nothing physical." I was reluctant about explaining too much of my business, but time was beginning to run out, and I felt that I had to vent a little before I went crazy on the inside. "I'm out here trying to stop a wedding."

"A wedding? Why are you trying to stop a wedding?"

I shook my head. "Because if I don't, I'll never be the same."

"Is it like that, Darrel?"

"You don't know the half."

"Where is this little event going down?"

"At Terrance Friday's luxurious abode."

"This wouldn't be the female that's marrying that character, is it?"

I nodded my head. "Yeap!"

"Well, why don't we pay Mr. Friday a visit. He has quite a few unpaid speeding tickets and a knack for thinking he's above the law."

My mouth dropped. "Are you serious?"

"Follow the cruiser, Darrel. It's the least I can do. You've helped me more than you know." He handed me my license and strolled to his car.

It was like the sun shining on my face for the very first time. Hope had resurfaced amongst my spirit. I jumped in my ride and high-tailed it behind the man once known as Spooky Collins by every bully and cool person in my high school days. Fate had a mysterious way of working out, indeed.

Once Friday's mansion became visible, my heart rate tripled. As I jumped out of the car, we were instantly bombarded by a mob of security.

"Is there a problem officer?" one of the guards questioned.

"No, we just got a late guest, that's all," Dexter quickly fired back as I rushed behind him.

"Where's his invitation?" another angry looking guard asked. He looked familiar. I quickly recognized him as the goon that had Friday's back the night before.

"This is his invitation," Dexter pointed his badge as we moved past the men. Feeling time was leaving me, I pushed ahead of Dexter and made my way through the entrance gate.

"Come back here," a guard demanded. I didn't hesitate one step as I kept pushing on. I was well on my way. I slid through cars, jumped over bushes and danced around barricades to get to my destiny. Suddenly, all my fears were forgotten. All I wanted to do was get my happiness back, to get Veronica back by my side.

As I approached the backyard, it was apparent that the wedding was on and going. There wasn't much noise, and all I could see was mounds of people's head in unison. My throat began to dry as what appeared next was the scariest thing I ever saw. Friday and Veronica were standing before the reverend with their eyes locked on one another as bride and groom. It almost appeared that I was too late as they were holding each other's hands. She was so beautiful in her gown, I wished it was me in Friday's place at that moment. With my feelings of fear reemerging, I did the first thing that came to mind.

"Stop!" I yelled.

Every head at the ceremony turned around to me. Complete and utter silence overwhelmed the area.

"Who the hell are you?" a partially bald old man jumped up and yelled from the front row.

"Darrel?" Veronica uttered.

"Walker, what the hell are you trying to prove?" Friday questioned. "Can't you see that there's a wedding going on? I didn't invite you anyway."

I didn't pay him any attention as I approached the altar. Getting to Veronica was my only destination. "Veronica, I can't let you do this."

A rash of grunts and whispered comments was dispersed by the stunned crowd.

"The hell you can't," the old man yelled. "Terrance, you gonna let this boy come in here and break up your wedding? Where the hell is your security? You better do something about this."

"Don't worry, I got this Uncle Suge," Friday said as he started walking towards me. "Walker, what the hell are you doing here? You trying to spoil the TGIF experience? Because if you are, it ain't gonna work."

"Terrance, I didn't come to start any trouble. I just came for what's mine," I said. Veronica's eyes rested on me, but I couldn't grasp what she was feeling from her expression. She had a worried look on her face, almost like she was about to cry.

"Well, you've found trouble," he said as he shoved me on my shoulder.

"That's right, nephew, kick his ass," the old man screamed. More grunts and whispers followed, as people began to stand.

"Friday, you're gonna have to kill me because I'm not gonna let this go down."

"It'll be all my pleasure," he smiled.

Just when he was about to swing and as I prepared to retaliate, she spoke, "Terrance, stop!"

"What?" he asked.

All eyes were on the bride. And a beautiful bride she was. All I could do was look at her in awe. It should be a crime to be so beautiful.

"Don't hit him," she said approaching us. Her maid of honor almost fell on her face trying to catch the back of her gown. "You just couldn't do it, could you?" she asked.

"Will somebody tell me what the hell is going on?" Friday's uncle asked.

"Let me smash his face in, disrespecting me like this," Friday griped.

"You just couldn't let me go off and be happy, could you? You had to make one last selfish attempt, didn't you?"

"I couldn't let you do this, Veronica. All of this is wrong. You don't belong with him and deep down inside you know it. You should be with me. I love you. And he can't love you like I can. He can't stop loving himself long enough to do so."

"Boy, what are you waiting for? This sucka' is at your wedding courting your chick. You better not stand there looking like a jackass. You better kick that nigga's ass," the old man ordered Friday.

"Sir, watch your mouth," the reverend advised the man.

"I'm sorry, Rev. This is just some bull, that's all," he replied.

"Nah, he got about two seconds to get up out of here before I have to lay a TGIF ass whoopin' special on him," Friday swore.

"Darrel, I don't know what you were thinking when you decided to come here, but you thought wrong.

I've made up my mind, and there's nothing you or nobody else can do about it," she said.

"But you don't love him," I answered. "Stop lying to yourself. You know this is wrong."

"What's wrong is your ass standing on my property spoiling the TGIF experience. That's what the hell is wrong. Saxon!" he yelled for whom I assumed to be security. "I thought they were supposed to be guarding that damn gate."

"Darrel, you need to leave," she advised me.

"I won't, not without you, Veronica."

"Oh, your ass is about to leave alright," Friday promised. "Saxon!"

"Mr. Friday, were sorry," said the big guard as he and his entourage came running up behind me.

"Oh, y'all asses are sorry alright. You're going to be out of a fucking job if you don't get this nobody out of here. How in the hell did you let this jackass get through, anyway?"

"He came in with the police, sir," another guard yelled.

All I could do was stare at her. She was telling me to leave with her mouth, but deep down inside I knew she didn't want me to go. I was hoping I would break through to her, but she wouldn't look at me long enough.

"Get his ass out of here, now," Friday demanded.

"Come on, dawg. Show's over." The guard tugged my arm.

"I'm not going anywhere. Not without Veronica," I vowed. "Baby, don't let me leave without you."

"This nigga's crazy!" Friday chuckled. "This cat better be glad I wanna get married today because I swear I'd give you a good old fashioned TGIF ass whoopin' if I didn't!"

"You may have to try and issue one because I'm not going anywhere."

"Darrel, just leave, please!" Veronica cried. "I'm where I want to be."

"Come on, dawg," the guard requested as he and the other guards began dragging me backwards. I was trying to put up a good fight, but their might overwhelmed me as I continued my attempts to move towards her.

"Veronica, you don't mean that. You know where you belong. Don't let me leave here without you," I pleaded with my legs dragging.

"Darrel, go home," she replied.

"Get out of here, chump," Friday laughed. "His dumb ass don't even know when to quit."

"I love you! You know I do. And you love me, that's why you can't look at me."

"Get his ass out of here," Friday yelled.

"Go home, Darrel," she advised.

"I can't! I need you like a turtle needs the shell on his back," I screamed out.

Instantly the crowd began laughing at me. "This nigga talking about turtles. Is he on crack?" the old man laughed. They laughed even harder after his comment.

"You're such a loser, Walker," Friday said with an arrogant grin. He knew he had won. He probably didn't know what went down between his bride and myself, but he knew whatever it was, he had won.

She stood motionless as the guardsmen took me away. She wasn't laughing like the others. She just stared at me sadly. It was almost like my honest gesture made some type of connection, but apparently it was too little, too late. A tear slid down her face as she turned away. Security proceeded to drag me off of the premises.

"Don't even think about bringing your punk ass back here again," the guard advised me as he shoved me onto the police cruiser where Dexter stood.

"And take that toy cop with you," one guard laughed. "Before we have his fuckin' badge."

272

"He probably got it from Wal-Mart, anyway," another man joked. They made their way back behind the gate as they all laughed.

"It didn't go as planned, huh?" Dexter asked.

"Nah," I answered, as I a got up and brushed myself off. I took in a deep breath as failure sunk in. "Not at all like I planned."

"Well, at least you tried."

"It wasn't good enough," I said walking to Rex's car. "She's about to make the biggest mistake of her life, and I helped her."

"You did more than the average man would've done."

I opened the car door. "The average man wouldn't have let someone that precious slip away."

"Well, you won't have to worry about asking yourself, what if? All you could do was try."

I just shook my head, mad as hell with myself. "Thanks for helping me, Dexter. I know you put a lot on the line by trying to get me here. You could've lost your job, for goodness sake."

He approached me and extended his hand. "And if I had to do it again, I wouldn't have any problem with it at all. Besides, what would life be like without a little bit of adventure?"

"I don't know, but without her, I'll probably find out." I shook his hand.

"You're alright, Darrel Walker."

"Thanks, Dexter."

"See you around. And make sure you watch that speed."

He walked to his car and drove off.

I gave Friday's estate one last stare as I sadly visualized Veronica accepting his hand in marriage. That Jagged Edge song started playing inside my head. All hope was officially gone. I jumped in the car and drove off.

They say that nice guys always finish last. That's one statement I didn't quite know where I fitted in at all. With my past, if I thought of myself as a nice guy, one could probably argue that I was thinking too highly of myself. I guess it really didn't matter where I was placed in that statement because I didn't win. Not this time.

My heart had left me and married probably the most arrogant man on the planet. I could just see him, rejoicing in himself on a cruise somewhere with a woman that was just too damn good for him.

And then there was me. Back on my park bench with the birds and the bums, all by myself waiting for the sun to sink below Metro Atlanta's tall buildings. It was like a cycle I just couldn't find myself out of somehow. A never ending cycle. I felt like dirt. And maybe Terrance Friday was right when he called me a loser.

"It had to be the dumbest thing I've ever heard, yet I understood every word of it. Turtles and shells."

I looked up and my heart almost jumped out of my body. She was standing before me. Veronica was standing right in front of me.

"I wanted to be mad at you forever. But I thought that, if he could get in front of all of those people and say something so outlandish to please me, I could at least give him one more chance."

"How'd you know, I..."

She smiled, "I know you, Darrel."

"I didn't sleep with her."

"I know now."

I immediately jumped up, hugged and kissed her.

"Wait just one minute," she said. "We have to get a few things straight before we go any further."

"Okay. Whatever you want," I said gleefully, as I took a step back.

"Darrel, I can't play ga..." I placed my finger over

her lips.

"You don't have to say another word. All I want is you. You don't have to worry about my lying, cheating or anything else. I know where my heart is and it's with you, baby."

"When I thought you betrayed my trust I didn't know what to do. I was so hurt."

"I know, and I'm sorry for letting things even look that way. You mean too much to me for me to go out like that. It's not in me to jeopardize being with you. It took me too long to find you."

"I'm sorry for being scared to tell Terrance about us. I just didn't know how to."

"Well, I'm sorry for the whole Brandi incident. I should've been man enough to tell her to leave from the beginning."

"We both made mistakes. All we can do is move on."

"I want that. You just don't realize how bad I want it."

"Well, you can have it. Only if you really want it, though."

"Oh, I want it. I want it more than life itself."

She giggled, "So I guess that makes me your shell."

"Baby, you're my shell and everything else."

"I told you I wasn't gonna let you be out here by yourself again."

"And I'm so glad you didn't," I hugged her "Wait a minute. How does Mr. TGIF feel about this?"

"Let's just say his ego took a huge dip when he got left at the altar."

I laughed, "You left him there. Oh, I wish…"

"We're moving on, right?"

"Yeah."

"Then we don't have time to talk about either one of our ex's."

"You have never been so right," I replied.

"Besides, I had to follow my heart, and it's with you."

"I love you," I told her.

"I love you, too."

"Give me a kiss," I requested.

"Why don't you come and get it? You know how to track down everything else."

"I don't mind if I do." I took a step forward and kissed the softest, sweetest lips I've ever kissed. The last lips I would ever kiss. The only lips that I wanted to ever kiss again.

There was nothing in the world that could pull me away from her. Not Rex, not Brandi Brown, not even my own stupidity. I was right where I wanted to be. Right where I needed to be. I was in it for the long haul, and at last, I was single no more.

The End

If you enjoyed
Single Again
please let the world know it and place
your review for this book on Amazon.com.

Thank you For Purchasing
Single Again

More Akirim Press Books

Books by Rod Cornelius

Diggin' Gold

The Trusted

Single Again

Ghetto Eyes

The Best Kept Secrets

Ugly

Books by Mirika Mayo Cornelius

Secret

Colored Lily: Poppa Took My Innocence

Ain't Quite What I Thought

Sunny Sides of My Shade

Murders At Gabriel's Trails: An Alexis &
Bain Love Story

Murders At Gabriel's II: Trails Sons
Sacrifice

Murders at Gabriel's Trails III: Paths of Revenge

Murders at Gabriel's Trails IV: Littered Deception

Books by Cyan Deane

Dead Man's Mayhem

Execution's Karma

Preview <u>Diggin' Gold</u>, an Akirim Press book written by Rod Cornelius

Trent slowly cruised his late model, cherry red Jaguar into the driveway of his two story abode. It was a quiet night out in the ritzy neighborhood.

"So we're here," Trent announced. He turned his car off and slouched back in his leather seat. He turned to his sexy companion, Kizzy, who was draped in much sexier attire than her restaurant clothing–a short sun dress that revealed a generous view of her smooth caramel thighs. Trent licked his lips as he undressed her with his eyes. "My, my, my, you're looking good tonight."

She blushed, "I swear you've said that about a million times already."

"Baby, when does the truth ever get played out?"

"I guess it never does," she replied.

"Alright then. As long as you're holding it down the way that you do, then I'm going to continue with my bombardment of compliments. I want you to know that I like what I see, baby."

"You stupid," she said as she peered through the windshield at the humongous home. His two-story brick house was immaculate, and it impressed her. "All that house just for you, huh?"

"Baby, you know I do everything big. It wouldn't be me if I didn't." Her questions gave him the perfect opportunity to do his favorite thing–talk about himself.

280

"I see. You don't ever get lonely in there with all that space to yourself?"

"Yeah, it can get a little lonely at times, but for the most part, I don't have much time to think about being lonely because I'm always out there trying to make that cheddar," he chuckled. "But you know I got enough room for a roommate, or even a wife, if you play your cards right."

"Oh wow, if I play my cards right. Aren't you the confident one," she grinned.

"Sweetheart, confidence is a man's doorway to success. Without it, failure is inevitable."

"So does that make me some kind of conquest to you?"

"Of course not. I'm in search for the right partner. One that I can overcome my conquests with. You just happen to be in the running, and your lead is overwhelming right about now."

"You're smooth, Trent, but I'll have you know that I'm not one of those little hookers out there that melt and ooze to any smooth words a handsome brotha' spits out at me."

"Oh, I know that. That's why when I first laid eyes on you, I knew I had to have you. I mean, seriously, I've had my share of fun and all, but I've gotten to the point where I just want to settle down."

She gave him a petite smile while shaking her head. "Now picture that - Trent Jackson calling himself settling down."

"You know I can do it, right?"

"Hey," she shrugged her shoulders. "I'm not disputing that."

"I can do it with you," he laughed. "Now I want you to picture yourself in that big ole' house of mine wearing nothing but a tee-shirt and some panties, fixing me up some pancakes and bacon right after I just got finished putting it down on you just before sunrise."

"Oh my God," she said as she burst out laughing. "You are so damn cocky." She gazed at him, while shaking her head. He simply stared at her with his big, boastful grin. "But you're so damn cute with it."

"That's me, baby. Cocky and cute with it," he said as he eased his hand onto her thigh and began caressing it. He had enough of talking, he was ready to get down to business.

"Did you lose something down there, Mr. Ego?" she asked.

"No, but I want to put something special down there."

"Yeah, I bet you do."

"You know last night was off the chain, right?" he said. "I mean seriously."

"So you think it was?"

"Hell yeah, it was," Trent declared. "So did you tell that clown about us yet?"

"No, not yet, but when did *we* become an us?"

He chuckled, "You gotta be kidding me right?"

"Well...," she held both hands out, in attempt to have Trent explain himself.

"Shit, every since I was beating that thang on top of your bathroom sink last night," he recalled. "*More, Trent. Right there, Trent. Don't stop, Trent. It's yours, Trent.*"

"Oh, so it's like that?"

"Hell yeah. Just like that," he laughed. "Last night, I put my name on it, baby. You know that. Why don't you slide that dress up and let me get a peak at my imprint."

"You're a funny guy, Trent Jackson. I'm not mad at you though. A sister has to admit, you most certainly handled your business. I don't know about your name being on it...yet, but you did your thing."

"Damn right, I did. I got to handle mine. That's exactly why there won't be any lady of mine working up in somebody's restaurant as the help. You're gonna be right there in my spot, beside me, handling shit."

"Oh really?" She liked the way he talked about them working together, but she wasn't entirely sold on the idea of completely leaving Jimmy. Jimmy was her bird in the hand.

"Yes, really. How can that cat, Jimmy, call you his main lady, and he got you in his little drive thru shop waiting and bustin' on damn tables? That's weak as hell. Ain't nothing weak about Trent Jackson."

"Now, in Jimmy's defense, we weren't together when I first started working there. We just sort of evolved into something over time. Nothing serious."

"Well, now you've evolved into something else, and it's as serious as a mutha fucker." He continued to gently

283

allow his hand to caress her inner thigh as he leaned over and began to nibble on her neck. The sweet smell of her soft skin had his manhood rising, and he was finding it increasingly difficult to compose himself.

"Hmmm, you're acting like you want a repeat of last night," she said as she leaned slightly away from him.

She wanted him just as bad as he wanted her, but just not bad enough to get it on in the car. She also realized that another round with Trent meant another day of lying to Jimmy, but what he doesn't know wouldn't hurt him, she thought. Besides, she was trying to come up and Jimmy's stock was falling fast. Trent had tangible assets, and she was almost ready to go all in.

"I told you earlier that I had a lack of patience for you. Now how about let's get up out of this ride and take a no-holds barred tour of my humble abode. There won't be a piece of furniture off limits. I promise," he said as he continued feasting on her neck.

She observed his house again, "I don't know if you got a back strong enough for the kind of tour that you're talking about. Your place looks like it has a lot of ground to cover. It could take the whole night to get it all."

He pulled up and backed away from her. "There's only one way to find out."

"Then why are we still in your Jag?"

He backed away further with a smile as she smiled right back at him. "Baby, it ain't nothing but a word."

"Then what are you waiting on?"

"Shiiiiiit!" he said. She finally told him what his ears had been waiting all night to hear. The green light was lit. He knew he could have pretty much any woman he set his sights on but Kizzy carried an extra spiff. Not only was she sexy and a freak in between the sheets, but she was Jimmy's lady. She was the last thing he could take from Jimmy and that was worth more than its weight in gold.

He quickly hopped out of the automobile and danced around the vehicle to open her door. He grabbed her hand to assist her on her exodus. He shut the door, not releasing her hand as they made their way to his front door.

As she stood behind him, she looked up and admired the huge brick home. She had never been in a house as big as his, and she couldn't wait to serenade it with him. "This really is a nice place, Trent. I could see you making me some pancakes in bed here," she joked.

"Oh we 'bout to make something, but it's not going to pancakes, that's for sure." He pulled her into the dark house and slammed the door shut. Then he pulled her into him and gave her a passionate kiss.

"So I guess you mean business," she said as she pulled away from his lips and rested her arms around his neck.

"Do I?" he smiled. He placed both hands on her rump and gripped it tightly, pulling her up off of the floor as she wrapped her legs around his waist. As his tongue ran its slow, slippery course up and down her neck, he walked her through the dark living space and carried her to the leather couch. He laid her down and his tongue twirled around her bosom as his hands made their way down her legs as he began to inch her dress upwards.

"I'm gonna make that pretty little kitty purr tonight," he promised.

Her hands raced up and down his back. "Stop talking and get to work."

"Oh, I'm 'bout to work your ass off," he said as he eased down to her stomach and began massaging it with his lips. She took her hands and forcefully pushed his head between her legs.

The door bell rang.

"What the hell?" his head popped up from her crouch.

"Just ignore it," she replied, wanting him to get back to business.

The door bell rang again.

"Nah, nobody comes to my crib this late. Anyone that knows me, knows better." He was pissed and was ready to share a few choice words with whomever stood on the other side of his front door. He came to his feet and stomped towards the door.

She let out a huge grunt and scooted up on his couch. She rolled up her panties and began straightening out her dress. "It's probably just somebody lost."

"Lost in this neighborhood? Hell nah," he said as he flicked on the lights. "Who the hell is it?" he barked towards the door.

"Davis County police department," recited a faint voice from the other side of the door.

Trent peeked through the peephole, "Who?"

Preview <u>SECRET</u>, an Akirim Press book written by author Mirika Mayo Cornelius

"I told you your aunt is resting, didn't I?"

I reach my leg back and kick him in his mouth. He yanks his head back and stares at me like he's gonna kill me, so I kick him again with both of my legs swinging like a wild bat. He jumps on top of me holding my right leg with his hand and ducking away from my other leg while its kicking. He starts to unbuckle his pants with his other hand.

"Yeah, it's present time now. You done asked for it. I heard about your momma. A nice piece of work there."

He rips off my pajamas after he gets his pants down. My heart fills up with scary feelings when I just now figure out why my Aunt May said what she told me all the time. Where's Aunt Janie?

"Aunt Janie! Your friend is in my room! He's not supposed to be in here, Aunt Janie!" I yell the loudest I can yell.

Sam reaches back with his right hand and hits me on the side of my stomach. I curl up in a ball.

"Guess what, Secret. She ain't coming so ain't no use in you calling for her. You act like I'm about to hurt you. I wouldn't have hit you like that if you didn't try to wake up your aunt, so I'm sorry. Now hold still."

He feels up my back with his naked hand. My stomach is aching. He keeps acting like he ain't gonna do nothing to me, but this don't feel right. I keep thinking about Aunt May while his hand is going up my leg. I feel

287

something wet on my leg, too. I yank away, but he jerks me in front of him. Jesus, please, help me, Lord. Tears are falling every which way down my face, but then I see it. I fell asleep with my pencil beside me in my bed. It's halfway covered up with my sheets.

"Touch it."

I look back at him, and he closes his eyes.

"Look down and touch it."

That's when I look down and see what he's talking about. I panic.

"Get off of me! No! I'm not touching that thing- ever! What is that? Aunt Janie, please!" I reach for the pencil real fast, but I don't know what to do with it yet. My hand grips the pencil like somebody else got it for me. My other hand grabs that long, ugly thing, and my hand, with the pencil in it, reaches all the way back and stabs that big, ugly thing right in the center.

He lets out the loudest holler I ever heard from a man in my life, and his eyes fly open. I jump up off the bed, and run towards the other end of my room. I look back at his ugly thing and see that the pencil is still stuck in there while he's tumbling around on the floor. His hands are around it, but he ain't pulling it out. It's hurtin' him so bad that I pick up my lamp so that I can aim for his head so I can bang some more pain into him. He justa hollering. Betcha he won't come in my room no more.

www.ingramcontent.com/pod-product-compliance
Lightning Source LLC
Chambersburg PA
CBHW070315260626
47160CB00003B/850